LIVING THE SUITE LIFE

THE DECKER CONNECTION
BOOK 3

CHERYL CAMPBELL

This book is for anyone who uses their swear jar as a savings account.

LIVING THE SUITE LIFE

by Cheryl Campbell

———

Stress and pressure come with the territory when you're the youngest General Manager in the MLB. Add in my self-appointed role as the protector of the Decker Connection, my tight-knit group of siblings and friends, and it's no wonder they say I'm grumpy.

I'm facing down a public relations nightmare after one of my players assaults someone at a local food festival, and this PR problem is about to push me over the edge. Then I meet this full-of-sunshine, rainbows from storm clouds, heart-full-of-kindness, single mother, and I'm in more trouble than I ever imagined. There's absolutely no saving me from falling now.

CHAPTER ONE

ALEXANDER

———

My legal team and the public relations consultants we keep on retainer for precisely this kind of nightmare fill the Reaper's board room. There are way too many people in here for my liking. I hate this shit.

"Jess, I don't care! It breached his Image Clause, and I refuse to pay out his contract. He's done. If someone wants to pick him up, that's fine with me, but he'll never play ball as a Carolina Reaper again." Lawyers are a necessary part of my life, but even those working for me get under my skin.

"I understand your stance, Mr. Decker, but until he's found guilty, he's still innocent in the eyes of the law. We can put him on administrative paid leave for ninety days, and let it play out in court," Jessica Whitcomb says, her voice trailing off when she looks at me. She's a newer front office team member and a prominent labor lawyer, but I can tell she's nervous standing up to contradict me. It's probably the look on my face that has her rattled. While most people are used to my normal, resting scowl face, I'm sure my current expression is beyond my usual irritated. I'm pissed. Anger, frustration, and outrage swirl in my gut, creating a whole new level of loathing.

While I respect her opinion, this situation isn't just about the contract. I fucking hate contracts. They're binding, and I don't like to be confined to someone else's rules. I need people to live by my rules. Show up. Do your job. And don't be an asshole and assault a fan. Is that too much to ask? Apparently so.

Fucking contracts. They're my least favorite part of my job, and there are days that's all I deal with. There's too much negotiation and interpretation with contracts. And too many people and opinions. Sometimes, I want to do something fast, decisive. Like now. Contracts slow everything down. My irritation is boiling over, and everyone in the room is on heightened alert. My leg is bouncing under the table, and when the pen in my hand snaps in two and skitters across the table, I shut my eyes and count to five but only make it to three. I gather myself and continue with the meeting.

I look toward Jack Manning, head of our legal department and an old friend. We were housemates back in college, and if anyone can get me what I want legally, it's Jack. He knows me and will get me there, working within the confines of the law, of course.

"What do you think, Jack?" I focus all my attention on him and he doesn't flinch. He knows me better than most and understands why I'm seething.

"Alexander, I know where you're coming from. I want the bastard gone, too. I doubt his legal troubles are going to go away easily. Pauly's agent tried to quiet it with money almost immediately, and this Danny Franklin held firm on principle. Trying to teach a lesson or something, said money can't fix everything. Either way, I agree with Jess. Let this play out in the legal system. Public opinion won't be in his favor. Pulling him immediately was the right move. Work with the PR team and keep focusing on family values. We communicate to his agent he's done. If they can get someone else to take the contract, we let him go. If not, we send him to our Low A team and bury him there if it doesn't resolve quickly. It's only been forty-eight hours. Let's see where it goes."

I let out an audible sigh and swipe my hand down my face. Patience is not my strong suit. I tried to work out my bad mood in the gym this morning, but even double time on the punching bag didn't help release my frustrations.

"Fine. Jack, handle it. You know what I want. Keep the details out of the press." I direct my last comments to the PR team. "That's all for now. Thank you."

Everyone quietly leaves the room, with Jack hanging back.

"Hey, great to see you, Ash. By the way, congratulations on your engagement," Jack says when he gets to the door.

Ashleigh steps from the corner and stands beside me, her hand on my shoulder. "Thanks, Jack. Good seeing you too. Give my love to Lucy and the twins. I might be in town for a while until this blows over. Tell her to call me. Maybe we can do lunch."

"She'd love that. See you around." Jack leaves the room, and I spin my chair and look at her with a huge grin on her face.

"How can you smile in the middle of this shit storm?"

"I love watching my big brother command a room. Especially when it's not directed at me for once."

Ashleigh is my kid sister and a social media genius. I wanted her to work for the Reapers after college, but she followed her heart, got engaged, and started her own social media company working with star athletes.

She was with me when I got the news about our starting third baseman being charged with assault and drug possession. The Reapers are a family organization, and we rally when the family's in trouble. Ashleigh came home with me to help ride out the storm. When she offered her services, I accepted. We need all the help we can get.

My family owns the Carolina Reapers, a Major League Baseball team. My father bought the expansion franchise when I was two years old and we've run this organization as a family for thirty-two years. Dad's semiretired now, and although he might come in the office occasionally, he's handed the reins over to me as the General Manager and President of the organization. We thought my siblings would work for the team alongside me, but they had other plans.

We also have a strait-laced image we want to project. All employees of the Reapers sign a contract: from the players to the front office staff, to the grounds crew. We expect our players to be role models. That includes their appearance, a required number of philanthropic hours, and maintaining an all-American superhero image. Drugs and assault do not fit that image. Fucking Pauly Jackson.

"I appreciate your support, Ash. Cole okay with you staying in enemy territory?"

She throws her head back and laughs. Her bouncy, blonde waves remind me of our mom, and I give her a wistful smile. A smile reserved only for her.

"The Reapers may be the Liberties on-field rival, but us, this team, will never be his enemy. You may not have drafted him, but he's part of this team nonetheless. I mean, Matt just made his MLB debut last night for you, and his sister threw out the first pitch. The Liberties may pay him, but his heart is a Reaper." Matt Hartman is Cole's best friend and my new starting third baseman because of this disaster.

"Yeah, yeah, I know. He's a good guy, and he makes you happy. That's the important thing. He back in Nashville?"

"No, they have another week on the road before he comes home. He'll never miss me."

"Oh, I think he'll miss you." That boy thinks the sun rises and sets by my sister. And it does.

She smiles brightly. "Yeah, he'll miss me. You know what I mean. Besides, I think you need me more right now."

I stand up and wrap her in my arms. "Thanks for being here, Ash. Means the world to me."

"I'll always be here for you, Xander. You know that. You, Jules, Dad, the Reapers. I'd do anything for you."

My brother, Julian, is a few years younger than me and struck out on his own too. He's one of the most successful sports agents in the country. I'll admit, that role suits him. Julian is more of a free spirit, and the structure of franchise leadership would break him. He's happiest when he represents one of my players and gets to "make me pay." Even though it's probably a considerable conflict of interest, we make it work. The Reapers are honest and pay their players what they're worth. Maybe more than we should when I think of Pauly Jackson.

"Speaking of Jules, is he still in town?"

"Yeah, we're staying at Dad's since he gave his apartment to Matt and Darcy until they get settled. Let's all do dinner tonight and work on a plan to clean up this mess. Maybe turn it into something positive."

"I know you're a miracle worker, but I don't think that's possible. What have you got in mind?"

"Well, for starters, one reason the victim won't take a payoff was because it was in front of his kid. It's a teachable moment."

"A kid. Aw fuck." Family friendly. That's who the Reapers are, so an assault by one of our players in front of a kid is unforgivable.

"Exactly. I'm going to offer them VIP tickets to the game tomorrow. By the way, can you get me a workspace for the week? It'll be easier to charm your employees face-to-face when I need something."

I think about bringing the victim to the game. "Won't that look like we're trying to buy his silence?"

"We'll ensure he knows it's an apology with no strings attached. We aren't asking for anything. It's just our way of letting him know who we are. We aren't covering up, more like owning up."

I kiss her on top of her head. "Thanks, Ash. And you can take the office by mine. It was going to be yours, anyway. Welcome home."

CHAPTER
TWO

DANI

_____

I keep my phone on speaker so I can switch out laundry and talk at the same time. Multi-tasking at its finest. Jenny's voice fills the room as we chat, and she conducts her daily check in.

"I just want to make sure you're okay. I mean, what's a best friend for if she isn't sending you funny TikToks to make you smile?"

"Jenny, I'm fine. Really. Although, don't stop sending the TikToks. I love the animal ones. We watched the one with the baby goat enough times to make it go viral." She giggles at my approval of her distraction efforts.

Jenny is my best friend, fellow third-grade teacher, and eternal optimist like me. Although, her energy and positivity make my sunny disposition look like Debbie Downer. She's over the top, and I love her. Right now, given her volume and tone, her happiness level is off the scale.

"I'm just embarrassed and angry he got the best of me. I would have taken him down if you and Tyler hadn't walked up." I chuckle because I may look weak, but I'm mighty. As a female military brat growing up surrounded by lots of guys, my dad, the Colonel, made sure I was well-versed in self-defense. I'm not above a kick to the junk. I can take down a guy twice my size without breaking a sweat.

"No doubt. I know you were about to put him in his place. I could see it in your eyes and feel horrible that we walked up and, well, that it happened at all." Her enthusiasm for making me laugh leaves, and her tone sobers.

"It's okay, I'm fine, and the swelling is almost gone. There's barely a mark. We can put this entire thing behind us."

Tyler yells at me because the doorbell isn't enough of a notification. "Mom, there's someone at the door!"

"Don't open the door! Wait for me, please." Like most six-year-olds, Tyler is fearless. And also bad at listening.

"Jen, I gotta run. I'll chat later!" I hang up and push the start button on the washer. As a single mother and teacher, the struggle is real. I reach the front door, where I find Tyler talking to a beautiful young woman. This isn't the neighborhood a pretty blonde like her should go door to door. She's stooped down to talk to him at his eye level.

"Tyler, what did I tell you about answering the door?" I try to use my teacher voice, but it's summer, and I'm out of practice. He's not even phased.

"Mom, this lady asked me if I like baseball. You know I love baseball, right? She said I could get a baseball if we came to a game. Isn't that cool?" His words are fast, and although I'm fluent in Tyler speak, I have no idea what he's talking about.

Tyler just finished his first season of T-ball this spring and is ready to start again in the fall. He loves everything about the game, and it's nearly year-round when you live in North Carolina. It's a perfect outlet for all of his energy too.

"Very cool, Tyler." I finally address the woman at my door. "May I help you?" She stands to her full height, and I'm greeted by a warm smile. She's wearing a Reapers polo, a white skort, and a cute pair of tennis shoes with a leopard print. Very professional and casual, the perfect look to put someone at ease. She extends her hand.

"Hi, I'm Ashleigh with the Carolina Reapers. I'm looking for Danny Franklin. Is he home?"

I shake her hand and return her smile. I always laugh when people think I'm a guy. It's been like this my entire life. "I'm Dani. How can I help you?"

She looks shocked. "You're Dani? Wow. Okay, then. Sorry," she stutters. She's clearly thrown by this revelation. "I only had the police report, and it had Danny spelled like a male," she mutters as a way of explanation. At the mention of the police report, I automatically raise my hand to cover the bruise on my cheek. She catches herself and focuses. "Wow. I'm sorry to drop in on you unexpectedly. Do you have a minute to talk?"

It's a hot July day in Charlotte at almost a hundred degrees, and she looks safe enough. "Sure, why don't you come in? Sorry for the mess. It's laundry day. Can I offer you some tea? I'm sweating more than a whore in church." I wipe the sweat from my brow with the back of my hand.

"Mom, what's a whore?" Tyler asks.

I roll my eyes at myself because I forgot he's standing next to me. "It's, um, someone who gets really hot in church because they wear so many clothes," I try to explain. Lying is a bad habit I don't want him to have, but sometimes I have to with him. The fact that I used the phrase in front of him goes to show I'm a little frazzled today. Why would someone from the Reapers be looking for me?

Ashleigh laughs. "I don't mean to intrude, but tea would be nice. It's definitely hot out." She gives me a little wink and a disarming smile.

"Sure, come on in. Tyler, why don't you gather your towels and bring them to the laundry room, please." It'll take him several trips, but at least it will keep him busy while I find out what she wants. We walk into the kitchen, and I pour us each a glass of iced tea. We lean against the counters and take a sip, appreciating the refreshing, cool, sweet tea and the reprieve from the heat.

"Thanks," she says. "This hits the spot. Again, I apologize for the drop-in and the mix-up. I don't have the details, as you can probably guess by my assumption with your name, but I know that one of our players was charged with assault on a Dani Franklin. On behalf of the Reapers, I want to apologize for what happened. We pride ourselves on being a family organization, and hitting a woman most definitely violates our code of conduct. He's no longer on our team, and we're working to ensure he's not associated with our organization." Sincerity and regret fill her face. "I'm sorry. Are you okay?" She glances at my bruise and tries not to stare.

I'm shocked at her apology. I've seen so many athletes misbehave, and everyone still puts them on a pedestal because they can do something with a ball. For her to tell me they fired him is surprising and against the norms I'm used to. Concern fills her voice. She's more than a mouthpiece for the team, and she's obviously upset.

"Thanks. I'm okay." My hand reaches for my face, but I catch myself and give her a reassuring smile instead.

Tyler comes back into the kitchen, towels dragging behind him. We both laugh as he proudly wrangles the laundry to the washer.

"Well, we would like to invite you and your family to a game this Friday. VIP access. You'll be treated to behind-the-scenes tours, sit in the owner's suite, and be our guests. I'd bet Tyler would love it." She looks toward the laundry room and suppresses her laughter as she watches him fight to untangle himself from the towels.

"Oh, he'd more than love it, but it's unnecessary. I don't blame the team for the actions of one person." I really don't. I wasn't even going to press charges, but my father insisted. He said the man should be held accountable. He went down to the police station that night, and they had the video footage from some bystander. I was the missing piece of the puzzle. They categorized it as domestic violence, and therefore the police didn't need the victim, me apparently, to press charges, so they had already arrested him when my father showed up. I had no idea he was a hotshot baseball player. To me, he was an entitled man who thought I would fall at his feet. He thought wrong.

We were at the uptown food festival when Jenny took Tyler to get a churro while I finished my lunch. Can't a girl just mind her own business and enjoy her food without being harassed these days? Apparently not. This guy approached me and insisted he knew me. He reeked of alcohol and privilege. When I politely told him I'd never seen him before he became indignant. He kept repeating, "you know me." Then he changed tactics and decided he would refresh my memory.

I used the usual deflection moves, including a firm no, but it was obvious that was a word he wasn't used to hearing. It was fine until it wasn't. Jenny and Tyler were coming back when I had just told him douchebags weren't my type. That's when he hit me. I had just turned my head to see where Tyler was, and he grazed my left cheek with his fist. I was shocked, but Tyler was upset, and I made it my number one priority to get him away from the scene.

Mr. Entitled stumbled off, and some guy grabbed him and told him it wasn't cool. They had another altercation, and we scurried out of there as the police rushed toward the ruckus.

My cheek didn't even hurt until I got home, probably because of the adrenaline coursing through my body. The swelling has subsided but there's still a slight bruise, but it looks better now that a few days have passed. No permanent damage, although I'm aware it could have been worse. Nothing a little ice and concealer can't fix. Tyler has been a little clingy, and when he touches my face, I do my best not to wince. He's the one I worry about. Always.

Ashleigh smiles and reminds me the world is filled with

better people than Mr. Entitled. "It would be our pleasure to host you. Please come. I'd love to share my family with you."

"Your family?" This girl takes her job seriously.

"Yeah, sorry. I'm Ashleigh Decker. My family owns the Reapers." She gives me a huge smile, and it's hard to believe anyone can say no to her. "And I'd like you and your family to be my guests at the game on Friday. We'll have fun, I promise."

"Can we go, Mom? Please? Pretty please?" Tyler begs at my side.

I smile down at him and rub his head. Excitement becomes Tyler's entire personality. At this point, I'd be a monster if I said no. "We'd love to come. Can I bring my parents too? My dad's a huge fan."

"Absolutely. Anyone else you want to bring, you let me know. Here's my number." She hands me a business card. "I'll meet you at the main entrance an hour and a half before the game. That'll give us time for a tour, a little shopping for all the gear, and dinner before the first pitch. Sound good?"

"Sounds great. We can't wait, can we, Tyler?"

"Woo hoo! I'm going to a Reapers game! I'm going to a Reapers game!" He runs around the kitchen, shouting his chant.

Looks like we're going to a Reapers game. I've always said that in everything, there is good. Even in bad, dark times, there's always gratitude to be found. Here's to the good blooming from the bad.

CHAPTER
THREE

ALEXANDER

———

I text Ashleigh to let her know I won't be able to do the tour with the Franklins.

> Meet you and the Franklins in our suite after the first inning. Hope that's okay.

ASH

Sure, we'll take care of them until then. I still remember my way around. It's nice to know you haven't cut my access off.

> Nope. Still hoping you'll forget about love and come back home.

Not a chance 😊

Multitasking tonight - making sure Darcy meets the other WAGs. It's a twofer kind of night.

> Can't think of a better wingman for her. Have
> fun. See you later.

————

My brother Julian knocks on the door and lets himself into my office. He drops down on the couch and puts his feet on the coffee table.

"Is that how you treat the furniture in your office?" I scowl at him, hoping it's enough of a hint to move his feet. In typical Jullian fashion, he ignores me. He knows exactly how to push my buttons, and he does it regularly.

Before I meet Ashleigh, I still need to wrap up a few things and drop into the other suites for quick "grin and grips," as I call them. The pressing of the flesh to our sponsors and leaders in the community. Fortunately, I make the rounds with Scoville, our hot pepper mascot. Everyone would rather have their picture with him than me, which suits me just fine.

"So, how're you doing today?" Julian asks.

"Fine."

"Seriously? One-word answers? I need you to loosen up and turn up the charm. Nobody likes the grumpy guy." I hate his grumpy label. I'm not. Not really. I'm busy. Serious. Under a lot of pressure. Not all of us can gallivant around the country and spend weeks in Mexico "working remote." Good thing he can't see my internal eye roll.

"Jules, I'm glad you're here. You've always had the people skills you like to point out that I lack. So why don't you use those skills to help Ash and let me finish reviewing these financials?" I love my brother, but I don't have the patience to deal with him right now.

"Whoa, whoa. Sorry to show concern for my brother." He takes his feet off the table, and I let my shoulders relax a little.

"Look, I appreciate you being here. It was generous of you to give Matt and Darcy your apartment until they get settled. Usually, I have someone to help with that, but right now, it's all hands on deck dealing with this asshole, Pauly Jackson." It's not how I'd usually welcome a new player, so add a side dish of guilt to my plate while we're at it.

"It's no problem. After all, Matt's my client, and Darcy's practically family since Ash is marrying her brother. Now that I say that aloud, our family tree probably needs to branch out a little more, huh?" He shoots his million-dollar smile in my direction, and I loosen up a little more. Jules has a charm about him that puts people at ease. It's probably what makes him so successful as an agent. Everyone trusts him, and honestly, they should. He's an honorable bastard.

I chuckle at his realization regarding our circle of friends. Glancing at the picture on my desk of us at Ash's engagement party makes me smile. We have a tight inner circle that expanded to include Cole, Darcy, and Matt. I admit they not only lower the median age, they're excellent additions to the group. Our group. The Decker Connection.

"Probably a good idea, but we can't let just anyone in. Not everyone can be privy to your girls' nights." I enjoy teasing Julian about his status with the girls in the group.

Jules doubles over in laughter. "You're just jealous that the girls like me best." Everyone likes him best, so I'm used to it.

"Go get the party started. I'll be down shortly." Hopefully, my dismissal will allow me a few minutes of peace before I have to drain my social battery.

"I'll have a cold beer waiting for you. I'm buying." He gets up to leave and makes it to the door when I realize what he said.

"How are you buying when it's my suite, you jackass!" I yell at him as he leaves my office.

His laughter drifts down the hall as he calls back, "Whoops! Guess it's on you then, brother!"

———

I take a deep breath and put on my public smile before I enter the owner's suite to meet Mr. Franklin. I can hear the laughter in the hallway, and my smile grows from forced to genuine. Ashleigh said this was the right move, and once again, she proves to me she knows best. I'm so damn proud of my little sister. She's amazing.

I open the door and find the suite filled to the brim with people. The Franklins must have invited everyone they know. Children are running around, and everyone seems to be having a good time. A few people are even seated watching the game. I see an older, dark-skinned man standing back, taking it all in. He's got this stiff posture like he's always in charge, but this suite is pure chaos, and he seems a little uncomfortable. It's something we have in common. He has his arm around a stunning, older, white woman with beautiful silver hair. I approach him and extend my hand.

"Mr. Franklin?"

He takes my hand. "Yes sir, that's me," he responds with a smile and a tilt of his head.

"Hi. I'm Alexander Decker, General Manager of the Reapers. I'm so glad you could make it tonight."

"Me too. It was quite a surprise, but we've had a good time so far. Thanks for having us. This is my wife, Carol."

"It's a pleasure to meet you, Mrs. Franklin. I'm so glad you're enjoying the Reaper hospitality. It was the least we could do. I also want to apologize for the behavior of one of our ex-players. I'm embarrassed and ashamed that he represented our team and my family. I hope he didn't cause you any harm."

"I appreciate your apology, young man, but I'm not the one he hit. That would be Dani."

I scan the suite and don't see any other men. Upon further inspection, it looks like the suite is filled with our players' wives, girlfriends, and kids. "Was Danny not able to come tonight?"

"Dani's watching the game with my grandson, Tyler. He loves the Reapers and playing baseball. I'll never be able to bring him to a game and sit in the cheap seats again after today. He's being spoiled rotten by your charming sister."

"I'm glad we could do it. I'll make sure Ashleigh gives you my assistant's number so you can bring Tyler anytime. Excuse me while I make my apologies to Danny. It was nice to meet you, Mr. Franklin. Mrs. Franklin."

He shakes my hand. "You're an impressive man, Alexander. You run a top-tier team. I appreciate you held this athlete accountable. I don't want Tyler looking up to men like him."

"Thank you, sir. I agree, if athletes are going to be role models, they need to earn it."

I give them a slight nod of my head and make my way down to the front of the suite. The padded seats are open to the stadium, so you can still get the game's sights, sounds, and smells but still have climate control and private restrooms. It's the best of both worlds. Although, I cherish the rare occasion when I can catch a game sitting in the outfield with the fans. Mr. Franklin mentioned the cheap seats, and I admit, they're my favorites.

Two little boys are leaning against the rail, watching the field. "That's my dad down there," Archie Samuels says, pointing to his dad, Joey Samuels, our catcher, at bat.

The little boy I don't recognize and assume is Tyler, appears fascinated with the game.

"Do you think he'll sign my ball?"

"Sure," Archie says with a shrug, not fully understanding why someone would want his dad's signature.

"Mom, look, it's Matt's turn up to bat! That's Ashleigh and Darcy's friend. We met him, and he signed my ball," Tyler says, with so much animation that he doesn't even take a pause.

The stunning woman he addresses as mom practically takes my breath away. Her unruly, caramel-colored curls frame her face, and her expressive eyes are filled with unfettered joy. Her smile blooms when she takes in his excitement.

The boy pushes the ball toward me, and I'm not sure what he

wants me to do with it. "Look! See my ball! Matt and some other players signed it." I take the ball from him and carefully inspect his treasure. It has several Reaper signatures, most of whom have wives and kids in the suite today. Ashleigh must have had him in the middle of the Reaper family. That's what this sport should be about—family fun.

"You'll need to keep that ball safe. It'll be worth a lot someday." I grin, hand him his ball, and scan the suite again, looking for Danny and Ashleigh. "Is your dad here somewhere?"

"I don't have a dad," the boy responds matter-of-factly.

I'm a little confused. The person Pauly assaulted was Danny Franklin. If it wasn't the man I already met, and it wasn't the boy's father, then who was the victim?

"I'm sorry. I asked the wrong question. I was looking for Danny Franklin."

The gorgeous woman with the incredible smile turns in her seat and gives me her full attention.

"I'm Dani Franklin. Happens all the time." She laughs at my faux pas.

I'm shaken to my core. The person Pauly assaulted is a woman? I'm even more angry than I was before. I never asked Jack the details of the assault because I was focused on getting Pauly Jackson off my team. Now I take in the incredible woman beside me and see a faint bruise on her cheek. That bastard hit a woman! What else did he do to her? I need to step away and gather myself, but I can't be rude. I school my expression and give her my Reaper's owner smile.

She watches me take her in, detail by detail, and her ringless left hand covers her cheek. Her smile fades, and the light literally dims around me.

"I'm sorry. I didn't know. Are you okay? Did he, um, hurt you?" I'm grinding my molars to keep my cool. Of course, he hurt her, dumbass. Look at her beautiful face. Her glowing skin, marred only by a hidden bruise concealed by makeup, reveals the evidence of her injuries.

She smiles at me and stands. Her hand reaches for mine, and she gives it a gentle squeeze. I'm frozen in shock. Is she comforting me? "No, not really. It mostly scared Tyler. I'll be fine. He was drunk and had obviously never heard the word no before." She laughs. Fucking laughs. Is she for real? A man struck her, and she can laugh about it.

My hands go to my hair as I try to wrap my mind around this. I'm immediately aware of our broken connection when my hand released hers. "I'm sorry. How are you able to laugh about this?" I don't mean to sound harsh, but her behavior has me so confused. Who is this woman and why is she turning me upside down?

She does this little shrug thing, and her eyes, all bright and amber, meet mine. Her long lashes make her eyes look even more exotic. "I'll be fine, I promise. I'm an Aries. I see everything half-full. I mean, he caught me off guard, that's all. But with every storm cloud, there comes a rainbow, right?"

"I'm sorry, what?"

"If I hadn't had that unfortunate incident, I wouldn't be here watching my son have the best day of his life. So with every storm cloud comes a rainbow. Don't you see it?"

"Um, I guess?" Honestly, I have no idea what she's talking about. I watch her hair bounce around her face, adding to her animated expression. I want to run my hands through her curls to see if they're as soft and springy as they look. Her golden-brown eyes twinkle with happiness. She's captivating.

"Oh, I see you met Dani," Ashleigh says as she approaches us. "Isn't Tyler adorable?"

I glance toward the boy who's watching the game. "Absolutely." And he is. "Ash, can I talk to you for a minute? Dani, I'll be right back. Can I get you or Tyler anything?"

It's like he has super hearing because over the crowd's roar and the chatter in the suite, from ten feet away, he yells, "Mom, can I have another Capri Sun, please?"

"Sure." She looks at me. "That is, if you don't mind?"

"No problem. Can I get you anything?" An ice pack? Medical attention? Pauly's head on a platter?

She holds up her half-empty water bottle. "No thanks. I'm good. It's still half-full."

I have no idea how she sees life that way.

Ashleigh and I walk out of the suite and I pull her into a supply closet down the hall. I don't have time to go back to my office. My smile is a long-forgotten memory, and my blood's boiling.

"When were you going to tell me he hit a gorgeous woman!?" I whisper shout at Ash through gritted teeth.

"Calm down, will you? She's fantastic, isn't she? And you said gorgeous. Hmmm." Ashleigh is smiling like Dani. What's up with these women?

"I can't calm down. What the hell happened?" I'm regretting this supply closet because I need room to pace. I'm like a caged lion, and I don't like it.

"It's not my story to tell. It's Dani's. But I got a copy of the video if you want to see it. Some guy was filming the crowd and captured it."

"There's a fucking video?!" I try to keep my voice down, but I'm furious and can barely contain my rage. My pulse is hammering away like I just finished ten miles on the treadmill.

The door to the closet opens, and Julian's head pops in. "Family meeting, and I wasn't invited?" My brother will understand my frustration. "Did you know he hit a woman?" I try to keep my voice down, and it becomes more of a growl.

"No. Oh shit. Is she okay?" Julian's smile is gone, and I finally have an ally in my anger. Finally. Someone that understands.

Ashleigh smiles at us and puts a hand on each of our faces. Her hand is a calming reminder to keep my cool. "Whoever says chivalry is dead has never met the Decker brothers. I love you guys, but once you spend some time with her, you'll realize she's fine. Now, I need you both to go in there and charm the pants off of her."

Jules wiggles his eyebrows, and she playfully pops his face. "Figuratively, not literally. Her father, the retired Colonel, will have you in front of a firing squad if you try anything."

"And why is our suite full of WAGs?" Not that I mind, but it's unusual to have the wives and girlfriends in the suite.

"When we toured, I was introducing them and Darcy to everyone, and it occurred to me that if we wanted to show them our family values, we should share the Reapers' family with them too."

"Brilliant, Ash," Jules comments. He seems to be more accepting of this than I am. I'm still not appeased.

"Send me the video," I order as I storm out of the closet and head to my office.

Ashleigh and Julian have this under control for now.

CHAPTER FOUR

DANI

———

The suite attendant approaches us and offers Tyler a Capri Sun, and I look around for Ashleigh and the mystery man who left with her.

Archie's mom, Casey, sits down beside me and offers me her nachos as we watch our boys discussing the game.

"Isn't this the sweet life?" She laughs at herself. "Suite life? Get it?"

Jenny's next to me and reaches across to offer her a high-five. "Good one. I love homophones."

"Mom, what's a homophone?" Tyler asks. I swear, that kid has supersonic hearing. I thought he was watching the game and talking to Archie.

"It's a word that sounds like another word, but it's spelled differently, and it has a different meaning."

"Huh? Never mind." Tyler goes back to watching the game with Archie, peppering him with questions too. Tyler is at that stage where he questions everything. Constantly. He's so curious, taking everything in around him. I feel sorry for his teacher when school starts in a few weeks.

"I take it you don't watch every game from the suites?" I try to get the conversation back on track.

"Are you kidding? No, this is a treat. We usually sit in the family section closer to the field or the mother's room downstairs where we can take fussy kids or nurse. We're beyond blessed Joey got traded to the Reapers two years ago. They take care of their players and families."

"Where were you before Charlotte?"

"Chicago. It was fun, but the winters were brutal. I'm from Alabama, so I'm used to snow as a novelty, not a seasonal thing."

"I admit, I'm partial to the mild winters too. Snow should be measured in inches instead of feet." I've lived all over the world and never found a place that felt like home until we settled here in Charlotte. Moving from Washington, DC to here two years ago was quite the culture shock, but in a good way.

"So, Darcy, tell me about you and Matt. Have you been together for a long time?" I ask.

She laughs. "Well, it's complicated. Childhood crush on my brother's best friend that came to fruition recently. A few days ago." She blows out a breath. "Has it only been a few days?" she says to herself. She shakes her head, and her dark locks fan around her head. She tucks her hair behind her ear and smiles. "Well, a few days ago, I had the best day of my life, and we came to Charlotte. It's been a whirlwind ever since."

"Yeah, it was crazy he got called up so quickly," Casey says. "Lucky you getting to skip those minor league years." She gives Darcy a warm smile.

"I guess," she responds with a shrug.

"That is a lot in a short period of time," I add. "Try to enjoy the moments, even in the chaos." I met Darcy today with Ashleigh, and she's a doll.

"Why was he called up so quickly?" Jenny asks.

Darcy bites her lip and sneaks a quick glance at me. I know.

I'm the reason Darcy and Matt are here. I give her a sincere smile and reach over Casey to grab her hand. "Hey, I'm so happy there was a good outcome. It wasn't that big of a deal. Look at all the good things that came from it. I wouldn't undo it if I could."

Ashleigh joins us and sits behind Darcy. Her hands go to Darcy's shoulders, and she gives a little squeeze. "I'm so sorry for the how, but I'm with Dani. Blessings abound."

Casey's face lights up, and she gets wide-eyed when it clicks. I'm sure she knows about the incident, but had no idea it was me. "Wow. Are you okay?" Her concern makes my smile dim a little. I hate people fretting and worrying about me. The last thing I ever want from people is pity.

"Yeah, I'm fine. Really." I look over to Tyler and Archie as they chat and watch the game, Archie occasionally pointing to something on the field. "Looks like Tyler's made a new friend."

Casey laughs. "I need Tyler at every game. Archie's seven-year-old energy usually starts rearing its head about now, and tonight, he's been a gem."

I laugh because I know exactly what she means.

"Dani, can I get you anything?" Ashleigh asks. I look around the suite again for the man she left with.

He was incredibly handsome with his chiseled jaw and perfect nose. I couldn't take my eyes off his luscious lips, which looked soft and kissable. His styled, wavy, dark blonde hair was perfect, but I wanted to run my hands through it and mess it up a little. He did that himself when he let go of my hand, and it was hot. The rumpled look is sexy, and I wouldn't mind seeing more of it.

He dressed impeccably, especially for a baseball game. His look was more boardroom than ballpark, and he had an aura of someone used to being in control. His smile was forced but not fake, like he didn't do it often, and his cologne was so intoxicating that I'm convinced it was pure pheromones. I've never had such a strong, immediate, physical reaction to anyone, and I'm curious to talk to him again.

"Lose something?" Casey asks.

"I'm sorry?" Did I miss part of the conversation?

"You seem to be looking for someone?" Casey questions. She's giving me a *I know but won't out you* look. Casey just moved up the friend list with that gesture.

I blush, caught in the act.

Jenny, the best friend ever, catches on to my secret. She wiggles her eyebrows at me and gives me a not-so-subtle wink.

"Hey Ashleigh, who was that dreamy guy you left with? He didn't introduce himself," Jenny asks. I'm going to kill her for outing me.

Ashleigh laughs. "Dreamy? Not quite. I apologize for his lack of manners. I can assure you he was raised with them. He should have introduced himself, but I think he was caught off guard." I knew the moment it happened because his mood shifted. It was when he realized I was the "victim" of the assault. "That was my brother, Alexander. He's the General Manager for the Reapers."

Casey giggles too. "Girl, I know he's your brother, and I'm happily married, but I think Jenny's right. You can't deny he's dreamy. I mean, he's been on *People Magazine's* hottest bachelor list for several years now. Between him and Chance Fuller, I don't know which one has more appearances on there." Her attention sweeps over to the boys. "Archie, do not throw popcorn at people." He gives her a *sorry, but mostly sorry I got caught* look and smiles at her. He blows her a kiss, and I laugh. That kid's a charmer.

At Archie's reprimand, Tyler approaches me, sits on my lap, and wraps his arms around me. He doesn't want to get in trouble by association. "Having fun, tiger?"

"Yeah. But I want to go closer to the game," he whines.

"You know what," Ashleigh starts. "I bet you and your grandfather would like seats closer to the action and away from all the girls, am I right?"

Tyler shakes his head enthusiastically. "Yeah."

"Well, I know just the place."

"Wow, you know all the good stuff, Ms. Ashleigh," Tyler says. He looks at her with a sense of wonder.

"Well, I kinda grew up here." Tyler gets up from my lap so he can focus his full attention on Ashleigh.

"You lived at the ballpark?" Archie asks in awe. His eyes grow wide, thinking of the possibilities of living here. I think Ashleigh has a fan club.

"Not exactly, but my dad kinda owns the place, so he worked here, and I got to hang out all the time." She gives them a small shrug, like it's no big deal.

Both boys give Ashleigh their undivided attention. "Wow. That's so cool. Did you get to eat hot dogs all the time?" Tyler asks.

"Yep." She texts someone, and her phone buzzes with a response. She smiles at whatever the message is. "How about we go check out those closer seats? My friend Scoville is waiting for us. Dani, do you mind?"

"Not a bit. Dad would probably be grateful."

"Can Archie come too?" Tyler asks.

Ashleigh looks to Casey, seeking permission. "Please and thank you," Casey says.

"Come on, boys. We'll be back before the game ends." She gives me a wicked smile. "And Xander has been on the list once more than Chance and my brother Julian more than both. Trust me, Julian brings it up every year." She holds out a hand for each boy, and they each take one. No complaints that they're too old to hold hands this time. Tyler grips his prized autographed ball in his other hand. "Come on, Darcy, let's get you closer to Matt."

She gives us a wink and heads toward my dad. I can't hear the conversation, but see Dad's face light up. He and Mom leave the suite with Ashleigh, Darcy, and two very excited boys.

As I watch them leave, another extremely handsome man watches me from the bar. He has the same dark blonde hair as Alexander, but his shoulders aren't as broad, and his smile looks more natural. He raises his beer to me and gives a wink. I twist around in my seat and slide down a little, trying to hide.

"What?" Jenny asks, noticing my behavior.

"Nothing. Let's watch the game," I say in a hushed tone. You would have thought that Casey and Jenny thought I said, "Turn around and stare" because that's what they both do. Casey turns back around and gives me a light elbow in the ribs, and Jenny makes noises that are somewhere between a purr and a moan.

Casey stage whispers, "And that would be the other Decker brother, Julian. Always has some actress or model on his arm, but he's the nicest guy I've ever met. The total opposite of Alexander's brooding, Julian is charming as hell. I didn't know he was in town." She stops and gives a brief pause. "Their family is tight, so I'm not surprised they're all here to work through this PR nightmare." She realizes what she said and touches my knee. "Sorry, I didn't mean that you're a nightmare. They have high expectations, and Pauly left them a mess to clean up in the media and with the fans." Casey panics, embarrassed by what she said.

"No, it's okay. I get it." I put my hand on top of hers. Casey has been nothing but friendly and kind. She cares for her Reaper family, too. Who knew the behavior of one person would affect this many people? "It's not their fault, but they're dealing with the unfortunate fallout. I wish I could help."

How can I help Alexander Decker? Many ideas come to mind, but most aren't for sharing. No. I don't think I want to share him at all.

CHAPTER
FIVE

ALEXANDER

———

For the last hour, I've watched the video on a loop of this motherfucker hitting her, and every time I notice another detail.

There's too much crowd noise to hear what's said, but I can guess. Her body language speaks volumes.

The first few times I hit play, I watched the drunk motherfucker come on to her. She politely says no several times, but he ignores her. He finally starts to walk away, and then she says something to him. He spins around and hits her across the face. The entire video is less than a minute.

After each view, I want to do something different to him. Instead, I focus on what I can do. I can make sure he never plays ball again. Anywhere. That's not nearly enough punishment, but it's something I can make happen. A quick email to the Commissioner with this video should do it. I send a draft for Jack to review and tell him to send it first thing in the morning.

I watch the video again. And again. I'll have to trust the

justice system to take care of the rest. I hit pause and send another text to Jack, telling him to contact the top law firms in the city and ask them to refuse to represent Pauly, regardless of how much money he's willing to pay. I try not to throw around the Decker name for favors, but this is one time when I'm making an exception. Sorry motherfucker, but I hope your smug smile and entitlement are attractive to your cellmate, and he doesn't believe in the *no means no* rule either.

After the tenth view or so, my attention to detail shifts. I focus on her. Dani Franklin. She's not some nameless victim. No. She's strong, not just physically, but a woman who can stand up for herself. When she says no to him, there's no flirty smile sending a mixed signal. Nothing to be confused about. She's firm. Serious. It's obvious her no means no.

She deflects his advances without being aggressive. She turns her body and moves from sitting at a high-top table to standing, so she has more choice in movement. Aware. The chair becomes a barrier between her and him. Smart. All great self-defense moves. He says something and takes half a step back. Then she seems to get the last word, and a small smile of satisfaction graces her luscious lips. I bet it was something sassy. She seems sassy. Full of sunshine and fire.

She never loses focus on her attacker until she does. There's a split second where Tyler barely enters the frame, taking her attention from Pauly, and she shifts her attention to her son. Her look turns from satisfaction to panic in a millisecond. She doesn't want Tyler near this situation and steps toward him, another defensive move. Mama Bear is protecting her cub.

That's when the motherfucker strikes. She's caught off guard. He hits her across her left cheek with a cheap shot. She shifts slightly to deflect the blow, but there's still enough force to knock her off balance, and she falls to the ground.

The video then shifts from her to him, a smug smile on his face. You don't have to be a lip-reading expert to see him call her a bitch. The person who took the video gets jostled around, and it ends a few seconds later.

I watch the video over and over, and each time, I'm more intrigued and captivated by this woman. The curve of her neck. The focus of her amber eyes. Her delicate fingers as they carefully remove his hand from her thigh. Her devotion toward her son.

My guilt weighs heavier each time I watch. I punish myself and watch it one more time. Then another. I played a part in this. I paid him millions to play a game and feed into this motherfucker's entitlement. How many other women did he accost? I'm willing to bet she wasn't his first.

I fire off a text to Jack and Jessica requiring sexual harassment training for everyone immediately, and request to review the employment contracts to make sure they have zero tolerance for this behavior. As much as I hate contracts, I'll use them to my advantage when I can.

I think about Ashleigh. What if someone like Pauly hit on her? Could she defend herself? I send another message to Jack and Jessica asking for a self-defense course for all female Reaper personnel, the WAGS, and their friends. Immediately.

I feel a little better after sending those texts. Jack confirms he'll make it happen. Then he asks if I'm okay. I send him the video as my response. He's been radio silent ever since. He knows me well. I'm not fucking okay. Far from it.

I've taken action and done what I can control in this out-of-control situation. I jot down a few other items to follow up on tomorrow, making a note to ask how we can sponsor women's shelters for domestic violence and offer these self-defense classes monthly to the community. Women should be safe from motherfuckers like Pauly Jackson, and I will do my part in making that happen. I'm disgusted that men behave this way and, worse yet, get away with it.

I pull up the internal coverage of the game. We have cameras everywhere. It's the bottom of the fifth, and the Reapers are up by two. The promotions team is doing a between-innings activity on the field near the first base line involving Scoville and some kids. The camera pans to Ashleigh and Darcy, laughing with Tyler's grandparents. I look back at the kids, realizing they are Archie and Tyler. They're trying to pop a balloon tied to the mascot's foot. I don't see Dani. I text Ash and watch as she pulls her phone from her pocket.

> Where's Dani?

ASH

> Suite. Boys wanted to be closer to the action.

> I guess you can't get any closer. Is she okay? You left her by herself?

> She's fine. She's not alone. She's with her friend Jenny and Casey Samuels. Besides, Jules is there.

> Great.

I'm glad she met Casey Samuels tonight. Casey is a lovely woman, a devoted wife, and an adoring mother. I think she's a book editor or something. Her relationship with Joey seems good. They've been together for years, and despite the demanding travel schedule, they appear to be a solid family. Archie's a great kid, and Joey is an involved father, helping coach his little league team when he can.

But Jules? The thought of the charming bastard in the same suite with Dani makes me stop my self-torture, turn off the video, and head back downstairs.

When I get closer to the suite, I regret how I acted toward her. I practically interrogated her and left. I didn't even notice she was there with a friend. Fuck. I was so rude, but knew I had to get out of there before I lost my temper. She'll think this industry is full of assholes like Pauly Jackson. That's no excuse for my unacceptable behavior, though. I guess I need classes on how to treat women too.

Miss glass-half-full, overflowing with sunshine, sass, and love, Dani Franklin. She's stunning and exciting and someone I need to apologize to. Again.

CHAPTER
SIX

DANI

———

I laugh so hard I'm crying. Tyler and Archie are on the Jumbotron playing a game with an oversized pepper mascot while Dad shouts pointers to him. He still can't stand to lose even years after his military retirement. My heart's full as I watch my parents and Tyler have such a carefree, fun time. Yeah, the assault sucked, but I'm mostly mad he got the better of me. I guess my dad's relentless fight to win didn't fall far from the tree.

I'm having a blast too. The ball game, the food, the people. Today's absolutely perfect.

"Is it bad if I say thank you for getting assaulted?" Jenny asks. She knocks against me, shoulder to shoulder. "I mean, I hate he hurt you, but thank you for bringing me on this apology tour."

"You know I couldn't do this without you, right? Soul sisters." I hold my hand out with my pinky extended. She hooks her finger with mine.

"Soul sisters," she repeats. "Hey, where did Casey go?"

"She's talking to some of the other spouses." I look behind us and see her with Julian Decker. Whatever they're talking about appears to be more serious than casual acquaintances. Casey's talking, and Julian is typing on his phone, practically taking notes. There's so much of this life I don't understand.

"I like her," Jenny says.

"Yeah, me too." I take a sip of my beer. I rarely drink, but Jenny convinced me having a beer at a baseball game is practically a requirement. This is my second. I don't remember the words of "Take Me Out to the Ballgame" mentioning a cold one, but when in Rome and all. It's cold and tastes pretty good on this warm evening, so it works.

I focus on the game and watch Matt catch a pop-up foul ball. "Good catch, Matt!" I yell from my seat. Knowing a player makes this game even more enjoyable, even if I just met him.

"He's playing a good game, isn't he?" I startle at the deep, baritone voice behind me and jump, sloshing my beer in my lap. "Sorry, hold on. Let me get you some napkins." I look over my shoulder to see the backside of Alexander Decker go up the four steps and ask the bartender for a towel. I admire the backside, forgetting about my beer-soaked lap.

He rushes back with a clean bar towel in his hand. "Here, I'm sorry." He starts to blot the spill, notices it's between my legs, and seems to think better of it. His hand hovers for a second above the scene of the crime. He hands the towel to me with an embarrassed grin. He appears flustered, which I'd bet is an unfamiliar feeling for him.

I take the towel from him, and as our hands brush, I swear I feel a spark. Maybe it's static electricity or what happens when a hot guy almost pats my crotch, but the tingle practically runs up my arm. I hope I'm not having a heart attack.

I blot at my white shorts, realizing with the wet material, I now have see-through shorts, and my pink strawberry panties are on full display. Jenny looks over, her eyes getting bigger when she sees my dilemma.

"Maybe if you untuck your shirt, it'll cover it up?" she whispers.

Alexander Decker glances at my crotch, a slight blush filling his cheeks.

"Ms. Franklin, I'm so sorry. I can't apologize enough." He runs his hand down his face in frustration. He types something on his phone and turns his attention back to me, concern filling his face.

"It's okay, really. It's my fault. When I'm focused on something, I can really focus. I got jumpy. Please, no apology necessary. They'll dry." I stop blotting at the wetness and drape the towel over my lap. I really should pay more attention to my surroundings. With Tyler under the watchful eye of my parents, I allowed myself to relax and let my guard down. Shame on me. You'd think I'd learned my lesson last week.

He points to the seat next to me. "May I?"

"Of course. It's your suite." His formality throws me. Ashleigh is polite but not nearly this formal. "You're so different from Ashleigh. Are you sure you're related?" I blurt out and slap my hand over my mouth. I probably shouldn't have drunk that beer because it appears my filter's loose.

His deep chuckle resonates around me. "Very sure." He looks at his phone and puts it face down on his muscular thigh. His tailored black dress pants hug his legs, leaving little to my imagination. "In what ways are you referring?"

Ugh. "Well, um, she seems." I'm struggling because I've spent less than five minutes with this man, and I'm already making assessments and assumptions. What if I'm wrong? I struggle to find something to say.

"Hi! I'm Jenny, Dani's very single best friend. I don't think we've met." Jenny stretches her hand across my chest, and Alexander reaches to shake her hand. The back of his hand barely brushes my breast, and I gasp. He quickly withdraws his hand, realizing what he touched, adding to his blush.

"Again, I apologize. I didn't properly introduce myself. I'm Alexander Decker." He makes eye contact with Jenny, then directs his attention to me. "And I'm usually not this rude. I promise I know more words than I'm sorry."

Another male laugh breaks into the conversation. Hands grip Alexander's shoulders and give him a shake. "He knows lots of other words, and if you got an apology out of him, you must be extra special because those are rare words in his vocabulary. I can't ever get one out of him."

Alexander glares at his brother. "Because you never deserve them," he mumbles under his breath.

A bartender appears behind Julian and offers him a tray of beers. "I'm Julian Decker. Alexander's younger and much more fun brother. We're glad you lovely ladies could join us today. It's made the evening much more interesting." He hands Jenny and me a fresh beer, takes my cup that was a spill hazard, gives one to Alexander, and takes one for himself.

Unlike my half-spilled draft beer, these beers are in bottles, so there's less chance of another accident. I examine the label and notice it has the Reapers logo, and I hesitate to drink it. I'm not a fan of spice. Julian seems to notice my hesitation. "It's our own brand. It's a pale blonde, but you, my lovely, could inspire me to have them come up with a smooth caramel blend." He gives me a wink and a smile.

"Julian," Alexander growls. "Enough."

"Lighten up, Xan. I meant it as the highest compliment. Beautiful women have always been an inspiration. Throughout history, men have fought wars, created art, and launched expeditions for beautiful women. I'm just saying Dani is an inspiration. Don't you agree?"

Alexander rubs his large hand across his forehead like he's trying to rub away a headache.

"Are you okay?" I lean over to look up at his face.

"I'm sorry, my brother can be a bit much. Most people can only take him in small doses." Alexander turns in his seat and gives Julian a look that communicates a message. His response? He laughs.

"Lighten up, Xander. We're at a baseball game. We're winning, by the way. The seats are full. The weather's perfect." He sweeps his arm around, pointing to everything around us. "The Reapers' WAGs are having a great time, and we're in the company of these charming ladies. How can it get any better?"

"You back in New York?" Alexander responds.

We all laugh. This guy's funny, in an under his breath kind of way. I sip the beer and enjoy the light, cold liquid as it runs down my throat, instantly cooling me off. I like this beer even more than the one I spilled.

The banter between these two is fun, even if it's a little intense. I want to help Alexander out of this conversation.

"First, please don't apologize to me anymore. About anything. We're having a great time." I look at Jenny and find Tyler and my parents in the crowd. "All of us. So thank you. Thank you for tonight. No apology needed, but certainly accepted."

I get a small smile from Alexander and a nod of acknowledgment.

"Hey Jenny, want to come with me to see the clubhouse?" Julian's grin and twinkle in his eye make me uncertain if he's serious.

"Absolutely!" Jenny hops ups, abandons her beer in the drink holder, and scoots in front of me and Alexander to Julian's extended hand.

"Do. Not." Alexander starts.

"You know I gotta, Xan. Matt needs a proper Reaper's welcome, and Tripp pitched a near-perfect game. I need them to know their agent is proud of them." His laugh fills the suite as he leads my best friend away. Her smile is so bright she could light up an entire neighborhood.

"Don't get caught!" I yell as they depart. I look at Alexander, and he's not joining in my laughter. "What?"

"Julian never needs encouragement." He takes another drink from his beer and scans the stands. A king surveying his kingdom.

"I'm definitely not a king," he says.

"What?" Oh no, did I say that out loud?

"I'm far from royalty." He continues to watch the game. His focus anywhere but here.

"I didn't mean anything by it. You must be proud of everything. It sure seems like a lot of moving parts." It's an impressive organization. I can't imagine what it takes to keep it running.

I get a gentle nod. Okay then. I'll try again.

I lean in close, his intoxicating scent nearly overwhelming my brain to think of something, anything, to say. "So, which player's your favorite? I promise not to tell."

He slowly turns and looks at me, seemingly surprised by my question. Thousands of people may surround us, but I feel like we're in our own private bubble. His eyes scan my face, studying every detail, and I feel a little self-conscious under his intense scrutiny. I nervously tuck my hair behind my ear, and he stares at my cheek. Damn. The bruise is fading, and I covered it with makeup, but it's still noticeable, and he seems to zero in on it. Again. He reaches for my face and catches himself, dropping his hand to the armrest between us.

"I know who my least favorite player is. Or should I say ex-player? I've requested he never play ball again, at least not in the MLB. It makes me sick to think about someone hurting you."

I untuck my hair in a feeble attempt to hide my cheek. "It's in the past. I'm fine. Really. I wish everyone would quit making a fuss about it."

"How can you act like it's no big deal?" His tone changes, showing a bit of anger or irritation.

"Because there's no sense living in the past. Live and let live. I wasn't seriously hurt, there were no lingering side effects, and I signed up for a Krav Maga course as a result. It should be fun." I have a lilt in my voice, signaling I'm really fine with the class. I need to get more exercise, anyway. See, a rainbow from the storm.

"Learning self-defense won't be fun because it's become necessary," he practically growls, the tension just below the surface.

"No, it's unnecessary, but my dad insisted. I've learned how to pick my battles with him, and this isn't one I'm willing to fight. Growing up like I did, I've learned to protect myself."

His frown deepens as he looks me over head to toe, his eyes lingering on the towel draped over my wet lap. "What, exactly, was in your past that would require you to know self-defense?" Uncertainty fills his eyes. He looks like he is about to go all caveman. I know the look.

I sigh. "Would you dial it down, please?" His brow furrows, like he doesn't understand what I'm referring to. I rub my thumb between his brows, smoothing the lines. My contact with him breaks his scowl, and he gives me a half-smirk.

"Self-defense?" He's persistent, that's for sure.

I sip my liquid courage and turn my attention to the field. I look toward where I think Tyler is sitting. The only way to get him to move on is to tell him and let the chips fall where they may. With an audible exhale, I start. "We moved around a lot because my dad was in the military." I glance at him, and his eyes are fixed on me. I look away. "It's hard sometimes, picking up and moving across the world. It's hard to make friends, real friends. Kids tend to run in packs. The officers' sons can be real assholes."

I feel him tense beside me, and when I steal a glance, his scowl is back. I smile at him and rub my finger between those gorgeous ocean-blue eyes that are dark and stormy. His smirk doesn't return. I drop my hand on my lap. I overstepped and touched him without consent. Am I just as bad as those assholes?

"Did?" His intense gaze practically melts me into a puddle of goo. I'm not sure my shorts will dry anytime soon at this rate, and not from the beer spill. "Did someone," he pauses. "Hurt you?" he whispers.

I stare into his eyes, intent on making him understand.

With more conviction than I feel, I say, "No."

His shoulders relax as he gives me a slight nod. He takes a drink from his bottle, his thumb scraping at the label, shredding it.

I give him my best smile. "It wasn't easy. I hate conflict and hierarchy and most things with structure. So growing up in the military, well, you can see how that wasn't ideal. I mean, I love people and wish everyone could be kind to one another. And it was tough being biracial, too. I didn't fit into any category, so I kept to myself. Loners become vulnerable in the pack world, so I learned how to fight back. I hate it, but it is what it is." I shrug my shoulders and take another sip of my almost empty beer. Despite my urge to set it down, I hold on like it's a security blanket. This bottle is doing its duty by keeping my hands occupied. Otherwise, I'd be reaching over to wipe those deep worry lines away from his face. I feel horrible that I'm causing him distress.

"Have you had to defend yourself often?" He's not back to neutral yet, because I can still feel the tension roll off of him.

"Could I get a water?" Between the look in his eyes and the determined set of his chiseled jaw, I can tell he's a protector. Hopefully, he'll offer to get it himself and break this standoff.

He types something on his phone, and the bartender appears at his shoulder before I can count to five. The bartender reaches for my empty beer bottle, and I exchange it for the water bottle, giving him a smile of thanks. Alexander reaches over and opens it for me. His intensity doesn't stop. Is he always this way?

I take a long drink and a deep breath, pulling myself together. I'm a lightweight with alcohol and shouldn't have had that last beer.

A young guy appears at his side and hands him a Reapers

bag from the team store. They don't say anything to each other, but the guy gives me a little wink. Alexander peeks in the bag and hands it to me.

So he texts and things just happen. Amazing.

"What's this?"

"I know this won't look as good on you as your shorts, but I wanted you to be comfortable. I'm sorry..."

I interrupt him. "Stop saying you're sorry. And this is totally unnecessary. I'm fine. Things happen. Live and let live."

His scowl tells me he doesn't agree. "There's a restroom at the back of the suite where you can change."

His change in tone lets me know this conversation is over, so I take the bag and put on the Reapers track pants. With luck, this will put an end to the argument we both want, but neither has started. The pants are lightweight and luxurious and honestly better than my see through shorts. I'll give him this, he seems to make decent decisions.

As I go back to my seat, the crowd erupts, and I hear the announcer saying something about a Reapers' grand slam. I look at the field, too distracted to focus on anything down there. The crowd is on their feet, cheering for the players as they round the bases. When I realize Matt hit the home run, I can't keep the smile from my face. He's greeted at home plate by the entire team and lost in his teammates' embrace. Way to go, Matt!

"He seems like a great guy," I say as I sit down next to Alexander. "Darcy must be going crazy."

"Yeah, he's had a pretty good week. He's a solid ballplayer, and Ash thinks the world of him," Alexander says. He scans me from head to toe, and his scowl lessens.

"Ashleigh's a total sweetheart."

He nods, his tension releasing a little more. He gives an involuntary smile when he thinks about his sister.

"And Cole plays for the Liberties?"

"He does." Alexander pauses. "He makes her happy. I've

enjoyed having her home this week. Might have to reconsider my thoughts on making him a Reaper."

She's here because of this crisis. Because of me. A blessing for Alexander, but I bet Cole is missing her. "Was it his dream to be a Liberty?"

"Nope." He pops his p. There's a story behind that one-word sentence. Because of my need for him to relax, I decide to let this discussion go. Unfortunately, he isn't as courteous.

"So, have you had to defend yourself often?" Shit. We're back to this. My exasperated sigh doesn't go unnoticed.

"I'm sorry," he says. His voice wraps over me, seeping down to my bones. "I'm making you uncomfortable. I'll leave you to enjoy the game."

He goes to leave, and my hand instinctively touches his thigh, pushing him back down. My hand connects with the solid muscle and he pauses. Even though I couldn't physically stop him from leaving, he understands my intention and stops mid-stand in some awkward squat. The control he has over his body is intriguing.

"Please don't go." He lowers himself back to his seat and looks at my hand. I move it so quickly you would think I touched a hot iron. "You promised to stop apologizing to me. So stop." I say that with some frustration, either because he keeps asking the same question or because I'm really into him, I don't know.

"I'm," he starts, and I tsk at him. He lowers his head like one of my third graders when I catch them at something. I laugh at him.

"I've still got it!" I laugh louder. No silly giggles for me.

"Got what?" He gives me a curious look. He must think I'm nuts.

"My teacher's voice. It may be summer break, but I can still put a kid in their place with one look."

He looks at me with another scowl.

"You're a teacher?"

"Yep. Third grade. I love that age. Still young and impressionable, full of curiosity and wonder. Just developing the sass. And the math isn't that hard yet." I smile, thinking about my job. I hope I get a wonderful group of kids this year. Only a few more weeks before school starts. I mentally start the countdown until we report to school.

"I never had a teacher like you, that's for sure."

"No? What were your teachers like?"

"Old and mean," he says quickly.

"Oh, I seriously doubt that. But at that age, anyone over the age of sixteen is old and haggard. I'm sure my kids think the same of me. I mean, I'm a mom, so I'm automatically ancient." I'm acutely aware he's staring at me again.

"I promise you, they don't think that." We sit in comfortable silence and watch the game.

My phone vibrates after standing and singing "Take me out the Ballgame" during the seventh-inning stretch. I look at the pictures Jenny sends me and gasp. She and Julian wrapped every item in Matt's locker in Christmas paper and put an enormous bow on his nameplate. Does that wrapping paper have Santa in lewd poses?

"Something wrong?" He's alert again.

I show him the pictures, and a small smile threatens to break free.

"Where did Julian find Christmas paper in July?"

He shakes his head because he knows. "In my office closet. That's the paper I used for the team gag gifts last year. Maybe this will steer the players off the scent. They still don't know where the gifts came from, but they know for certain this prank wasn't me." He laughs genuinely, and it's the best sound I've ever heard.

"Do I want to ask? What did you get?"

"Can't say."

"Can't or won't?"

"Both."

I'm loving this banter between us, how he's showing me another side of himself. I get a feeling it's not something he shows many people. And it makes me feel very special. Maybe his grumpy, won't let it drop, over-protectiveness isn't the primary makeup of his personality. He gave gag gifts to the team and wrapped them himself. There's a fun side under the stiff business suit. I'm curious to see more of it.

Too bad this is a one-time encounter. He's a rich guy who runs in famous circles, and I'm a single mom and third-grade teacher. Nope. Not even in the same game. Not even on the same playing field.

"Oh, so he can have fun." I lean over and bump into him with my shoulder.

He gives me a magazine-worthy smile, and I see why he's one of the hottest bachelors in America. His blue eyes glimmer with mischief, and his smile is wickedly sinful.

He wiggles his eyebrows at me. "Oh, I can have fun." The innuendo hangs in the air, and unlike the thousands of other women who probably throw themselves at him, I blush. Like a damn shy schoolgirl, I blush.

He clears his throat and focuses his attention on the game. We return to watching in companionable silence. The noise in the suite is almost gone, and I notice most of the other women left, so there aren't many people in here now. I glance at my host. I know that our time is ticking away with each batter that sits down.

"I'd like to see you again," he says. His sudden statement surprises me and leaves me with mixed feelings. Sure, I'm attracted to him, but my life isn't about me anymore. Everything I do affects Tyler. I haven't dated much since he was born and won't introduce anyone to him that won't be sticking around. I'd like to spend more time with him, but it isn't realistic.

"I'm not sure I can do that..." I start. We're interrupted by boisterous laughter entering the suite. Jenny and Julian come in, not looking the least bit guilty. They sit directly behind us.

"Dani, you ought to see it. That locker room is nicer than my apartment." I'm happy Jenny is having a great time. Their entrance breaks the tension between Alexander and me.

"Clubhouse," Julian corrects. "Locker rooms are for sweaty high school boys."

"Whatever," Jenny says and leans down to me. "It was seriously nice. So are the offices. You should see the views." I'm sure they're amazing. Another reminder of our different worlds.

Alexander's phone buzzes, and he looks at the message. He goes to stand, and I don't stop him this time, even though I want to. I stand at the same time and start to thank him for the evening.

"And the Reapers win!" the announcer booms over the loudspeaker.

Tyler bursts into our circle and wraps his arms around my legs, almost knocking me sideways. Alexander reaches out and takes my elbow to steady me. His hand slides down my arm and he holds my hand.

"Mom, Mom! It was awesome. Did you see me pop the pepper's balloon? His name is Scoville. He's named after how hot peppers are, and a reaper is super hot. And then Ashleigh got us Cracker Jacks, and I want to live here like she did."

We all focus on Tyler, and I take in the smiles. Ashleigh is standing at the bar with my parents, beaming at him. Jenny and Julian smile at him like he's the cutest kid ever. Even Alexander is smiling, but instead of looking at Tyler, he's looking at me. His fingers give mine a little squeeze before he drops his hand.

"I saw it all, tiger." I run my fingers through his dark curls. His hair is unruly, like mine.

I look at Alexander. "Thank you. This was an incredible day, and I can't thank you enough."

"Anytime. I mean that." He stoops down to meet Tyler at his height.

"Tyler, would you like to come back to the stadium and practice with the team?"

"That would be awesome," he says. His eyes sparkle with excitement. "Can we, Mom?"

"We'll see," I say, with a little more attitude than I mean. While I appreciate this invitation, I don't appreciate that he invited Tyler without asking me first. If we don't make it, then I'm the bad guy.

"Tyler, let me tell you what we did," Jenny tells him conspiratorially. The tension between Alexander and me is so intense others feel it. She knows from my tone that I'm not happy. Jenny reaches for Tyler's hand, and he leaves with her and Julian, going up to where my parents are watching us.

"I'm sorry. Did I say something wrong?" Worry furrows his brow again.

"Rule number one. Don't invite a kid to something before you run it past their parent first," I snap at him, my irritation rising. Is he using Tyler to get to me? Or am I so untrusting of men that I think they will use him to get to me? I hate feeling this way. Maybe the assault impacted me more than I want to believe.

"I didn't mean any disrespect." He looks truly sorry, and his hard exterior crumbles a little. "We have open practices once a month where families come, and the kids take batting practice with the guys. I just thought he'd enjoy it, that's all. But you're right. I should have asked you first, and I apologize."

I realize I was harsher than I should have been, and guilt washes over me. He was just trying to be nice and didn't mean anything by it. Probably. There's something about him that intrigues me. He's not the grumpy man he shows the world. It hides in the way he talks with pride about his brother. His glances and brief smiles at his sister. It's there, just waiting to be set free. Because no one intentionally scowls all the time, right?

"No more apologies, remember?" I give him a little smile. "I get it. You aren't used to being told no when you make such generous offers."

"That's not," he starts, but is interrupted by Ashleigh. She puts her hand on his chest and gives him a playful push. He doesn't budge.

"Everything okay here?" She asks us, but she's looking up at Alexander.

"It's fine." I smile at her. "Thank you all for a fantastic day. You guys royally rolled out the red carpet, and I appreciate it. Tyler will be flying on cloud nine for a while. Thanks again, but I'm going to get him home and attempt to get him to sleep."

Ashleigh wraps me in a hug. "You have my number," she whispers. "I'd love to hear from you again."

As tempting as that would be, I need to remember Cinderella only got one fantasy night. This was mine. It may not have been a fancy ball, but this ballpark was just as magical. I need to get home before the magic wears off and reality settles back in.

CHAPTER
SEVEN

ALEXANDER

———

"When was the last time it was just the three of us?" Ashleigh muses. We sit around the gas fire on the balcony of my penthouse and unwind after a long day. I pulled out Ashleigh's favorite wine and Jules and I sip on my expensive Kentucky bourbon. I gaze at the view that overlooks the stadium and reflect on the events of the day.

She's right. It's rarely just the three of us these days. We have a tight group of friends who are like extended family, and someone always has one friend or another with them. Not that I mind. I would lay down my life for Trevor, Chance, and maybe even Cole, Ashleigh's fiancé. Definitely Emma, her best girlfriend. Hell, our friends, our chosen family, are pretty special. But right now, I'm glad it's just us Deckers.

"I don't know if I can remember. Maybe after Mom's funeral?" Jules responds.

"That long?" That was over a decade ago. A life-altering time for all of us. I look over at Ashleigh and notice Jules watching her, too. She looks so much like Mom when she was younger and healthy. That last year drained the life out of her. Ash was so young then. Jules and I were both in college, but Ashleigh was still in middle school. My breathing hitches thinking about it. I clear my throat and take a sip of my bourbon.

"Yeah, me too," Jules says, acknowledging the unspoken. We miss her. So damn much.

Ashleigh drains her wine and starts heading inside for a refill. I finish my bourbon in one gulp and take her wine glass. "I got this." I glance at Julian and notice his drink is untouched. I refill our drinks and grab the charcuterie board Ash made because I don't like her drinking on an empty stomach. She may be an engaged woman, but it's still my responsibility to watch over her.

Julian and I stepped in to help raise Ashleigh after Mom's death. Dad was barely functioning those days, and as a result, we're both overprotective of her, but I'm working on loosening my grip. She has a fiancé now, and she's the center of his universe. I'm so damn proud of my sister. She's intelligent, beautiful, and in love. Mom would be unbelievably happy to see her now.

I settle back in my chair, cross my ankle over my knee, and take another sip of my drink. I relax for the first time in forever because I know where my siblings are and that they're safe. I can't help it. I'm always protective of people I care about.

"So, today was fun," Ash starts.

"I feel like I haven't been to a game in forever," Jules adds. "It's nice to be home."

"It felt like old times." Ash tucks her feet under her, and Jules gets up and drapes a light blanket around her. It may be July, but tonight, it feels unseasonably cool. He grabs a piece of cheese and holds it in front of her mouth, encouraging her to eat. I'm not the only one who cares for her, whether or not she likes it. She snaps at his fingers with her teeth but smiles as she takes a bite of cheese.

I nod in agreement.

"Matt sent me pictures of his locker. Everyone thought it was hysterical." She laughs at Jules. "Where did you get that lewd wrapping paper?"

"Ask him." He gestures to me, and her mouth drops open.

"Xander! What the hell?!"

I shrug and feign indifference. "I cannot confirm or deny knowledge of said wrapping paper."

We all laugh. I know I can be the hard ass. That's my role. Jules is the fun one. Ash is the precious one. But I can be fun too. I just don't flaunt it like my brother.

"Well, apparently, it sparked quite a debate in the locker room about a Secret Santa from last year, and they're still trying to figure out who it was. Spirits were high after the win, but they also had a bonus team-building exercise. Good job." She nods at me and lifts her wineglass with a mock toast.

I'm pleased knowing the team is bonding and having fun. Professional sports can be cutthroat and become more about the money and wins than the love of the game. I want the Reapers to have it all.

"There's the smile I love." Ash throws an almond my way. I catch it mid-air and pop it in my mouth. I may not play anymore, but I still have a ballplayer's reflexes. A torn rotator cuff ended my baseball career in college. I could never throw the heat after surgery, and my shoulder still acts up before it rains. Occasionally, I'll even workout and practice with the team for fun. I'm not MLB caliber anymore, but I could have been back in the day.

"It was a good day, Xan. A fantastic day." She throws another almond my way.

"I know." She's right. It was a good day. The team won, attendance was above average, and Matt and Tripp had incredible games.

"So, what did you think of Dani?" Jules asks. "You think she'll hold the Reapers responsible for Pauly?"

Dani's an incredible woman. She's beautiful — no, absolutely stunning. And intriguing. She's complex in a way I don't understand. She's a puzzle I feel compelled to solve. I want to know how she maintains her optimistic outlook on life when bad things happen. I'm fascinated, and I'd love to spend more time with her, preferably not apologizing with every other sentence.

"She's nice." If I let my siblings know I'm interested, I'll never hear the end of it. Besides, she shot me down. Hard.

"Nice? Really?" Ashleigh draws out her words, showing her apparent disbelief in my assessment.

"Yeah, she's nice. Seems like a great mom and friend. She's tough too. She held her own against Pauly."

Thinking about the video reminds me of what I put in motion tonight.

"By the way, I'm getting a self-defense class set up for all the Reapers staff and WAGs. We're going to offer it to the public once a month too. All the guys are going through a session on how to treat women. I'm looking at sponsoring shelters or resources for battered women, too."

"That's good stuff, bro." Jules smiles and lifts his drink to me.

"Which reminds me." I turn my attention to Ash. "I want you in that class before you leave. And if it's scheduled after you go home, I'll set up private lessons. Have you ever had to protect yourself from unwanted advances?" Because if she has, so help me, I'll track him down and promise he'll never force himself on another woman in his life.

She wilts a little under the scrutiny of both of us. Julian's usual playfulness is erased when we're discussing Ash's safety.

"No, not really," she mumbles.

I uncross my legs and lean forward. "What does not really mean? It's a yes or no question." I can feel tension fill my shoulders. My eyes don't leave hers, and she finally answers.

"I mean, guys are guys. No one's forced me to do anything or physically hurt me, but I've been in situations where I needed to get bailed out. At times, there were persistent guys, especially when they knew who I was. They saw me as their meal ticket, I guess." She shrugs. "That's what made Cole so different. He loved me when he only knew me as Leigh, some college girl who was good with social media." She gives us both a sweet smile, her love for Cole seeping from her pores. The guy is growing on me, I guess.

"Fuck," Jules mumbles under his breath.

"I'm getting you a personal security instructor this week." There's no arguing with me, and she knows it, but she tries one more time.

"That's not necessary, guys. I'm fine. Really. It's the way of the world. I'm smart, and I watch my surroundings. I can take care of myself." Her sweet demeanor switches to a tough girl in the blink of an eye. I admire her fighting until the bitter end. That's the Decker in her. We don't give up.

Jules sets his phone on the table. "Hey, what's up? Is Leigh okay?" Cole's voice comes from his phone, his tone on edge.

Ashleigh rolls her eyes and lets out a frustrated sound. "I'm fine," she grits out through her teeth. "My brothers are going all bodyguard on me."

"Why, what happened?" His voice is clipped and full of concern.

"Tell her she needs to meet with a personal safety instructor this week," I say, my eyes never leaving hers.

"Nothing happened," she says at the same time Jules goes inside. His contribution was to call Cole. Good move, but he's not getting in the middle. That's why he's her favorite, but she won't forget his part in this discussion.

She looks at me and says, "I'll think about it." She grabs Julian's phone and takes it off speaker. "I'm fine, but I miss you. How was your game?"

She goes back inside, leaving me stewing. Is that how women have to function? Is that the way of the world? I hate that Ashleigh and Dani have to worry about being safe.

Dani. She's a juxtaposition. Soft and tough. Sunshine and

sass. Strict and loving with Tyler. Instead of either/or, she's more like both/and. She's an interesting shade of gray, or even color, in my black and white, yes or no world. I'm not usually one to color outside of the lines, but with Dani, I might try.

Julian joins me back on the balcony.

"Smooth move calling Cole."

"Sometimes, the best way to get what you want is not head-on, but through a different route. You watch. Cole will have her meeting with that trainer before we will. Let's face it, brother, we are no longer the primary influencers in her life anymore."

I lean back into the cushions and admire the view. He's right. I tend to come on strong and hit things head-on. It's the most efficient and direct way to get me from point A to point B. Maybe, when dealing with the fairer sex, it's not about being direct.

"He's a good guy, right?" Julian spent more time around Cole than I have, and my dad seems to like him. I don't dislike him. It's just that I'm not sure anyone is good enough for my baby sister.

"He's perfect for her. That's what matters. But yeah, he's solid. Loyal, family focused. He's a little hotheaded, but that's more about his passion for the people he loves. And he loves our sister. I mean, hell, have you heard the latest gooey love song he wrote for her? Duncan Keller's new song? So damn sweet, I practically got a cavity just listening to it." He kicks back and gets comfortable on the recliner.

"I can't believe he writes love songs and plays baseball. I would think the guys would rag the shit out of him for that," I chuckle.

"Oh, they do. Until their girlfriends find out. Then the guys are asking him to help them out with sweet gestures. That boy can woo with the best of them. Maybe he can help you woo that gorgeous woman you met today?"

His comment catches me off guard. How did our conversation go from Cole to Dani? "Don't know what you're talking about."

"Oh, you don't? Let me guess. You've already got someone looking into her?"

"Why would I do that?" I ask defensively. Fuck, I hate he knows me so damn well. Of course, I've asked Jack to find out what he can about her.

"Because you need the facts to approach her head-on." He sits up. He swings his legs to the side of the recliner and looks directly at me. "Maybe you need a different tactic here. If you want to know about her, ask her." He gives me one of his half-smirks that makes me want to pop him upside his head. That smirk is usually accompanied by him being right and me being wrong. It doesn't happen often, but I hate that damn smirk.

"I just want to make sure she's okay. She had a traumatic incident, and I want her to have the resources she needs to, um, recover." That's partially true. I don't want to be that guy that doesn't know how to take no for an answer.

"She didn't look traumatized to me. Jenny told me she was more worried about Tyler being a witness to the entire thing. She's very protective of him."

"I noticed." She practically ripped my head off when I invited him to batting practice. "As she should be. She's an amazing mother. It can't be easy doing it all by herself." Tyler said he didn't have a dad. What does that mean? He's obviously not in the picture. "Did Jenny mention Tyler's dad at all?"

"Nope, didn't come up. Maybe if you want to know, you should, oh, I don't know, get to know her more. Novel idea, right?" His smirk is still there. I'd love to get to know her more, but she didn't act like she wanted to see me again. I'm not sure how to win her over, but maybe the background check Jack is running will give me some insight. With the information Jack gathers, I'll figure out the strategy to approach Dani Franklin. What does Julian know anyway? I'll do this my way. It's always worked before. Why not now?

CHAPTER
EIGHT

DANI

———

Tyler bounces in his seat so hard I'm afraid he'll break the shocks in the car. He can't contain his excitement as we park in front of the Reaper's stadium. Here we are again. I shake my head in disbelief. Casey Samuels surprised me when she called and practically begged me to bring Tyler to open practice today. Apparently, Archie wouldn't stop talking about Tyler, and he wanted his new friend at practice. After a little persuasion, I said yes, and well, here we are. I know Tyler will have a blast, and if it means a little awkwardness for me, then it's a price I'm willing to pay.

It's been over a week since we were here meeting the Deckers and their Reaper family. It was surreal. I'm riddled with guilt as I think about my harsh and dismissive tone with Alexander when he invited Tyler here today. And yet, here we sit, ready to attend because Casey invited us. Will Alexander take it personally? Do I care? That's probably the big question of the day. I won't deny I'm attracted to him. But any heterosexual female with working eyes couldn't help but be attracted to him. What kept me from saying yes? Probably temporary insanity fueled by fear and insecurity.

I'm usually the say yes, ask questions later kind of person. But with Alexander? He, well, he scared me. I'm not sure quite why. It's his, what? Formality? Intensity? Money? Not sure, but yet, there was a certain something just below the surface. Vulnerability, perhaps? And that vulnerability makes him sexy as hell. And deep down, I know that's what scared me. Once I see behind his self-imposed wall, I'm afraid I could fall. Hard.

I'm lost in my mini-self-therapy session when Tyler's bouncing speeds up, making me shake my head and let those errant thoughts go. I'd do anything for my kid and that includes facing Alexander Decker again. After parking the car, I steal a glance at my son in the back seat. Any amount of guilt evaporates when I look at his full-faced smile. I'm willing to endure the embarrassment for him. Maybe I won't even run into Alexander. I'm sure he was just being polite when he extended the initiation. He didn't really mean it, did he? Besides, I'm sure he's a very busy man who doesn't frequent open practice sessions with kids.

After our last encounter, I googled him. More than once. I became curious when his magazine appearances were mentioned. It's one hundred percent understandable. He's pure hotness. When I went to Google images, there was shot after shot of him at various charity galas, and, wow, does that man looks good in a tux. I turn the air conditioner to high just thinking about those images.

In some pictures, there were various women on his arm, all statuesque, beautiful, with long, straight hair, and the perfect figure. Most were socialites or successful business women. They weren't me, that's for sure. My hair is naturally curly, the tight ringlets more cute than sexy. People always think I'm younger than I am, and I attribute it to my curls. I sure don't feel young at thirty-two.

My reflection looks back at me from the side window, and I barely recognize myself today. I had time to kill this morning, and my anxiety got the best of me. While I listened to my favorite podcast, I straightened my hair. It was practically meditative, and while it was calming, I don't feel quite myself. With the new hair, I added makeup too. It's like I'm wearing a costume and playing pretend. Maybe I can hide behind this new persona.

"Mooooooooommmmmm," Tyler whines from the backseat. "I can't unbuckle until you turn off the car."

I glance at the clock. Casey told us to be here around nine-thirty, and I'm right on time. Not typical of me. I'm always late. Unsure of the protocol, I wanted to be fashionably late today. Oh well.

"Remember what we talked about. Be polite. Listen, and do exactly what you're told. Don't run off. Lots of please and thank yous. Most of all, have fun. Got it?"

"Yes ma'am. Got it." He's waving his glove, sending me the visual he's ready to go.

His grin is the validation I needed to know it's okay to be here. My mind wanders to Alexander again. He's sure living rent free in my head lately.

We make our way to the entrance, following Casey's instructions and follow several other people to the field.

"I'm so glad you made it! Ohmygod, you look fantastic." I'm embraced by Casey, swinging us side to side. Tyler sees Archie and runs to the dugout where the kids are gathered. So much for staying by me.

"I should say a little prayer for the players. Tyler is wound up." Casey laughs and loops her arm in mine.

"Oh, they'll be fine. They like this, especially since it keeps the coaches off their ass for today. Joey will keep an eye on them. Come on, let's go sit in the shade." She leads me to a place in the stands where a few other women I met in the suite are seated and offer various greetings. I'm watching Tyler and Archie run the bases with the other kids. We sit behind home plate and next to a tunnel that must connect to the locker room because players keep appearing one and two at a time. Everyone appears to be happy and relaxed.

We watch the practice, and I'm not sure who is having more fun, the kids or the players. Tyler's smile takes up his entire face. This was a good decision and my heart is full.

"Thanks again for inviting us. Tyler is having the time of his life."

"I'm so glad y'all could come. I wasn't sure you would."

"Why do you say that?" She's right. I said no more times than I could count before I gave in and said yes.

She gives me a sly smile. "They're just guys who have talent with a ball and a stick. Their job happens to be a game. They still leave their underwear on the bathroom floor and have to be reminded to take out the trash. Marriage is marriage. Men are men, regardless of the job." She laughs at her husband as he runs backwards to catch a pop-up ball. "Good job, honey," she yells when he crashes into the fence, ball in his glove. The rest of the team responds with wolf whistles and teasing.

"How long have you and Joey been married?" They're cute. It's obvious he's an adoring husband and father. Even if he leaves his underwear on the floor. It's a good reminder that they are people that have different circumstances than I do, but they're still people. My mind flits to Alexander. I doubt he leaves his underwear on the floor.

"We got married right out of college, a week before the draft. I needed him to understand that I was all in, no matter what happened with the pro offer. I wasn't a cleat chaser." She smiles at the memory. "That was eight years ago."

"Cleat chaser?" Now I sound like Tyler, asking questions for words I don't know.

"Yeah, girls that hitch themselves to college athletes hoping they go pro, and when they don't get the call, the girls drop them and find another one. They chase money and fame. Let me tell you, minor league ball is not all that. Joey's been in the show for the past four years. But those first three in the minors? Not easy, especially with a baby."

"Cleat chasers are the worst," Darcy says as she joins our conversation. "Almost as bad as those people telling you that your guy has a girl in every city and can't be faithful."

"Is that a thing?" I ask. Are these guys players on the field and off? I wonder if Alexander has a woman in every city?

She winces. "There might be a few guys like that. Some of the bachelors, but not all. Most of the guys are solid, family men. Especially on this team. The Reapers don't put up with that." Family values are important to this team. That's something I can stand behind.

I'm enjoying Casey's company, and we've already planned for Archie and Tyler to get together for a pool day before school starts back. From storms come rainbows. I'll add Casey Samuels and her family to that list of rainbows.

CHAPTER
NINE

ALEXANDER

———

I'm wrapping up a meeting with the Operations Team and glance at the clock. The open practice is about halfway through, but I have just enough time to change and join them for a quick batting practice.

I grew up around baseball and starting playing when I was four. I always enjoyed the game. I was an all-star pitcher in high school and a starting pitcher my sophomore year in college. I had my first injury that summer. After surgery my junior year, my arm was never quite the same. I'm lucky to get to work in the sport I love and appreciate that the team humors me during open practice, allowing me to relive my glory days.

I walk out of the tunnel into the bright sun and stop to look around the field. It never gets old. I'm still filled with awe when I step out and feel the fine dirt under my shoes. The smell of the fresh-cut grass fills my lungs, and I exhale all the stress of running this ballpark and team. The pitchers are playing catch with a few kids near the bullpen while the rest of the team has a kid next to them at their position. The kids vary in age from around five to thirteen, but all play well together.

Freddy Swanson is at first base sporting a bright pink glove, embracing his girl dad role. His thirteen-year-old daughter, Maddie, is next to him, ready for the next batter.

"Hey boss," Freddy calls out. "Want to take some swings so Maddie can practice tagging your sorry butt out at first? You're getting slow."

"Better watch it Swanson, or I'll drop you and sign her," I tease. She's a softball superstar. I know because Freddy tells everyone, and I'll never discourage parental pride.

I grab a batting helmet and take a few practice swings. Tripp is on the mound, and if the kids weren't out here, I know he'd strike me out in three pitches. Instead, he lobs a slow pitch in my strike zone, and I hit the ball and take off for first base. Luis Rodriguez throws the ball to Maddie, and she catches it, but I was a little faster and round to second. Maddie tosses the ball to Archie Samuels, who drops it, and I jog to third. Archie runs with the ball instead of throwing it and tags me out at third.

"YOUUUURRRREEE OUT!" the kid on third calls. I don't immediately recognize him, his face hidden under the oversized brim of his hat.

"Great job, Tyler," Matt says. And it clicks. Tyler Franklin is here. Which hopefully that means his mother is here too. I can't contain my spontaneous grin.

I tap the bill of his hat. "Wicked call, Tyler. Having fun?"

His grin speaks volumes. "Yes sir. I'm gonna be a Reaper someday."

"Sooner than later, I'm sure." I'm tempted to ask about his mom, but I can't risk Matt jumping to conclusions. The right conclusions, but nothing he needs to be involved in.

I look up at Matt. "Enjoying your first open practice?"

"Sure am." His grin rivals Tyler's.

I relieve Tripp at the mound and call all the kids in to bat. It gives the guys extra cardio because they have to run farther infield to catch the ball. And the unofficial rules are to run with the ball so they can tag the runner instead of making the out on base. The kids bat, some with Reaper help, and the bases are loaded. Laughter fills the air, and everyone is having fun. It's a reminder of what this should be about. Not ticket sales and contracts, but love of the game.

We wrap it up after all the kids get a chance to bat. The players still have an afternoon of meetings and film to watch, but they make time to greet the family members at the tunnel entrance who are there to gather their kids. I walk with Tyler because I'd love to talk to Dani. I can't deny she's been on my mind. And in my dreams. She's consumed my thoughts more than I'd care to admit.

When Tyler stops and wraps his arms around her legs, I'm stunned.

"What did you do to your hair?" I internally smack myself as the words leave my mouth.

Her smile quickly vanishes. "Excuse me?"

"I mean, I barely recognized you." I'm trying to recover, but I'm afraid this blunder will cost me.

Her hand goes to her sleek, long hair, and her fingers slowly move through the straight strands. Where are those bouncy curls that I loved so much? My hands itch to play with them, wrap my finger around a ringlet and, hell, I really liked her curls. This Dani looks sexy, seductive, beautiful, but maybe a little cold. Her light isn't as bright as before. I worry something's happened to the woman I've come to think of as my sunshine.

"That sounds like a you problem," she snaps back. Yep, there's that sass I knew she had. I have mixed emotions when it's directed at me. Her fire turns me on, but it's because I hurt her feelings, and that is the last thing I ever want to do. I never want her to hurt again.

"Mom, did you see me with Matt? Did you watch?" Tyler interrupts.

"Of course I was watching. You ready to go? We're going to

have lunch with Archie and his mom." She gives him a half smile. Yep. I dimmed her smile down a few notches. Fuck.

"Hey, look, I'm sorry. I didn't mean...".

"No more apologies, Mr. Decker. I appreciate you letting Tyler come. He had fun, didn't you, tiger?" She gives him a little squeeze.

"Yeah Mom, it was the best day ever." He's bouncing, filled with pent up energy.

"Hey Tyler, want to go run the bases one more time before you leave? Grab Archie, and you can race." I look at her, and she's scowling at me. It's a new look for her but goes with the hair, I guess. Yes, I'm aware I asked him something without asking her. I know it's against the rules, but I need some time with her. It's a calculated risk. One I'm hoping will pay off.

Tyler takes off, calling to Archie as he runs. I only have a minute to make one last attempt at resetting this.

"Dani, I'm sorry. I didn't mean to," I start.

"No, that's okay. I get it." Gets what? My brain isn't fast enough to keep up with the shifting conversation.

"No, no, listen. You caught me by surprise, that's all. Let me explain. Will you go out with me? Dinner? Coffee? You can wear your hair however you want. I just want," I say before she interrupts me.

"Thanks for the permission, but I'm good."

Tyler joins us. She puts her hand on his shoulder and turns him around. His big brown eyes look at me like he knows I'm in trouble, and he feels sorry for me. Yeah kid, I know.

"Dani, wait." I reach for her and catch myself. I don't want to be the man who grabs at her. She pauses, but doesn't turn around. "I'm glad you and Tyler were here today. You're welcome anytime."

"Thanks." She nods as they walk away.

I squat down, my legs not willing to hold me upright. I slam my hat on the ground and run my hands through my sweaty hair. How did I fuck this up so bad? I've never had an issue with women. But this one? I'm an idiot.

I'm calling it a day. I grab my things from my office and go home. After showering, I'm still stewing over my interaction with Dani. I don't know what to do, but I know I need to do something. I reach for my phone, and he picks up almost immediately.

"Jules, I fucked up."

I tell him what happened, and he laughs at me. "Are you really asking me for help? After all the shit you give me for Team True Love?"

Jules is a hopeless romantic. He claims responsibility for helping couples find their happily ever after with the help of him and our busybody friends he's dubbed Team True Love. Maybe that's why I called him, but I'll never admit it.

"I'm asking for help," I concede. Me asking for help is as rare as a perfect game. It doesn't happen often, and when it does, it's a big fucking deal. But my way isn't working and I'm a big enough person to admit when I've failed.

Julian's laughter stops, and he clears his throat. I brace myself for the serious advice he's about to dish out. "Have you ever heard of a grand gesture?"

CHAPTER
TEN

DANI

_____

When August hits, it's time to go back to work. Other parts of the country don't start as early, but I won't complain about our school schedule since we're done in May. I will always complain about the early mornings though.

Tyler slept over at my parent's last night to enjoy his last few days of summer before we are both awakened by alarm clocks. I don't like early mornings, and this is the first time I've had to set an alarm since May. Why does a teacher's workday have to start so darn early? I hit my favorite smoothie place on my way in, a treat to myself.

Today is a real work day. Time to set up my classroom. It's hard work, but incredibly fulfilling at the same time. I need to add color and function to a cinderblock room to make it an optimal learning environment for my students. Today's the first day back for teachers to start that task.

We received a message to report to the auditorium before heading to our classrooms this morning. That's a little unusual, but I welcome seeing all my fellow teachers in one place before the work begins.

I'm dressed in overalls and a crop top with my unruly curls held back in a bandana. Today's look is about manual labor, not fashion. I have so much work to do in my room to transform it into a warm and safe space for my students. I've loaded my car with the few boxes of leftover supplies from last year, but I need to see what I'm working with before purchasing additional supplies.

"Don't you look totes adorbs?" Jenny sashays up to me in the hall. Her long, dark ponytail sways with her walk. She's wearing a Reapers t-shirt and cargo pants. Since when did she start sporting Reaper's gear?

"You know I'm getting a new room this year, so it's starting from scratch. A girl's gotta do what a girl's gotta do."

"Worth it to be next door to me! You know I'll help," she squeals.

Jenny and I have classrooms next to each other this year, and I'm thrilled to be a door away.

"And I'll take you up on it too." I throw my arm around her shoulders and give her a half hug. "Any idea what the meeting is about?"

Lisa, another third-grade teacher, answers my question as she approaches. She's way too perky for this time of morning. "I heard we got a huge donation of supplies. Nothing better than school supplies for a teacher. Beats flowers, hands down. Am I right, ladies?"

We all laugh because she speaks the truth. Back to school is expensive, and many of us use our own money to stock our rooms. It's even harder when you teach in a low-income school. I can't allow the parents to decide between school supplies and food, so I do what I can. My kids and their families need a hand up. I'm blessed to do that for them.

My phone buzzes in my pocket. "Hey, let me get this. I'll meet you guys in there."

I take a quick call from Mom to get an update on Tyler. I hang up and pull the door open to an auditorium full of people. The buzz is electric as the voices blend into a low roar.

I stop at the top of the ramp and look around to get my bearings. I recognize many of my fellow teachers, but there are dozens of people I don't recognize. There are a lot more men than I remember working here last year. We rarely get a male elementary teacher, let alone this many. And they all look fine.

I scan the room for Jenny and do a double take when I see her talking to Matt and Darcy. That can't be. Then Casey Samuels waves at me. I tilt my head, trying to figure it out. What are they doing here? Am I in the right place? I'm at my school, not at the Reaper's Stadium, right?

"Hi."

His rich baritone voice sweeps over me, and I practically melt. I slowly turn to see Alexander Decker standing next to me. He's wearing a Reapers baseball shirt, tailor-made jeans, and a backward baseball hat. If those ocean-blue eyes weren't seared into my soul, I wouldn't have recognized him at all.

"Hi. Um, what's going on?" I ask, still stunned.

He gives me a panty-dropping smile and shrugs. "A little community outreach." His eyes move over my body, checking me out. The skin that peeps through the overalls warms just from his eyes.

"Huh." I'm struck with the realization I look a mess, much different from our last encounter. I put my hand to my head and remember I'm wearing a bandana. "I bet I'm a sight," I mumble.

"You are." He smiles at me, making me think his comment isn't negative. "I love your curls. I didn't say that right last time."

My cheeks heat with embarrassment. He loves my curls? I thought he liked the sleek and polished look since all his red-carpet dates look like that. Maybe he isn't as he seems?

I can't believe he's here, and I look like I'm about to scrub bathrooms. Meanwhile, his muscles are well-defined underneath his tight shirt. Even his casual look is magazine worthy. His fore-arms flex as his hands fist at his side.

Mr. Davis, our principal, calls for us to take a seat. Everyone moves toward the front of the auditorium and sits scattered throughout the room. I don't know if I'm up to walking down the ramp to the front, so I scoot into a seat next to where I'm standing. Alexander doesn't sit with me but goes down to Mr. Davis.

I slink down, wondering if I can escape and go home with no one noticing me. Mr. Davis gives us all a quick welcome back and then hands the microphone to Alexander.

"Thank you, Mr. Davis. I'm Alexander Decker, General Manager with the Carolina Reapers. It's our pleasure to be here with you all today. Teaching our future generations is a noble and often thankless job. I know that teachers often spend their own time, money, and energy on their classrooms. Well, we wanted to pitch in. I've brought my Reapers family here to help you get your rooms ready. There are supplies, paint, furniture, and anything you need to get you started this school year. And just as important as the supplies, I brought people power. We're here to work, so whatever you need, you tell us, and we'll do it. Thank you for allowing us the privilege to give back." Alexander hands Mr. Davis the microphone as the room breaks out into applause. My phone buzzes with a text.

JENNY
SOOOOOO much better than flowers 🙄

Huh?

"Hey, Dani!" I look up to see Darcy dancing, shifting her weight from side to side from excitement.

I stand up and hug her. "Darcy, I'm surprised to see you. Why are you guys here?"

"The Reapers do a lot of community outreach. Alexander asked if I'd help, and, well, here I am." Her eyes twinkle. "You get me today. Tell me your vision for your room, and I'll make it happen." She winks at me. "Designing is my jam."

"Wow. I'm just surprised, but this is fantastic. I have a new room this year and haven't even checked it out yet. That's why I'm dressed this way." I'm dying a thousand deaths thinking about how I look. I didn't put on any makeup. My hair is covered in a bandana. My overalls are baggy but oh-so-comfortable. I can't believe I'm seeing all these people looking like this. "It's going to be a lot of work."

"Well, I think you look great. Really. I'm dressed to work too." She's wearing an oversized Reapers t-shirt with leggings and Converse high-tops. It may be casual, but she still looks put together. Her coolness is effortless. It's just Darcy, and I'm a little jealous. "Let's go check out this room and get started." She loops her arm around mine and pulls me toward the doors. Darcy Davidson is a force to be obeyed.

We go to my classroom, and it's more drab than I thought. I look around and am underwhelmed. I sit on the old metal desk and scan the room. There's a pile of stuff in the back. Great. We need to clean it out before we start. I try to imagine it with bright faces and think about what they need to feel comfortable and safe.

"I can see a reading alcove here," she starts as she walks around the room. "A nice soft rug, a comfortable chair for you. Lots of low shelves and books. What do third graders read these days?"

"My kids are a little behind in reading, so anything that will keep their attention. *Dog Man*, graphic novels, fantasy, humor. Some even like biographies. I have a decent stash from last year, but I send books home with them for the summer, so I need to replenish every year."

"Got it. Consider it done." She types something into her phone and focuses back on me. "What's your favorite color?"

"What?"

"Your favorite color. I know this is for the kids, but you spend so much time here. This room is for you, too."

"Oh, okay. I like yellow." I feel the need to clarify. "Not the yucky brown-mustard color, but the French's mustard that's pure yellow. It's so yellow, Crayola should name a crayon after it. Oh, like the cornsilk crayon. I used to love the dandelion crayon, but they discontinued them in 2017, but I still search for them sometimes. I'm not as fanatical as that girl on TikTok but, gah, I miss dandelion crayons." I pop my hand over my mouth. When I get excited, I ramble.

She beams at me. "Yellow. Figures. Happiness, warmth, and sunshine. Dandelion yellow, huh?" She nods her head like she's agreeing with someone, but we're the only ones in the room.

"What?" I've gone overboard with my rambling. "That was too much, wasn't it?"

"No, not at all. It's perfect. Just ignore me. Okay. Tell me more about your students. What do they need?"

"Well, this is a low-income school. Most of these kids come from this neighborhood. Often single-parent homes who are working and don't have time to help with homework. They're just trying to get by. Food insecurity is real for a lot of them. I make sure they get decent snacks at the end of the day, in case they don't get dinner. They don't have extra money for school supplies, especially the nice-to-have items." I look out the cracked window and sigh. "They need to feel safe here."

Darcy sniffles, and she has tears in her eyes.

"I didn't mean to make it sound sad. The kids are great! They're like sponges, ready to learn. They're loving and kind, for the most part. Occasionally I get one on their way to a hardened heart, but with enough love and encouragement, I can keep that away for another year. I love my students. They're fantastic, tiny humans."

"You're so beautiful." She squeezes my hand. "Thank you for what you do."

I blush. "I'm just doing a job."

"No, it's more than that." A tear slips down her cheek.

There's a knock at the door, and we both look up to find Matt in the doorway. "Hey, Dani." He looks at Darcy, comes in, and wraps her in his arms, kissing her at her temple. "Hey, pretty girl. What's got you all teary?"

At his touch, her tears seem to evaporate. "Dani is a saint." She looks at me and smiles. She pulls away from Matt and kicks back into work gear. "Let's get her room ready. I'll need three painters, someone for furniture assembly, and a shopper."

"On it. I'll be back with a team in a minute." He starts to leave and turns back. "Hey Dani, thanks for letting us do this for you. My girl is over the moon with this project. Don't let her Sigmund Freud you with her color mumbo jumbo." He winks and practically leaves the room at a jog.

"He's just the cutest," I comment. "He's got such golden retriever energy."

We both laugh.

"He really does," she agrees.

"Have you guys found a place to live yet?" When I met them a few weeks ago, they had just moved to Charlotte and were temporarily staying at Julian Decker's place.

"I've looked at several places. Julian said we could stay as long as we want, but we've determined we are not high-rise, luxury-living type of people. I'm looking for something with potential and a yard to make ours. I want a charming neighborhood."

"It's exciting to start this new chapter. I'm happy for both of you." I think back to when I was Darcy's age. I finished college and started my first teaching job in Washington, DC. It's where I fell in love with low-income schools. It was, well, it was before.

True to his word, Matt reappears with Tripp Stevenson, a superstar Reaper pitcher, Casey and Joey Samuels, and Alexander. Everyone enters my drab room and looks around at the task before us. It's daunting.

I introduce myself to Tripp and Joey, but they both say they remember me. Tripp gives me a wink, and I think I hear Alexander growl. I giggle like a schoolgirl.

"Okay, listen up," Darcy commands. "Tripp, Matt, and Joey, I need you to be the painters. Tripp and Joey start taping the edges and putting down the drop cloths while I order the paint. Matt, come with me." I swear he gives her a wicked smile. "Casey, can you put together a few simple shelves?"

"Of course." She practically sounds offended.

"I can," I start to volunteer.

"Nope. Just wait for your assignment." Darcy smiles and slowly spins around the room one more time. I'm surprised at her bossy side because she seems so sweet.

"Alexander, I'm going to text you a shopping list. I need you and Dani to hit Costco and stock up on a few things. Can you handle that?"

"But I want to help here," I say weakly.

"You are helping, trust me. When you get back, you won't recognize this place."

"If you aren't comfortable going with me, I'll switch with Casey," Alexander says to me. He looks at me with apprehension. Does he think I'm still mad at him? Does he still think I'm afraid of men? Of him? Please.

"What? No. No. It's not that." I lean against my rusty desk, my hand catching on the nicked faux-wood top. "I feel bad asking everyone to do the heavy lifting."

Tripp walks by with several rolls of blue painter's tape. "This beats time in the weight room, hands down. Now that's heavy lifting." Matt and Joey laugh, and Alexander gives them a scolding look. "I'm excited to get to do this. I'd gladly come back and read to the kids if you want. Just let me know how I can help." I picture Tripp reading to my kids, and my heart swells. The kids will love him.

Joey slaps him on the shoulder. "Painting is a good workout for that arm. Reading should be easy for you. Don't you still read kid's books?"

"Manga are not kid's books," Tripp says with an edge.

"If you say so. They still have pictures. Dani, don't come back until that truck is so full it'll take the entire team to empty it, got it?" Joey quickly kisses his wife as he passes by her with an arm full of drop cloths he grabbed from somewhere in the back of the room.

I look at these people who are genuinely happy to be helping me. I'm so full of joy that it leaks out as a tear.

"Please don't cry." Alexander reaches toward my face but catches himself and drops his hand. My bruise is long gone, but I know he still sees it. Is he always going to see me as a victim?

"You guys make me so happy, it can't stay contained." I give them all my best smile. I grab my purse. "This should be fun." I look at Alexander Decker and give him an evil grin. He may be in casual mode, but I'll bet he's never been to a Costco.

"Why are you looking at me like you know something I don't?" He's cautious, which is smart.

"You ever been to Costco?" My grin deepens.

"No, it's just a big-box store, right?"

The entire room breaks out in laughter.

This is going to be fun.

CHAPTER
ELEVEN

ALEXANDER

———

We walk down the hall toward the administration area I entered last week when I met with Mr. Davis. Julian was right, and if I wanted to see Dani, it needed to be in a meaningful way. She isn't some basic girl that will be swayed by flowers and a nice dinner. She has more substance than that. Dani has a purpose. When I learned she taught in a low-income school, I knew exactly what I needed to do.

The Reapers do a good bit of community outreach. We often focus on kids or areas that our players are passionate about. One player, Josh Harley, supports free mammograms for the community every year in honor of his mother, who died from breast cancer. The Reapers stand beside him, matching his financial donation and providing hands to help at the event. We pay for the advertising to get the word out, too. We support the community and our players. Their cause is our cause.

When I said I wanted the Reapers to sponsor a school, it wasn't out of character for our brand. The fact that I was specific about the school and arranged it myself may have been a little suspect. I asked Nikki, our Community Outreach Director, to accompany me to meet with Mr. Davis, but I made it clear that I wanted to take the lead on this.

I asked what the students needed, and he rattled off the usual paper, pencils, and backpacks list. I wanted to know what the teachers needed, and he casually mentioned how they have classroom prep days that include manual labor. That I could provide. And all the other stuff. The Reapers are providing lots of supplies for the students and teachers today. We have full trucks to unload.

The guys were more than happy to skip the usual workouts for the outreach day. The coaches weren't thrilled with me, but I pulled rank. We're calling it a team-building day. I made sure the entire Reaper payroll is here. The front office, coaching staff, players, and stadium crew. I saw a mixture of disbelief as they looked at the state of the school when we pulled up, but when they got their assignments before the school staff showed up, their smiles said it all. They're happy to be here.

This school is in an underdeveloped neighborhood. The landscaping needs a little TLC, and our grounds crew are working on that this morning. The playground was a broken mess, so that's where I sent the trainers. The new playground equipment is being assembled now, and my guys will make sure it's safe. These kids may not come from much, but this neighborhood deserves a school they can be proud of.

The Reapers Foundation is funding this day, except for one room. This room is mine. I made sure Darcy understood the assignment. Make it a reflection of Dani. Sky's the limit. I sent Darcy a few pictures last week when Mr. Davis showed me around. I asked to see Jenny and Dani's rooms, specifically, to understand what we needed. I figured asking about two teachers would shift suspicion and motivation. Not sure it worked, but I don't care. Jenny's room is getting a total makeover too. Have to take care of the best friend. Everyone knows that.

I fire off a quick text to ensure Dani is getting a new desk. That rusty box is a tetanus shot waiting to happen. Darcy sends me a picture of the new desk that's in a truck. She's waiting for us to leave to get everything moved in.

Then Darcy sent me the shopping list she promised. She tells me Dani's students have food insecurity. Get lots of food. Snacks. Canned goods to send home. Grocery gift cards. Darcy says Dani tries to provide snacks in case they don't get dinner.

Fuck. These kids don't have food? That shouldn't be happening anywhere. But Dani takes care of them.

We pass two players carrying boxes toward a classroom.

"Boss," Harley says as he passes us. He gives me a nod and winks after glancing at Dani.

"So you just snap your fingers, and they do what you want?" she asks.

I give her a small smile. "Not exactly." She gives me a questioning look. "Well, sometimes." Guilty as charged.

"Hey, do you mind waiting here for a minute? I need to see Mr. Davis about something."

"Sure, no problem. I'll keep watching these players work." A few more guys come down the hall carrying rolled-up rugs. She watches them pass, checking out their asses.

I give her a loud sigh and a slight shake of my head, letting her know I saw what she was doing. Deep down, I'd like her to look at me like that, but I need to have a quick conversation with the principal about building a food pantry somewhere in the school for the neighborhood. We'll provide the food. He'll provide the place. With those details worked out, I shoot another text to Darcy asking her to make it happen. She tells me she'll have her contractor friend, Jay, come up from Charleston and build it out this weekend.

I meet Dani back in the hall where she's leaning against the wall, looking down at her phone. She's so damn cute in her overalls today. I want to tug her by the bib and pull her close. That hint of skin underneath teases my fingers to reach out and skim her smooth waist. But I won't touch her. She's already had one man touch her without her permission. I won't add to that.

She's taken her bandana off and pulled her hair into a ponytail, leaving a few errant curls to frame her face. I'm desperate to wrap one of those curls around my finger. Her hair looks so soft I'm dying to touch it. Down, boy. Don't be that guy.

I clear my throat to get her attention. She looks up, but her smile is gone.

"Everything alright?"

"Um, yeah. It's Tyler. He's not feeling well."

"Do you need to go home and take care of him?" Her kid comes first. Always. My mom always put us first, and I know that's rule number one for Dani, too.

"No, he's fine. He's with Mom and Dad. I hate that he's missing one of his last days of summer before he starts school. Poor guy."

"Do we need to go by their house so you can check on him?"

"No, he'll be okay in a few hours. Come on. I can't wait to pop your Costco cherry. They're going to know you're a virgin before you even grab the oversized cart." She rubs her hands together.

"You look like a villain watching their plan come together. Just missing that twirl of a mustache to finish the look." When she looks at me like that and talks about popping my cherry, a rush of heat goes up my neck to my cheeks. Is this girl making me blush?

She looks at me, throws her head back, and laughs. Her laugher mixes with the other sounds of happiness throughout the school. It's a good day. I try to relax into that.

She wraps her arm around mine and tugs me toward the front doors. I guess I'm about to see what makes her so maniacal about Costco.

Holy Hell. This place is huge. And everything they sell is enormous. Who needs that much salsa in one container? She's right. This place is getting the best of me. The chaos of it all. Is there any organization or method to what's next to what? Pants are next to books which are next to TVs which are next to watermelons. What is this place?We push oversized carts through the aisles. Everything she stops to look at, considers, and puts back, goes in my cart. We're stocking her room with snacks for the kids. Prizes for her treasure box are all food related too. We get lots of protein bars, and I make a mental note to reach out to our suppliers to deliver to the school on the same schedule they deliver to the stadium.

"I told you, get what you want. Be extravagant. The kids deserve it." I wouldn't have made it this long in here if it weren't for her childlike wonder over a pack of special edition crayons and her lament of the discontinued crayon that didn't even make it thirty years. I got her ten boxes of the special crayons because it contained cornsilk, which, according to her, is the second best yellow.

She looks in her cart. "But this is going to cost a fortune."

"Not your problem, sunshine. Get anything you want. We're going to make sure these kids love coming to school, even if we have to bribe them with candy." I take a box of full-size candy bars and throw them in my cart. I reconsider and throw in four more boxes. Her eyes grow big when she focuses on my over-filled cart, compared to her conservative, half-empty cart. "Get to work." I nudge her with my cart.

She shakes her head at me and starts down the next aisle.

"If you could have anything for your classroom, what would it be?"

I tried asking questions about her life, but didn't make much progress. Jules was right. Direct isn't the tactic here. She's more than chatty about her job.

"Anything?"

"Anything." I figure she'll say books or finger paints. Easy. I'll fill her room with them.

"A class pet."

"A pet?" I honestly wasn't prepared for this answer. She's always full of surprises.

"Yep. Like a guinea pig or a chinchilla or something. So many of the kids don't have pets, and studies have shown that having pets can be effective for emotional growth." Chinchilla? I've never had a pet or even considered it. There's enough stress caring for my family and friends and I can only imagine the mess a pet brings, too. "Are you a big animal lover? Do you have a pet at home?"

"I love animals. We never had a pet growing up. We moved often, and the Colonel thought it was hard enough to move a wife and child. I've thought about getting Tyler a dog, but I don't think he's ready to help take care of him. A classroom pet could come home with us on the weekends sometimes. So yeah. A class pet. But they're expensive, and I'd rather spend money on food. We can't have luxury items when we don't have the basics, you know?"

I nod and listen. Damn, this woman is killing me with her kindness to others. How is she so optimistic when she sees the saddest part of society every day?

I swallow hard. "Yeah, makes sense. Hey, let's finish this shopping. We've got a few more stops to make."

"Oh, like where?"

It's my turn to look like an evil villain. "You'll see. Just get moving."

We get to the checkout and they ask for a card. I hand the cashier my black AmEx, and she rolls her eyes at me and sighs.

"First time?" she asks me. I'm confused, and before I can answer, Dani is next to me, knocking me with her shoulder, trying to push me out of the way. Does she think I'm going to let her pay? I'm questioning her sanity.

"He's a virgin," Dani says, hiding her mouth with her hand.

Virgin? Not hardly, sunshine. What the hell are they talking about?

The cashier looks at our carts and gives a little whistle. "He's a big one, isn't he?" What the fuck?

"The biggest," Dani says with a giggle. She's got my normally can't-be-rattled mind running in overdrive. I put my hands through my hair and tug. I'm literally pulling my hair out here.

"Got a card?" She looks at Dani like they know something I don't. Apparently, they do, because Dani whips something out of her purse and hands it to the cashier.

"What are you doing?" I grumble. My frustration level is growing, the enjoyment I felt while watching her shop, a long-forgotten memory. She's killing me here.

"Showing her my membership card," she says casually, like I should have known.

"Your membership card?" What is she a member of?

"Yeah, silly. You think just anyone can shop here and get these bargains. You have to be a member. Duh."

"Did you just say duh at me?" Something about the way she put her hand on her hip and rolled her eyes at me, flips a switch and now I'm chuckling at her. She's making me have more mood swings than a hormonal teenager. She hip checks me, and I play-fully push her aside. I freeze when I realize what I did, and panic fills my chest. She wraps her arms around my bicep and squeezes. When I realize I didn't hurt her, I relax.

I watch her eyes grow wide as the total climbs. When it hit four digits, she insists we put things back. She tries to let go of my arm to reach for things on the conveyor belt, and I put my hand over hers. I'm all for consent and would never force myself or desires on her, but in this scenario, I absolutely will not listen or comply. She won't get her way when it comes to me spending money on her or her class.

"It's too much," she repeats for the tenth time.

"It's not. It's for the kids. Share it with Jenny if it makes you feel better." Little does she know Jenny's room is equally stocked.

It took three employees to ring up and box our purchases. I'm ready to leave this place and never return.

"Let's get out of here. We aren't done with our errands."

"No." She stops pushing her cart and refuses to move, her arms crossed over her chest. I'll need to add stubbornness to her list of qualities.

I can't help but smirk at her. She thinks she has the upper hand with me? I stop and glare at her. "I've already paid for this, and it's not going back." Fine. She wants a showdown? I'll give her one.

"Nah, I let you win this round. But we aren't leaving until I buy you a hot dog." She let me win? Interesting perspective.

"I have a catered lunch back at the school." I try to reason with her.

"Nope. Over here. I'm not leaving until this happens."

"What's so magical about this hot dog?"

"Did you know Costco sells more hot dogs a year than all MLB ballparks combined?"

"What kind of Wikipedia bullshit is that?" If I know one thing, it's the numbers around my ballpark. We sell over nine thousand hot dogs a game. There's no way this warehouse store sells more.

She continues like she didn't even hear me. "And the hot dog combo is still a dollar-fifty. Hasn't gone up since the eighties. It's a cultural phenomenon. And to top off your Costco deflowering, I insist." She puts her hand out, inviting me to join her. I put my hand in hers because I will accept any invitation she extends.

"Can you not talk about deflowering in public?" I mumble. She drags my unwilling body to a food stand, and we order a hot dog combo. I reach for my wallet, and she slaps my hand, the pop loud and clear.

"My treat. Let me enjoy this. Please?" She looks at me with those pleading, beautiful eyes, and I realize at that moment, there's nothing I wouldn't give this woman. Including letting her pay for my hot dog.

"Fine. Why didn't you get one?"

"No way. I'm saving room for the catered lunch." Her laughter echoes in the cavernous room, and my life's mission is to hear that sound as often as possible. I swear my chest practically explodes at the sound. She's so damn happy and excited about everything. I'm fascinated, and my need to know more about her is insatiable. How does she do it?

We fill the back of the G Wagon with the snacks and candy we bought. It looks like the supply closet for one of our concession stands.

I open the door for Dani and make sure she's buckled up. I start the car and blast the air conditioner. August in Charlotte is sweltering.

"Hey, I'm going to step out to make a quick call. Why don't you see if Tyler is feeling better? Maybe we can pick him up and take him to see your new classroom? That is, if you want him to. Your call, of course." When it comes to him, I've learned my lesson to always defer to her. I'm the first to admit I know nothing about parenting.

"I don't want you to go out of your way or anything."

"Not out of the way at all. Today is about you and your kids. That includes Tyler. He's a cute kid. Check on him, and I'll be right back." I give her a smile and close the driver's door.

"Hey, boss."

"Darcy, not you too," I groan.

She giggles. "Sorry, couldn't resist. Calling for a status update?"

"Yep." She flips our call to FaceTime and shows me around the room.

"It looks great. You're magical." The room is bright and cheerful, a far cry from the drab place we left a few hours ago.

"Well, if their baseball careers end, they'll need to find a different backup plan. They are the messiest painters I've ever worked with. But they got the job done." Her smile fills the screen.

Yeah, I hate I didn't get to watch Tripp do manual labor. He's the most pampered guy I've ever met. "I hope the paint didn't mess up Tripp's manicure."

"Hey, I heard that, you bastard." Darcy pans to Tripp, hanging white, gauzy curtains that look like clouds against the bright yellow walls. His shirt looks like he got into a fight with a paintball gun and lost.

"Everything looks great. She's going to love it. We'll be back in a few more hours. Is that enough time?"

"Yep. The other rooms weren't as labor intensive, so the crew tackled our two special rooms. Both are almost finished."

Nikki's face fills the screen next to Darcy. "And the playground is installed. The landscaping looks great, and it's relatively childproof. They are setting up the lunch for the teachers in the cafeteria shortly. You think you'll be back for that?"

"Maybe. Hey, you think there's a space for one other thing in her room?"

Nothing like throwing a wrench in Darcy's design. Seems I'll be apologizing again.

CHAPTER
TWELVE

DANI

———

"Mr. Decker, is this your car?" Tyler asks from the back seat.

"It is. Why?" Alexander looks at Tyler in the rearview mirror.

"My grandpa thought you'd drive a, what was it? Oh yeah, a splashy car. Is this a splashy car?"

Alexander gives a full-belly laugh while I die of embarrassment in the front seat. Not only did Dad speculate on Alexander's flashy European sports car, but he was also sure Alexander was a womanizer. Not my words, his. That Tyler is repeating part of the conversation has me cringing inside. Please don't say anything else, Tyler. He's said enough. He's also let Alexander know he's been a topic of conversation.

After our day at the Reapers game, Mom commented on how charming the Decker family is, especially Alexander. She thought their emphasis on family was refreshing. Dad liked him but didn't have the same thoughts. He thought Alexander was impressive, but with an agenda. He thought his stoic and formal presence was suspect. This was fresh coming from the most stoic man I know.

At Costco, Alexander shed his buttoned up and formal facade and showed a glimpse of his fun side. I'd catch him smiling at me or laughing at some outrageous tub of mayonnaise. He was enjoying himself. I'm not sure if it was because of me, or the insanity of Costco, but either way, I liked it.

"Out of the mouth of babes," I mumble.

Alexander's eyes sparkle with mischief. "No, I don't think this car is splashy, do you?" Tyler gives him a little shrug. He has no idea what a splashy or flashy car would be. He's used to the practical Honda I drive. Safe. Affordable. Boring.

"What color do you think a splashy car is?" Alexander asks Tyler.

"Um, red?"

Alexander chuckles. "Yeah, red is pretty splashy. But a splashy car wouldn't be very practical for taking little boys and their pretty moms out shopping, would it?" He gives Tyler a wink.

Oh god, I'm dying. This guy whipped out his black credit card at Costco and didn't blink twice at the almost four-thousand-dollar total. I gulped. He has this gorgeous black G Wagon SUV with the most buttery leather seats I've ever touched. They're so soft and luxurious, definitely not like my juice stained car seats.

Tyler shrugs.

"Hey Tyler, what grade will you be in this year?"

"First! I'm going to big boy school with Mom."

Alexander looks over at me with a questioning look. "He'll go to your school?"

"Yeah, he'll go to Bellwood. Tiffany will be his teacher. I made sure he got the best class in the school, didn't I, tiger?"

"My mom says only the best for me." My heart swells at the sweet smile from my angel.

"So you live near the school?" His voice is deep, concern dripping in his tone.

Oh, I get it now. He's concerned because it's in a pretty rough neighborhood. Always the protector.

"No, we live near South End. It's easier for me to keep him at school with me."

He seems to visibly exhale. "Oh, that makes sense."

"Mr. Decker, are we going to see Mom's room now?"

"One more stop." I'm so distracted by Alexander's captivating eyes and praying Tyler doesn't say anything else incriminating that I'm not paying attention to where we're going until he pulls into the parking lot of a strip mall with an assortment of stores. There's a clothing boutique, a gourmet grocery store, and a coffee shop, and then I see it. A pet store.

What is he up to? "Why are we here?"

"Well, I thought Tyler would like to help pick out the class pet since he's going to help care for it." Alexander made sure to cover all the basics and now he's spoiling me with luxury items. He puts the car in park and looks at me.

"Are you serious?" My tone is a little incredulous. Who does this guy think he is?

"What? Is this not okay?" Panic crosses his face. "Fuck, I mean, fudge." He glances back at Tyler. "I'm sorry. You said you wanted one, and I thought that meant it was okay."

I reach across the center console and reach for his hand. "I'd hug you, but the seat belt has other ideas," I mumble. "This is amazing. Thank you."

The panic subsides, and he looks relieved. He turns around and looks at Tyler, who bounces in his booster seat. "You ready to pick out your new friend?"

"I want a snake." His eyes are wild with excitement.

We both shout "No!" at the same time. At least we agree on that.

———

We spend an hour looking at all the possible classroom pets. We asked the shop owner, researched online, and debated each animal's merits with Tyler. While lizards and snakes are popular, they're not coming into my house. We look at guinea pigs, hamsters, and even ferrets. Tyler is in heaven, playing with all the cuddly fur balls.

We finally settle on two, hopefully male, hedgehogs. My heart melts watching Tyler and Alexander playing with the adorable creatures. I won't deny I snapped a pic and sent it to Jenny with a caption about my ovaries exploding.

I tasked the boys with selecting appropriate names. Tyler decided they looked like baseballs and asked Alexander who his favorite baseball players of all time were. We now have two hedgehogs aptly named Joe DiMaggio and Mickey Mantle.

It's become crystal clear Alexander does nothing halfway. After asking permission from me away from super hearing ears, he bought two identical setups, one for the classroom and one for Tyler's room. Alexander decided we needed two hedgehogs because one just seemed lonely. The setup is a two-story condo with plenty of play areas, heat lamps, a dining room, and an easy-to-clean bathroom area. It's over the top and completely adorable. He bought a travel case to bring them from school to home. He also bought several months' worth of bedding, food, and treats.

The kids are going to love Joe and Mickey.

We get back to the school, and I barely recognize the place. The front landscaping is beautiful. The bushes are all trimmed up, and we've got big pots of flowers lining the walkway. The grass has some spots of sod, so it looks kind of patchy, but it'll even out.

A welcoming committee greets us at the car. Whoever said

many hands make light work knew what they were talking about. The team empties the car in ten seconds flat.

Matt opens my door before I unbuckle my seatbelt. "I hear a special piece needs to be installed before the big reveal." I look at him like he has two heads. What is he talking about?

"Yep, just take one set. The other is for their house." Alexander points to the box on the back passenger floorboard. The car is packed to the brim.

Alexander helps me out of the car and stands beside Matt as he grabs the pet supplies.

"Darcy is going to flip. If you ever need a sitter, give us a call." Matt gives me a wink, ruffles Tyler's hair, and grabs the hedgehog condo and bag of accessories. He hands it to another guy and gently takes the box with Mickey and Joe.

Tyler's eyes are enormous as he realizes who's leaning in the car and rubbing his head.

"Mom! Mom! Do you know who that is?" He doesn't even give me a chance to answer before he continues. "Mom, that's Matt, the baseball player." He's in shock to see the players out of uniform and at our school. I get it because I'm still processing myself.

"Mr. Decker has the entire team here to help us get ready for school. Isn't that amazing?" Amazing doesn't even describe this generous gesture.

Alexander leans in to unbuckle Tyler. "Mr. Decker, can we go see Joe and Mickey now?"

"Absolutely!" He helps Tyler from his seat. That simple gesture makes my heart melt.

He looks at me with a slight smile. "Hey, if it's okay with you, I'd prefer he not call me Mr. Decker. I keep looking over my shoulder for my dad. But I don't want to override your wishes."

"Oh, that's sweet. Do you want him to call you Mr. Alex?"

He visibly shudders. "No. My friends call me Xander. Is that okay with you?"

I nod. Xander. I like it. It suits him.

He helps Tyler out of the car. "Hey bud, if it's okay with you, why don't you call me Xander? That's what all the cool people call me."

Tyler looks at me, seeking permission. He only calls a few people by their first names. I give him a nod. "Xander is a cool name." Tyler grins from ear to ear, and Xander has one to match.

We walk into the school, Tyler in the middle, holding each of our hands. I can't knock the smile off my face. If people saw us, I'm sure they would think we're a family. For a brief moment, I like the idea.

Jenny greets us at that door, throws herself around Xander's waist, and gives him a hug to end all hugs. "Thank you, thank you, thank you." Her hurried words are muffled into his chest. He stiffly gives her a pat on the back, clearly uncomfortable by the spontaneous affection.

"You're welcome." I'm not sure why he's awkward with Jenny, but then I hear the snickers from the guys. The entire team is lining the hall, waiting to greet their leader.

"Jenny," I stage whisper. "Stop. You're embarrassing him."

She pulls away and looks guilty.

"Better than flowers any day." She looks at Alexander and gives him a quick peck on the cheek. The team can't hold it in any longer, and several have turned their backs on us to hide their laughter.

He needs a rescue. "Come on. I want to see what y'all have done. This place doesn't even feel like the same school. The kids will say this place is lit."

We walk down the hall, and the smell of fresh paint fills the air. Tyler gets a high-five from most of the guys, and when we get to Matt, he reaches down and puts Tyler on his back. Darcy greets us at my door, and everyone else gathers to watch my reaction. I feel like I'm on one of those surprise designer shows. Just then, several cell phones begin filming.

"I hope you got some amazing pictures and stories for the

team's social media," I say to one girl with a camera. I think her name is Nikki and seems to be the one coordinating today.

"No, ma'am. This wasn't for press or marketing. It was just because. We may use the footage for our end-of-the-year recap, though." Wow. Not that I questioned their intentions. But why wouldn't you get credit and good press while doing a good deed? Isn't that what most organizations do these days? The Reapers continue to surpass my expectations.

"Ready to see your room?" Darcy asks.

"Absolutely."

"I won't use a blindfold, but will you close your eyes for me? You too, Tyler. Hands over your eyes." I put my hands over my eyes and feel Darcy guide me by my elbow while a large hand guides me by the small of my back.

I like the feel of his hand there. It's the first time he's touched me, and the sensation electrifies me. When Jenny embraced him, I admit I had violent thoughts.

"Duck, buddy," Matt instructs Tyler.

"Okay, you can look!" Darcy proclaims.

I first notice the bright yellow walls, full of sunshine and fun. Dandelion yellow? How did she do it? She transformed the drab room into a place of happiness and joy. The contrasting color is black. Not what I would have picked. It's the opposite of the sunny yellow, but it makes the yellow pop. I love it! Gauzy white curtains drape the windows, giving the room a feeling of lightness and air. A gorgeous white desk is in the corner, with a large black swivel chair. I sit in the chair and spin around. The plush velvet envelopes me in a soft caress.

"While I wanted a white chair, I figured black was a little more childproof," Darcy comments.

"Absolutely. White is a no-go color in elementary school."

"I've never designed a classroom, but I hope it's okay. I tried to keep it as washable and child friendly as I could. This wall is whiteboard paint so that you can write on it."

I see the Erin Condren gift card on my desk and squeal. I haven't ordered my planner and can get all the upgrades with this. I'll buy Jenny's too. I look at Darcy, and she gives me a shrug, signaling me to go with it.

I get up and walk around, needing it to take it all in. The desks are sharp black tables for two, with yellow chairs, a perfect size for third graders. Each chair has a Reapers book bag that looks so full it can barely zip. I run my hand over it and try to pick it up. It must weigh thirty pounds.

"Every seat in the school has the same book bag filled with supplies, including a Chromebook or tablet for the younger kids," Alexander says.

"Each child gets a computer?" I'm stunned—five-hundred computers, just like that. The cost and the speed at which this happened aren't lost on me. This guy lives in a different world than me. Cinderella, remember? I had my moment. This world where we spend time together and have a happily ever after? Yeah, I may be a glass-half-full girl, but I'm not delusional. My life isn't a Hallmark movie.

"Yeah, they're preloaded with age-appropriate apps so they can work on homework and won't need help if their parents can't be there for them."

The amount of money spent today is more than the entire school budget for ten years. The generosity is overwhelming.

I take another moment to look at the details of the room. Bees adorn the walls, dotted lines showing their journey around the room to each station. I follow the bees, my hand trailing along to touch every fabric, label, and detail. The bees pull the yellow and black theme together perfectly. The room has a high-end designer touch but doesn't feel like a *look, don't touch* space. That's good, considering the kids don't believe in that concept.

As I wander around the room, I come to the reading corner. The large, black, plush area rug is nicer than anything I've ever had in my house. I lean down and run my hand across the silky fibers. I want to curl up on it and never leave. Three walls of low shelves surround the area, packed full. There must be hundreds of books here. I try to read some titles, but the freely flowing tears blur my vision. Xander leads me to the bright yellow whisper glide rocker and encourages me to sit.

He kneels in front of me, concern filling his face. "You okay? You're leaking again." He reaches up and brushes a tear away. "I'm sorry if I made you cry."

"No more apologies, remember?" I'm overwhelmed. I take a deep breath and give him my best smile.

"So, do you like it?"

I nod my head several times. "No words."

He graces me with the biggest smile I've ever seen, making him even more handsome. He goes to cup my cheek and pauses. That little motion might as well have been a slap across the face. It's a reminder I'm the victim. I need to get back to reality.

I take a deep breath, gather myself, and check out the rest of the room. Darcy used the space efficiently and practically, making even the messy coat area look like a designer showcase. Although it's hotter than Hades outside, several coats already hang there. The sign above the coat rack says, "Need a coat? Take a coat." She thought of everything.

The supply closet bursts at the seams with all the items we bought from Costco.

Tyler is on another area rug under the big window at the side of the room. He's rolling on the floor, his giggles bouncing off the walls while he plays with Joe and Mickey.

"Look, Mom! They like running in their balls." We got them extra large hamster balls so they could roam freely without getting injured in the classroom. They can also serve as carriers in an emergency.

"I see. Do they like their house?"

"I think so," he says, clearly enamored with the fur balls.

I turn to Darcy, Alexander, Matt, and the rest of the crowd gathered in the room and lingering out in the hall.

"Thank you from the bottom of my heart. When I got out of bed this morning, at a time much earlier than I would have liked, might I add, I could never have imagined in my wildest dreams my school, my students," I look at Tyler and take a steadying breath, "my kid would be blessed like this by a bunch of hot baseball players." The room erupts in laughter. I shake my head in embarrassment. "Hot *pepper* baseball players. You know what I meant. Don't let it go to your heads." They all laugh even harder.

"Thank you doesn't begin to express my gratitude. You guys have no idea how much you guys have touched these these kids' lives this year. Like it or not, you have five hundred kiddos you just adopted. Thanks for stepping up."

Some guys high-five each other. Others are clearly humbled by the kids we teach.

"Hey, there's a catered lunch in the cafeteria for everyone. You guys earned a cheat day," Alexander addresses the group. His boss persona takes over. His smile is gone, his tone serious. "Good job. See you at the field tomorrow."

Guys file past one by one and thank me. I can't believe they're thanking me. They did all the work today.

"Ms. Dani." One player stops to shake my hand. He's handsome, and his smile is the kind that toothpaste companies pay millions to use in their ads. Maybe that's why he looks a little familiar. I feel bad I don't know all the players by name, but I vow to write each of them a personal thank-you note.

"I had a teacher like you when I was little. She saved my life. Literally. I want you to know you may not see the fruit from the seeds you plant and tend, but they're out there. Thank you for what you do."

I wrap my arms around him and give him the biggest, hardest hug of my life. This guy, who must have had a rough childhood, grew up to play in the MLB. He wouldn't be here if it weren't for a teacher. He didn't forget.

As I pull away, I realize I don't know his name. "I'm sorry, I don't think we've been introduced."

Xander steps beside him and puts his hand on his shoulder, pulling him back a step. "This is Luis Rodriquez. Future Hall of Famer and star of the Reapers outfield."

"Well, Luis, I'm your new number-one fan. Thanks for being here today."

"I'll be back," he says. "Even more after the season. I know some schools have room mothers. Well, I can't be claiming that dad thing, too much swagger for that, so I'll be your room *Tio*," he teases. "But I'll be glad to help any way I can."

"I'll take you up on it, Luis. Thanks!"

I need a moment alone before I embarrass myself further. "Hey, Tyler, do you want to go with Luis and see what they have for lunch? I'll be there in a few minutes. You can introduce him to Jenny." I look at Luis to see if he's okay with my request, and his smile lights up the room. He gives me a slight nod and a wink. I know I can trust him with Tyler.

"Can I bring Joe and Mickey?" Tyler asks.

Alexander glances at me and notices I'm about to lose my composure again. He squats down to talk to Tyler. "That might be too much excitement for them. I'll put them in their house and let them chill for a bit before you go home. Will that be okay?"

Tyler screws up his mouth as he thinks about the options. He looks from the hedgehogs to Luis's outstretched hand. "Yeah, that sounds good."

Tyler takes Luis's hand, and they head out of the room. I have a feeling Tyler went from having my dad as his only male role model to an entire MLB team in the blink of an eye.

Alexander puts the hedgehogs in their elaborate habitat, softly rubbing their backs as he gently sets them in the dining room of their multilevel condo. He follows through on what he says he'll do. He's giving me a minute to get myself together.

I take a deep breath and turn in a full circle where I'm standing to recenter myself. When I see Alexander, he's staring at me intensely. "They're adorable." He's adorable, I think. I didn't say that out loud, did I? "Thank you. I know this wasn't some coincidence and random Reaper outreach."

He looks at me sheepishly. "When I say it was my pleasure, I mean it. I can't remember when I had this much fun getting my cherry popped at a warehouse store."

I laugh so hard I snort. So there's that. I'm a snorter. Classy, right?

"Well, it was unnecessary, but very much appreciated. Thank you."

I want to hug him like Jenny did. I want to wrap my arms around him and feel his body next to mine. But I know if I do, I may not let go. And I can't let myself believe it's anything other than the kind and very generous gesture of a guy who feels bad for the victim of an assault.

"You're welcome."

We stand frozen, both unsure of what we should do next.

"Hey Dani, we're headed out," Darcy calls from the doorway, breaking our awkward, strange standoff. "I've got a few things that didn't come in before today, so I'll drop them off next week. Is that okay?"

"What? Um, yeah. Absolutely. Thanks again, Darcy. It's just perfect."

"I'm glad you like it." She looks around the room and lands back on me and Alexander. "Yep. I think it suits you perfectly. A lot of sunshine tempered with a little darkness to keep it interesting. Very balanced. Can't wait to see if I'm right."

"Huh?"

"Don't mind her. Told you, color mumbo jumbo. Bye, boss. Bye, Dani. Hope to see you and Tyler at the ballpark again," Matt calls as he pulls Darcy away.

"I'd better go check on Tyler."

"Yeah, I have a feeling we might need to rescue Jenny from Luis," Alexander says.

He puts his hand on the small of my back to lead me to the school cafeteria, and it's the best feeling I've had in forever.

"Oh, I'm sure Jenny is just fine. It's Luis we may need to worry about."

CHAPTER
THIRTEEN

ALEXANDER

———

Tips for the first day of school flood the morning news: warnings to watch out for school buses, weather updates on what to wear, and school supplies still needed. It's been a week since I saw her. It doesn't take a glance at my calendar to know the timeline. I'm more aware than I'd like to admit. Thinking about her welcoming her students into her bright classroom this morning makes me smile. When the kid's faces light up, she'll shine bright.

Today is Tyler's first day of first grade, which means it's likely to be an overwhelming day for her overall. I should do something, but I don't want to come on too strong. The last thing I need is to add to her stress.

Should I text to check on her? Although we never exchanged numbers, I entered hers in my phone when Jack pulled the background check.

The background check. It had holes. Holes I'm curious about. When I asked questions about her past, she always shared about someone else. She seems like an open book until I want to know about her, especially her past.

Julian's words play on a loop in my head. I can't be my usual direct self. But what can I do to see her again? I've made it through several department meetings today, and everyone is still discussing the school project. They enjoyed it so much that I'm going to add quarterly all-staff give-back days—validating why I need to expand our community outreach team.

It's three o'clock. School should be over. I call Mr. Davis to see how the first day went. That's a good follow-up, right?

"Mr. Decker, it's great to hear from you. Today is a little chaotic, but that's expected. I can't thank you enough. It feels like a different school." Mr. Davis sounds a little frantic. Maybe my call wasn't the best idea. The last thing I want to do is add stress to his day too.

"I hope in a good way?"

"In the absolute best way. The food pantry is amazing. We introduced it during the open house, and the few families that attended were excited. I think the Reapers have fans for life now."

"That isn't why we did it, but we enjoy taking care of our community." I've asked Nikki to keep some numbers from the food pantry. We're prepared to pivot and change strategies if we need to adjust how it operates. Do other schools need a food pantry? Kids without food are not acceptable in my book.

"Well, we appreciate everything. I hope you don't mind, but I called our local news channel to cover the excited kids getting their backpacks. I know you didn't do it for the press, but I think letting the community know is necessary." I knew he called them when our PR team started fielding media calls yesterday for comments. "It'll be in the evening news cycle. I'm sorry. I know you wanted to keep it low-key, but five hundred kids going home with laptops will not stay quiet for long."

I chuckle. He's probably right. "I understand. I'm just sorry I couldn't witness the day firsthand. How are the teachers handling it all?" Especially a particular third grade teacher?

"I've got a great team of dedicated teachers who do this because they love their jobs. They're good. Tired, but good."

"That's great to hear. What can I do for them?"

"Short of caffeine and prayers, nothing. They're running on pure adrenaline. But I appreciate you showing concern. It means a lot to all of us."

"It's the least I can do. I admire the work you all do. I'll arrange a little something for the staff tomorrow. And please, let me know if you have any other ideas. Nothing is off limits."

I'm focused on my emails when a chat from Elaine pops up, telling me I have a visitor.

It's at that moment I notice her. She's sitting in the waiting area, looking everywhere but in the vicinity of my office. From my vantage point, I watch her cross her long, lean legs. She's wearing a ruffled, flowy skirt that hits above her knee. The dark floral pattern is in contrast to her white t-shirt and denim jacket. She sure doesn't look like any teacher I ever had. Old and haggard, my ass. Those kids don't know what they're talking about.

I walk out of my office and take her in. She turns her head, and those eyes catch me looking. I put my professional face on and walk toward her, totally aware I'm under Elaine's watchful eye.

"Mr. Decker, Ms. Frankin doesn't have an appointment but wanted to drop something off for you. I asked her to wait because I knew you'd want to thank her personally." Elaine has a smirk on her face that lets me know this will be breakroom fodder tomorrow.

Elaine's been my assistant since I took the General Manager role three years ago. I'm the youngest GM in the league, and Dad wanted me to start with a team I selected that would help me succeed. I would be dead in the water without Elaine. But this smirk? It makes me rethink her employment status.

"Thanks, Elaine." I glare at her, hopeful her smirk will go away. It intensifies. Damn.

I take a few more steps closer to Dani, and her smile lights up the room. "Dani, it's great to see you. How was your first day of school?"

She takes another step toward me and catches me off guard by hugging me. I pat her back while being overwhelmed by the nearness. I inhale, taking in the smells of a tropical island, coconut, seawater, and sunshine, and relax into her hug more than I should. Our bodies fit together, her head tucking perfectly under my chin. She's like a puzzle piece snapping into place, and I wonder how long we can stay like this and not be awkward, or I get a hard-on. Like she hears my thoughts, she steps back.

"Are you blushing, Mr. Decker?" she teases.

Elaine snickers behind me. I give her my classic scowl. "I'm going to get some coffee. Can I get you two anything?"

I should reprimand her for her lack of subtleness, but her wicked smile tells me it won't be effective. Elaine knows how much she's valued, and no reprimand will be taken seriously.

"I'm fine, thank you," Dani replies. "I came by to drop these off for you and the Reapers." Dani holds out a stack of papers, folded in half and tied with a yellow ribbon. She hands me the bundle of handmade cards.

"From your class?"

"The top two are from Tyler; one for you and one for Matt. The rest are from my students and Jenny's class. It was their idea to thank the team who made this, and I quote, 'the best school ever.'" Her face lights up talking about her students. It's obvious they mean so much to her.

I motion to my office. "Please come in for a minute. I'd love to hear about your first day of school." It's then I realize she's alone, and thinking of the cards, I wonder where her son is. "Where's Tyler?"

"My dad took him out for ice cream after school. Something

about starting a new tradition? I don't know. But it gave me a chance to drop these off. I'm sorry for just stopping in. I don't want to keep you from your work."

"No, don't be silly. I was wrapping up for the day, anyway. Please, come in?"

Elaine returns with her afternoon coffee and scoffs. Yeah, wrapping up is a little white lie. I work too much, and Elaine knows all my secrets. But I don't have to stay tonight. Technically, I don't have to stay late any night.

"Okay. Thanks."

She comes into my office, and Elaine is right behind us with water bottles, a sly smile on her face.

"Thanks, Elaine. Why don't you head home too?"

"Oh, that's okay. I have a few more things I'd like to get done today." She winks at Dani and heads back to her desk, undoubtedly eavesdropping on me. If I close the door, it might make Dani uncomfortable and give Elaine's imagination something to work with.

I give a small sigh and a slight shake of my head.

I feel the need to explain myself. "I'm not a taskmaster, I promise."

Dani raises one eyebrow, giving me a skeptical look. "I don't know if I believe you, boss. I saw how everyone responded to you at the school." She opens her bottle of water and takes a sip, the action attempting to cover up her smile. It doesn't work.

I don't have a response for that, so I focus on the bundle of cards in front of me. I pull out my scissors and cut the ribbon, causing Dani to gasp.

"What?" I'm a little harsher than I intended to be, but I can't imagine what I did to get that reaction.

"Nothing," she whispers.

I give her my boardroom look, and she caves.

"You cut the ribbon. Most people would take their time and untie the bow."

I put my elbows on my desk and lean across, ready to tell her a not very secret piece of information. I quietly share something about myself that my inner circle already knows. "I'm not most people, Dani. And I'm direct when it comes to something I want. I don't let obstacles slow me down."

Her eyes grow wide at my words. Is she imagining the innuendo I intended?

I lift the ribbon to get her attention. "This ribbon was in the way. But rest assured. I can take my time unwrapping a beautiful package."

A blush fill her cheeks. Her attention goes to the water bottle in her hands. Suddenly, she finds it fascinating.

I take the first card and see a crayon drawing of Joe and Mickey. Their smiles are bigger than their bodies, but it's clear what they are. Inside, it reads, *Thank you for giving us a family.* The writing is neater than I expected from a six-year-old.

I set the second card aside since it's for Matt. I scan the other cards, appreciating the words from her students. Most say thank you for the school supplies, laptops, and other items. Several cards mention how much they love Joe and Mickey. One catches my eye, and I spend more time on it.

Thank you for the food. I can't wait to fix dinner for my sisters. It's signed by Jasmine. There's a picture of her cooking and two girls sitting around a table. I'm reminded of the hardships these kids face. And Jasmine is cooking dinner. She's like eight, right?

"Everything alright?" I look up to find Dani watching me.

"Um, yeah. Fine." I open my water and take a gulp, washing away the lump in my throat and the emotion this card evoked. "Jasmine's card just hit differently, that's all." I shake it off. "Tell me about your first day."

At the mention of her class, she lights up. "I have twenty kids, fourteen boys and six girls, so lots of energy in that room. They love Joe and Mickey. Those creatures must be grateful for the quiet night alone after being held and talked to all day. We spent some time learning about hedgehogs, what they eat, their behaviors, and their habits. I can't thank you enough for everything. We've enjoyed having them at home but decided it was best they stay at school and only come home on weekends." She points to my desk. "You can see Tyler just adores them."

I hold his card again. "These are great. I'll share them with the others tomorrow." I put Tyler's card on my desk, next to the group photo at Ash and Cole's engagement. This card means more to me than she'll ever know.

There's an awkward pause in the conversation, and we both make eye contact. I can't help but stare at her beauty. Her teeth bite her bottom lip, and it takes monumental effort to stay on my side of the desk. What the hell is wrong with me? She elicits a reaction from me I've never experienced before, and it's taking all my willpower to be a gentleman. I'm inexplicably drawn to her, like a moth to a flame.

"Um, I should go. I just wanted to say thank you." She stands, and I reach across my desk and grab her wrist.

"Wait! Let me walk you out." I don't want her to leave. I'm craving more time with her.

"I don't want to inconvenience you." She looks at where my hand is on her wrist, and I immediately release her.

Fuck. I'm grabbing at her like a desperate man. Am I any better than Pauly? I look down and apologize. "I'm sorry. I didn't mean to touch you like that. I..."

"What did I tell you about apologies, Alexander Decker?" Her tone is direct and authoritative.

"Did you just use your teacher voice on me?" I look at her, and she's smiling like I hung the moon. I don't want to tell her what that voice did to me, but it's definitely something she should spank me for.

"I did. You're a smart man. Those diplomas from Wake Forest and Harvard on the wall tell me that. Stop treating me like some sort of victim. I'm not a fragile doll that you need to be careful with. Nor am I someone you need to keep apologizing to. Got it, smart guy?"

This is the spitfire that fucking turns me on. I love the sass. A smile slowly creeps across my face. I hear you, beautiful. I hear you.

"Yes, ma'am." I give her a nod and a quick wink. I use my version of my teacher's voice, but it's the clubhouse "don't fuck with me or else" voice. "So let me walk down with you. Not because you need an escort, but because I want to, and I'm going that way anyway." I've left no question. I will walk her downstairs.

She looks at me and slowly shakes her head, but can't hide her shy smile. "Okay."

"Good." I grab my phone and step toward her, gesturing her toward the door. "After you, Ms. Franklin."

"Thank you, Mr. Decker." She fucking giggles, and I almost lose it. I did that. I made her giggle and I feel like I won the World Series single handedly. What the fuck is wrong with me?

We walk past Elaine, who is trying to look busy, but I know she's not. "Goodnight Elaine. I'll see you tomorrow morning."

"Don't forget you have that breakfast meeting with the County Commissioners in the morning." She tries to sound all business and professional, but she barely contains her laughter.

"Got it. Go home, Elaine." I sigh. I will not live this down. I know Elaine heard me get put in my place, and she enjoyed it. Ashleigh and Elaine are the only other women that try to do that, and it's rare either of them try.

"Goodnight, boss."

Dani and I walk down the administrative offices hallway, and I try to ignore the eyes that watch us. Yep, there will be talk in the morning.

"This place feels so different when it's empty," she comments. "It feels so much bigger. No game tonight?"

I walk over and look out over the field. The sprinklers are running, keeping the grass in pristine condition. "We have a west coast road trip, so away games for the next week."

"Do you ever travel with the team?" She's standing beside me, looking around the stadium.

"Sometimes, usually at the beginning of the season, to make sure the team is bonding, set behavioral expectations, that kind of thing. By this point in the season, they don't need me there. I may show up if I need to meet with another GM, scout a potential trade, or want to get away. Keeps them on their toes. They play one-hundred-sixty-two games, not including playoffs. Baseball is the longest season of any American professional sport, and it can be grueling."

"Wow. That's a lot of frequent flyer miles."

I want to explain we have a team plane, but I remember how she often comments about money. No need to bring up things like that.

"Yeah, something like that."

"What time do you have to pick up Tyler?" I need more time.

"He needs to get ready for bed by seven, so not for a few hours."

"Can I treat you to dinner to celebrate your first day of school? There are several great restaurants in the area. We could even walk."

She looks at her watch and gives a slight chuckle. "Are we really that old we need to get the early bird special?"

I look at my watch, and it's a few minutes after four o'clock. I'm not used to leaving work this early. "Oh, I wasn't thinking about the time."

"You know what? How about ice cream? If Tyler and my dad got ice cream, why shouldn't we?"

I was thinking of a nice bottle of wine and dinner, but ice cream is okay too. "That sounds good. Let's get my car, and I'll drive us to the best ice cream spot in town. Do you mind walking a block?" I know she's been on her feet all day, and even though her shoes don't have those spikes women like to wear, they do have a slight heel.

"Sure, it's a glorious day. Why not? But you don't park at the stadium? Or are you driven around like a big shot?" There she goes teasing me again.

"No, most days I just walk. I live over there." I point to my building, a high rise that overlooks the ballpark.

She lets out a low whistle. "Nice." She walks toward my building and I take a few steps to catch up. I gently move her over, so I'm walking on the sidewalk closest to the road.

She notices my gesture, and I brace myself for another lecture about not needing to be protected. Instead, I'm pleasantly surprised with one of her incredible smiles. A strange sensation fills my chest, and suddenly being rewarded by one of those smiles might be my new kink.

CHAPTER
FOURTEEN

DANI

We drive to this out-of-the-way, not fancy, nondescript place with a sign from decades gone by. He opens my door and walks me to the ice cream shop, another action from the gentleman's handbook. When we enter, Alexander is welcomed by name. He says hi to everyone, talking to some about baseball or asking about school or some other personal stuff. A red-haired boy that looks like Ron Weasley scoops his usual rocky road without even asking, then asks me what I want.

"There are too many flavors to pick. I don't know." Deciding on a flavor may take me a minute because they all look so good. Brady, the teenaged boy straight from Hogwarts, helps me narrow my selection by asking about my likes and then offering me samples of various flavors. This homemade ice cream is delicious, and I'm afraid if I pick one, I'll have FOMO for the other flavors. I settle on cherry vanilla with the perfect ratio of ice cream to cherries and chocolate chunks. Great choice.

When Alexander pulls out a frequent-buyer punch card, I

can't contain my surprise. The guy who drives the most incredible Mercedes I've ever seen has a punch card to an ice cream parlor. None of it adds up in my head. He's a conundrum, that's for sure.

"A punch card? Really?"

"Yeah, I'm here a lot." He says it like it makes sense. And for a broke teacher, it does. For him?

"Obviously," I say with some sarcasm.

"Are you judging me for having a punch card or being an ice cream addict?"

"Neither?" He doesn't believe me, and his glare is downright reproachful.

"Would it change your mind if I told you my mom used to bring us here as kids all the time? Best ice cream in the city, hands down." I bring my hand to my chest, attempting to hold my heart because he brought me somewhere meaningful to him.

He's not what I expected. "And the punch card?"

He shrugs as he tucks it back in his wallet. "I leave the filled punch cards at random places around town or give them to a person on a nearby bench. Everyone should enjoy this ice cream, don't you think?" Is this guy for real? He gives me a wink, and my stomach flips.

We sit at an outside table under the shade of a large oak tree. It's another hot day, so my ice cream melts quickly, dripping down the cone, causing me to lick it before it hits my fingers. I glance at him. and his eyes are burning, his resting scowl face filled with something new. Not quite anger, but he's upset about something.

"What?" I'm not sure what I did, but I feel the need to tread lightly.

"Why won't you tell me about yourself?" Is this an example of him being direct?

"What do you mean? I've told you tons." I feel like we've talked a lot. I don't always answer his questions directly. That's his style, not mine. I'll tell him anything he wants to know about me, but in a more you have to listen to what I say than here are the answers to a test. I'm not being coy, but I think getting to know someone is more than a quick interview.

"No, you really haven't. What's your favorite flower?"

"Why?" Now I'm just being stubborn, and he's going to have to work for it. I bet he's up to the challenge. And if he's not, well, then he's not the man I think he is. I'd bet most women fall at his feet, and I understand that. But that's not who I am. I suspect that's not what he wants, either. He thrives on the game, the chase, the competition. Will he still be interested once he catches me? That's the question, isn't it?

"Because I might want to send you flowers. What's your favorite? Something yellow? Sunflowers?"

While I like sunflowers, they aren't my favorite. "I don't want you to send me flowers, and for that reason alone, I refuse to answer." My smug smile resurfaces, and I focus my attention on my ice cream cone.

"Okay, I'll ask another question. Why did you say no when I asked you out?"

I nervously fidget. What do I say? I'm not entirely sure why I said no. Other than the obvious disparity in incomes and lifestyles, I'm attracted to him. No doubt. I haven't had a physical reaction to a man like this in years. Seven years, to be exact. Why did I say no? To protect Tyler? Myself? But protect us from what?

He wants to know about me, then I'll answer a question he didn't ask. It's more valuable information than my favorite flower. "I don't want you to feel sorry for me." I can't believe I said that, even if it's true.

"Why would I feel sorry for you?" He cocks his head to the side, like he's trying to solve a problem.

"I'm not a victim," I mumble, taking another lick of my ice cream cone.

"Never thought you were," he states matter-of-factly. "Now, can I have your number?"

"Why?" I wonder why he's asking. Surely, he can get it from Ashleigh. Is he being polite? Is he asking permission? I'm not sure why he's asking, but the thought of him using it to reach out to me makes my heart flutter.

"I might want to keep up with Joe and Mickey." He pokes his bottom lip out and pretends to pout.

How do I say no to that? I don't.

CHAPTER
FIFTEEN

ALEXANDER

————

"You're not pushing me out of this hospital like some invalid," Trevor argues.

"Sit your sorry ass in that wheelchair and quit being difficult. These nurses don't need to put up with more of your whining." We have a stare-down, and I win pretty quickly. Yeah, Trevor definitely isn't himself.

I had barely said goodbye to Dani after our ice cream date when I got the call. Trevor was in the hospital after a horrific motorcycle accident. A medically induced coma, two surgeries, a full-leg cast, and ten days later, I'm taking him home. Thank god for helmets.

In the past week, I've spent hours at the hospital, rented equipment for his recovery, and hired a nurse to help with the transition home. It's been non-stop with minimal sleep.

Trevor Lewis is my best friend, and while we don't live in the same city, we talk or text daily and see each other regularly. He owns a college summer league baseball team, the Savannah Pajamas, that has become widely popular because of Ashleigh's phenomenal social media and Trevor's unique take on baseball as entertainment. That's actually where Ashleigh met Cole and Matt. Still not sure if I should thank Trevor or kill him for that. I'm not mad. Anymore.

I get Trevor in the house, and we kick back on the sofa. Trevor has his leg propped up on pillows and tries to act like he's okay. His eyes tell another story.

"How much pain?" I've been by his side enough to know how the nurses ask. I also know to add three points to anything he says.

"Five. I'll be okay. Just give me a minute. That was a lot of jostling around."

"You sound like a grandpa," I tease. I've been a hard ass to him since I got to the hospital, and the medical team assured me he would be okay. I'm hard on him because that's our way. And he scared the life out of me, so he deserves it. He has a long recovery ahead, and I'll be beside him every step of the way.

What I won't let him see is how much I cried on the drive to Savannah. My insides twisted, thinking I could lose my best friend. We've been friends since freshman year at Wake Forest. He learned everything he knows about baseball from me. I've learned how to sell tickets from him. Honestly, Trevor taught me how to live life. He was with me when my mom was sick. He taught me how to grieve. Hell, he taught me how to cry. And now, I'd rather not use those life lessons on him.

I hand him his pain medication and a beer to wash it down. He quirks an eyebrow and takes it.

"You need to work on your bedside manner. It sucks." He takes a long pull on his beer. His normal humor gone.

"You need to be a better patient," I snap back. Both of us speak the truth.

He looks at me, his eyes glossing over with tears. I'll ignore them like he ignored mine when he first woke up.

"Thanks, man. You know, for dropping everything." He's choked up, the words difficult to get out.

I give him my usual head nod. It conveys everything I can't say. Of course I'd be here. You're my best friend and brother. I love you. And we will sue the truck driver that never even slowed down after he turned into you.

The front door bursts open, and the room fills with a delicious aroma that causes my stomach to growl. "Hi, boys. Thought you might be hungry."

Emma walks through the den and into the kitchen with a large tote. She's unpacking food before I can even get up.

"Hey there, Em," Trevor calls from the sofa, a little life in his voice. "I'd get up and help, but well, can't."

I greet Emma with a kiss on the top of her head. "Hey. Thanks for this. Why aren't you at school?"

Emma is Ashleigh's best friend. She's a schoolteacher in Savannah and has been with me at the hospital when she's not working. She's like another little sister to me and part of our inner circle of friends.

"I took the day off. I figured you needed a proper meal, and our patient over there needs to be well-fed so he won't abuse his nurse. Besides, if you need anything, I could get it." She gives me a wink, and I shake my head at her. She may be five foot nothing, but she stands up to us big guys like we're just bugs she can squish under her heel. Which we are, and she could, but we don't voice it out loud.

"Thanks. We just got home a few minutes ago. Smells great. What can I do to help?"

"Turn on the oven for the cookies. Everything else should be hot. I've got lasagna, salad, garlic bread. Figured you could put a few pounds back on after all that hospital food." She squeezes my arm and pretends its soft. It's not. I've been in the gym working out my stress when I haven't been at Trevor's side.

"I could say the same about you. You okay? You look tired." I put my hand under her chin and make her look at me. The purple under her eyes peeks through under her makeup.

"I'm fine, Xander," she whispers. "He just scared me to death, that's all."

"Yeah. Me too." I wrap her in my arms and give her a hug that we both need. I love this girl. She's been such a blessing to Ash and our family. Even though her last name isn't Decker, it might as well be. She's one of us.

A kiss on her head, a deep breath, and it's back to taking care of Trevor.

We make plates and take them into the den, where Trevor is dozing. Maybe washing the pain pill down with a beer wasn't the best idea, but he needs to rest.

"Let's eat at the bar and leave sleeping beauty alone. I'm sure peace and quiet won't last long," Emma whispers.

We get settled and tuck into our lunch. "This is so good. I appreciate it." I'm eating like I haven't eaten in days, and now that I think about it, I probably haven't. I've been living on wraps from the cafeteria and protein bars. This is my first hot meal in a while, and I'm eating like a teenaged boy with no table manners.

My phone buzzes. Probably Jules or Ash checking in. I've been horrible at keeping up with texts and emails. My phone died several times while I was at the hospital because I didn't have a charger. I'm not the best communicator in normal times, and this situation hasn't helped.

When I see the message, a spontaneous grin breaks free.

"Oh, this is interesting," Emma muses. "Do tell, what could make that elusive smile appear, hm?"

I flash my phone at her to share the picture that fills my screen. It's Joe and Mickey with a sign on their table with a big yellow smiley face that reads, "Thinking about you." Both hedgehogs are in the picture, one looking at the camera, one looking at the sign. It's adorable.

"Those are cute. Who's sending you animal memes, and why

do they make you smile? Not something I'd have on my Xander bingo card."

"It's from Dani." I'm not sure what Ash tells Emma, but I assume she knows about Dani.

"Dani, the hot, single mom?"

"Interesting, yet accurate description. She wanted a classroom pet, so I got her two. That's Joe DiMaggio and Mickey Mantle."

"Of course you did, you big softie." She punches me in the arm. "Darcy told us about it during our last virtual girl's night. We didn't know you were text buddies." She wiggles her eyebrows at me. It should be cute, but Emma can be scary, and I'm smart enough to stay on alert.

"We aren't. Not really. I saw her two Tuesdays ago, told her I'd text, and then." I give her a half-shrug. We both know what happened on Tuesday night.

Not that I don't think about her. I do. But I failed. I didn't reach out like I said I would. I couldn't exactly ask her out when I'm not there. Every day that passes, I figure it's more sand dropping in my hourglass, my window of time slipping away. The longer it goes, the more I think I've missed my moment.

What prompted her to reach out now? My phone buzzes with another text before I've decided how to respond to her picture.

SUNSHINE

Luis came to visit my class today. Kids adored him. Told me you were out of town with a family emergency. Just reaching out to say I hope everyone is okay.

Hope Luis behaved himself.

Did she ask Luis about me? How did I come up in conversation? Wait. What was he doing there on a game day? Is he moving in on Dani? She's gorgeous, but I thought Luis was smarter than that.

> Thanks. My best friend was in a bad motorcycle accident last Tuesday. I just brought him home from the hospital today. Him versus truck. Guess who won?

SUNSHINE

That had to be terrifying. Are you okay?

Am I okay? Has anyone asked me that? The fist that was squeezing my chest releases a little. Dani's sunshine breaks through the darkness from hundreds of miles away. I drop my shield a little. Test the waters.

> I am now.

SUNSHINE

Gotta run. Kiddos are coming back from lunch.
Let me know if you need anything.

> Thanks. I'm glad you reached out. I'm sorry I didn't. I wanted to.

I wait for the dots to show up, and they don't. I'm like a teenaged girl waiting for a text response. I sigh and put my phone down.

There might still be hope.

CHAPTER
SIXTEEN

ALEXANDER

———

We've been texting for a few days now. She said pictures are worth a thousand words, and I said I prefer clear, direct communication with words. So naturally, she sends mostly pictures that I have to interpret. It's much harder than direct words, and when I told her that, her picture game amped up. I think she enjoys giving me shit, and I kinda like it.

I growl at this latest picture of Luis waving at her from the field. She follows it up with a picture of the WAGs giving me cheers with their beers.

When I put together she was at the game, I asked my intern Corey to check on her, and before I knew it, she had me buying a round for the WAGs to pay for my mistake of sending Corey. She's at my ballpark. At the invitation of another. And it irritates me. That's twice now. She's hovering at the edge of my world, but I'd give anything to get her to jump in with me.

My need for information is gnawing away at my sanity. I'm

dying to know what's going on, so I contact Ash, who calls Darcy, to find out what was happening with Dani. When I ask Ash for a follow-up, she sends the laughing emoji a hundred times. She doesn't answer when I call. I know better than to ask Darcy directly. Now I'm frustrated while I watch the game with Trevor. These women are driving me crazy.

"Something bothering you?" Trevor got a new cast today, and he's mobile with crutches now. The cast is still above the knee, but it's better than the one he had that went to his hip. I got him an automatic recliner, and he's much more comfortable.

I swirl my bourbon around in the glass while I decide how to answer him. I'm irritated, but I'm not sure why. "Dani's at the game."

"Why does that bother you?"

I've told Trevor about Dani. He's up to speed with as much as I'm willing to admit. Which isn't much.

"It doesn't," I grumble. Does it bother me she's there? No, not really. I'm glad she's enjoying herself at my ballpark. Do I wish I was the one hosting her? Absolutely. Fuck. That's what's bothering me. She's there as Luis's guest.

Trevor lets me stew in my thoughts. He understands me and lets me think things through, and for that, I'm grateful. Trevor's a goofball, but he has extraordinary emotional intelligence. He can read people better than anyone I've ever seen.

"She's there as the guest of Luis Rodriquez." There. I say what's bothering me in a roundabout way. Evasiveness works.

"I thought you liked Luis. He's a good guy. What's the problem?" Why doesn't he get it? He should understand because it's so fucking obvious.

I don't say anything and gulp down the rest of my bourbon. I get up to pour another one.

"Oh, I get it. You like her, don't you? Like you want her to be your girlfriend, like her." He laughs at me in my misery.

"You're as bad as the girls. Are you joining them for girl's nights now?" I'm sure Ash and Darcy have already looped Emma into my desperate attempt for information.

Trevor lowers the recliner and sits up to talk. He keeps the game on but hits mute. At least I can watch the game without sound. They need to win to make it to the playoffs. Tonight, they're up against last year's series winners, so it's going to be sheer will and determination, with a bit of luck sprinkled in to get the win and move on.

"So spill. What's the story? Are you going to let Luis make his move?" Trevor's face lights up, and a spark of life shines in him, more than he's had since he's been home. He thrives on drama. Other people's drama, that is. My life is his entertainment. So for the sake of his healing and mental well-being, I bare my soul.

"I'll let her do whatever she wants. She deserves the absolute best in life. I mean, she's an incredible woman. Strong, brave, gorgeous. She's like bottled sunshine, always the optimist. I don't understand her, but I want to. Jules said I can't come on strong, or it'll turn her off. But I don't know any other way than to be direct. Besides, she thinks we come from two different worlds."

"You asked Jules for advice? Team True Love? This must be serious." He throws the remote at me to get me to look his way. "Well, buddy, I hate to tell you, but you do come from different worlds. But that doesn't mean it can't work out. I'm with Jules on this one. You can't buy her things or dazzle her with your stuff." I know what he's saying, but I need her to be comfortable in my world too.

Maybe that's part of the appeal? She's not chasing the money and lifestyle I can provide. I like that she's caring and giving. I mean, not every teacher is made to teach in underprivileged schools. That shows her character.

"I don't dazzle," I mumble.

My phone buzzes with a text. Maybe it's Ash with an

update? I see a picture overlooking the ballpark taken from my office. I give a low chuckle at Dani's reflection in the glass.

She's sitting in my chair, turned around with the desk behind her. The oversized leather chair embraces her as she leans back, relaxed. Her white tennis shoes are on display as she crosses her long, lean legs. It's hard to tell in the reflection, but it looks like she's wearing those sexy white shorts again with a tight under-shirt that shows off her perky breasts. She's wearing an unbut-toned, red home jersey that practically swallows her whole. I wonder if you can even see the shorts from behind. I don't need to think about that view now, because my dick is paying atten-tion. The jersey? It's fucking Luis Rodriquez's number four.

The grin on her face tells me she knows exactly what she's doing. This girl is a vixen, and I'm here for it.

I show Trevor the picture, and he laughs. "Xander, I think it's time for you to go home."

I sigh. I don't want to leave Trevor, but I'm tired of playing from the sidelines. It's time to get in the game. I give Trevor a nod.

"You're coming with me. No arguing. You know the line. Never leave your wingman."

Trevor laughs. "I got you. Let's go." He starts to stand and falls back into the recliner. "Maybe in the morning?"

I shake my head at him while I pick up my phone and send a group text asking for help to set up my place for Trevor. Now that he's more mobile, he's needs aren't as extensive. Since my penthouse is one floor, stairs are no longer an issue. Honestly, the layout is probably better than his brownstone, anyway. I should have brought him to Charlotte earlier.

His doctor gave me his number, which I used to ask if the relocation was safe. After some brief instructions and a connec-tion with a colleague in Charlotte, we get the green light to travel.

I have one more text to send.

"Oh, looks like Xander's ready to play," Trevor chuckles. "I'm in, brother. I'm in."

I give him a definitive nod. Yep. It's time to move this along.

> Nice view.

> Get ready. I'm coming for you, Dani Franklin.

Yes, I'm aware of the double entendre. Very aware.

CHAPTER
SEVENTEEN

DANI

———

The Reapers won, and the city is electric with fans filling all the bars and restaurants after the game. Luis texted Jenny and asked us to meet him at a brewery close to my house, so we go home, drop the car off, and walk a few blocks. Parking in this area is such a pain.

Casey warned us the guys would be hungry and hopped up on adrenaline, so be on high alert for anything. I'm caught up in the excitement and flying high after my banter with Alexander, so I know how they feel. I'm as nervous as a cat in a room full of rocking chairs.

I can't believe I sent that picture. He hasn't responded, and I'm worried I may have crossed the line. Corey was nervous about letting me into the offices, but I assured him it was fine. He trusts I'm not some rando. He saw me for the first time when he delivered the pants to the suite after my shorts were drenched. Then Alexander sent him to check on me tonight, and I made Alexander buy the WAGs a round of drinks for that stunt. If

Corey gets in trouble because of me, I'll call Ashleigh to help him. He's just an intern trying to do the right thing. Sweet kid.

Alexander's desk was neat, with nothing laying out or cluttering his space. He had one picture on his desk facing him. It was of a group of cheerful people, some smiling at the camera, others looking at each other. Ashleigh is kissing someone, and I assume he's her fiancé. Alexander and Julian looked at her with loving smiles, but it seemed like Alexander was being playfully held back from them by a handsome Black man. Everyone else was hamming for the camera. Darcy and Matt were in the picture too, but not next to each other. There was only one other girl, surrounded by lots of stunning men. I wonder who she is? Was that Chance Fuller, captain of the Raleigh Renegades? And Tripp Stevenson? His family.

Tyler's card was next to the picture. It was enough to make my heart melt when Tyler showed it to me. And now, it's one of the few things on his desk. Puddle of goo.

I feel a little bad for sending the picture, but I couldn't resist pushing his buttons. Was the jersey too much?

Jenny and I arrive at the crowded brewery. Most people are wearing Reapers shirts or hats. I see two large picnic tables outside with reserved signs, and we approach them where Casey and Darcy are already seated with a few other girls.

"The guys will be here soon," Darcy says. "Matt is excited to see y'all again."

"Tyler will kill me if he finds out I get to see Matt. He absolutely adores him."

"He is adorable," Casey giggles.

"Stop." Darcy playfully pushes against Casey. "But yeah, he is." Her smile lights up the room when she talks about Matt. They are the perfect couple and support each other with everything they have.

We order food and drinks while we wait for the guys. The place continues to fill up, and I'm amazed at how we can hold both tables. Cheers erupt from the other tables, and I look around to figure out why. That's when a group of guys walk up to our tables and greet their partners. I can't believe I'm sitting here with eight Reapers who just won their game.

Darcy hops up and runs to Matt. He spins her around and gives her a kiss that could melt steel.

"Hey, pretty girl," he says as he breaks the kiss.

"I'm so excited for you. You knocked in the winning run!" She gives him a quick kiss and drags him to our table.

Luis greets us with side hugs and sits between me and Jenny when Matt clears his throat. "Luis, why don't you sit on the other side of Jenny? I'm sitting here." Matt claims the spot beside me, with Darcy on his other side. I'm in a Jenny and Matt sandwich. He nods to Tripp Stevenson, who sits across from me. I'm not sure what this seating chart is about, but it's comical and a little suspicious.

Everyone chats and eats when an occasional fan breaks through the crowd to ask for an autograph or selfie. The guys are gracious and kind and have a polite way of letting them know they're with their significant other. There's a lot of laughing and joking, and everyone is having fun. Spirits are high.

The guys quickly devour the food we ordered, and someone orders another round of wings and beers. Casey wasn't kidding. These guys are putting away the food. I'm amazed at how they eat so much and still have the bodies they have. Okay, so yeah, I noticed their bodies. It's hard to ignore.

My look must give away my thoughts when Tripp says, "This is a cheat meal. We usually eat a lot cleaner than this during the season. But tonight? We celebrate." He lifts his hot wing to me in salute, and I crack up.

"Was I that obvious?"

"A little. It's cute. Most people have preconceived ideas about us. They aren't all correct." He gives me a wink, and I blush.

Tripp may be quiet, but he's clearly a leader on the team. He's one of the older players, according to the roster. It makes me sad that thirty-four is old, and your career is almost over.

Tripp pitched the first few innings, but they pulled him once the Reapers were ahead. The girls were telling me they need to save his arm, and that's why they limit his play. He's still got what it takes, but he wants to keep it going for another season or two.

The conversation flows, and every time Luis asks me a question, Tripp or Matt highjacks the conversation. Luis finally gives up and focuses all his attention on Jenny. I don't know what's up with them because he's clearly into Jenny, but they are acting like bodyguards or something.

Tripp is attentive and peppers me with questions about school and Tyler. He seems shy but works to keep me engaged in conversation. When he gives me a hard time about wearing Luis's jersey, Luis pretends to be offended, and I ask whose jersey I should wear. They discuss something about a custom jersey, and I laugh at their ridiculousness.

"Hey Dani, any new pictures of the hedgehogs?" Matt asks.

"Sure." I pull out my phone and see I have an unread text. I gasp when I read what it says and pull my phone to my chest, not wanting anyone to see the message.

Jenny turns to me, concern filling her face. "You okay? Tyler?"

The volume dies down while everyone waits for my response. My face flushes from the embarrassment. Or maybe from the text, I'm not sure. I swallow hard, take a deep breath, and nod. It's okay. Alexander Decker responded to my picture. And his response was not what I was expecting.

"Yeah, yeah. Fine." I give them all a reassuring smile. I drop the phone below the table to open my picture roll. Jenny peeks and sees my last picture is a view of the field from Alexander's office. She cocks her head and hits my thigh, letting me know we'll talk about it later. I pop her leg in response. I gather myself, scroll back a few pictures, and find some of the hedgehogs and Tyler.

"Here are my boys." I share the picture of Tyler with Joe and

Mickey cuddled in his arms. His smile must be contagious because everyone smiles. I know I'm biased, but he's adorable.

"Oh my god, I just want to squeeze them," Darcy says.

I scroll to find another one, and Matt sees one of Tyler with a bat at practice.

"Is Tyler playing fall ball?" Matt asks.

"Yeah, he is. I swear, the bat is bigger than he is. But he loves it. He wanted to play third base because he has a little hero worship going on, but the coach makes them rotate positions every game."

Matt laughs, and Luis reaches around and knocks his hat off his head. I'm amazed how his arm can reach around Jenny and me, but then I remember that incredible catch he made that seemed like he was ten feet away from the ball.

"Outfield is where it's at," Luis says.

"Catcher is the one calling the shots," Joey says.

"Pitching is where the money is," Tripp mumbles.

All the guys nod in agreement with Tripp.

"When I visited the school, I told Dani we would try to make a game or practice." Luis smiles. The players scowl at him. I knew he shouldn't insist. It's too much.

"Oh, no. No." All the players give me a stern look, and now I've officially crossed the line with them. "I hope you're too busy winning the playoffs and the trophy and don't have time for little league."

"I remember what it was like, watching my heroes, hoping for the chance to meet them someday." Matt looks at Tripp and laughs. Clearly, there's a story there. "If I can make it happen, I will. Drop me his schedule."

"Oh, you don't have to," I start.

"Drop him the schedule, Dani," Tripp says with more volume and authority than I've heard all night. "It will happen."

I look at the players, who all have a determined glare. "Okay," I whisper. "Thanks."

The party winds down, and everyone pairs off to head home.

"Can I take you ladies home?" Luis asks me and Jenny.

"I took the light rail," Jenny responds. "I can…"

"Nope, I'll drive you home. It's too late to be alone on the train. Dani?"

"Oh, I just live around the corner. I walked here. I'm fine."

"I'll drop you off," Luis says.

"No, Rodriquez. I've got her." Tripp's tone puts an end to the discussion. "You just make sure Jenny gets home safe. Jenny, is that okay with you?"

She looks at me, waiting for my approval. Funny that Jenny gets a choice, but apparently, I don't.

"Thanks, Tripp. Luis, be careful with her." I give him a hug and a kiss on the cheek. "And thanks for the tickets and this." I shake the jersey I'm wearing. "I think tonight was exactly what I needed."

Tripp scowls at Luis, and I laugh.

Tripp's phone buzzes. He excuses himself and steps a few feet away. He nods and says, "Yeah, I've got her," before he hangs up.

I can guess who's on the phone. I think back to the picture on his desk. I laugh to myself and shake my head. His family.

Yeah, I hear you, Alexander Decker.

Warning received. I'll be ready.

CHAPTER
EIGHTEEN

ALEXANDER

———

I've gotten Trevor settled at my place and returned to the office for a few hours today. I made the mistake of asking if he wanted to tag along to get him around other people again. Trevor is a social creature at heart, and I think my company isn't working for him or helping in his recovery. Meanwhile, he's driving me crazy.

I got him one of those old people scooters to get around because, frankly, watching him on crutches is pitiful. Along with a shattered leg, he broke three ribs and dislocated his shoulder. He tried to be a tough guy, but I couldn't take it anymore.

Bringing him to the office is worse than bringing a puppy to work. My office has been a revolving door of visitors wishing him well since we showed up late this morning.

Matt and Tripp took him to lunch after their workouts and meetings and have returned him back to me. I can hear them FaceTiming with Chance outside my door. I know it's Chance because he's the one person who makes Elaine giggle. Chance Fuller is Julian's best friend and part of my extended family.

"Hey, preseason starts next week. Let me see if I can get to Charlotte later this week, and we can do dinner. When are you guys free?" Chance's voice carries into my office.

"Does Friday work?" I shout. Hopefully, the team should be back on Thursday night with some wins to celebrate.

"Xander, where are you?" Chance says from Tripp's phone. Tripp tosses it to me, and I see more of Chance than I'd like.

"Do you ever wear a shirt?" It looks like he's in the Renegade's weight room. Chance's build differs from the baseball players I'm around because he's a hockey player. He's a bulky six-foot, three-inch hulk with a heart like a pre-teen girl, all gooey and sweet. Where Trevor and I are opposites, Jules and Chance are two peas in a pod.

"Hey, I hear we might need to assemble Team True Love again." The guys laugh while I decide how to torture Julian with his big mouth. Team True Love is what Chance and Jules call themselves. The last thing I need is for them to get involved in my life.

"No need for that, but it would be good to get the gang together, even if it's for a night. Let's shoot for Friday?" I toss Tripp's phone back to him.

Before we hang up, a group text calls everyone home for the weekend, including Ash and Jules.

Trevor and Tripp make themselves comfortable in my office. Matt stays standing.

"Take a seat, Hartman. If you'll be hanging with these two, you might as well join us. But hit the door, would you?" At the mention of Team True Love, I better nip the talk in the bud.

Trevor transfers from his scooter to the couch, releasing a reflexive sigh. He's in more pain than he lets on. Maybe bringing him was too much? I may give him shit all the time, but I worry more than I show.

"How's the pain?"

"I'm okay. I'll take some Tylenol when I get home. I'm trying to kick the hard stuff now that I'm operating a motorized vehicle." He lovingly rubs the handlebars of his new scooter. I blinged it out with handlebar streamers and a flowery basket as a joke, but he loves it.

I reach into my drawer and toss him a bottle of Tylenol. He takes four and washes them down with his milkshake from lunch.

"I need you to feel better so you can feel the pain I plan to inflict, asshole," I mumble loud enough for him to hear. His grin lets me know he heard the message.

"It'll be nice to get everyone together," Tripp says. He's always the diplomatic one, the peacemaker.

"Yeah, I haven't seen Cole since I got called up," Matt adds. "Is it bad I'm happy his season is over so he can be here?"

"Well, since we'll be playing the Liberties, it'll be his first chance to show where his true loyalties lie," Trevor says. He's always adding fuel to the drama.

The Liberties drafted Cole, and he's playing for their triple-A team in Nashville. Their season wrapped last week, so he's officially in his off-season.

"I would never ask him to choose," I say. I mean that. I expect my players to be loyal to the team they work for, and I would expect the same from Cole. I know he grew up a Reapers fan, but I won't hold it against him because he plays for another team. Hell, it's my fault he's not a Reaper to begin with.

"Fuck that, I do. When we play against each other, sure. But I expect him to cheer for me and my team when I'm on that field." Matt has that best friend's point of view that I can't argue with either.

"So, are you bringing a date Friday, Xan?" I look around for Julian as his voice fills my office. I look at Tripp, who is silently laughing. He flashes his phone to me, and I see Chance and Julian on the screen. That bastard didn't hang up. He added Jules to the call. Tripp is going to pay for that.

I flip Tripp off and think about answering the question.

"No. This crew can be a lot. But it doesn't mean I'm not ready to get off the bench and enter the game." I look at Matt and Tripp. "Tell me about Luis. Is he interested?"

Tripp smiles. "Is this what Team True Love looks like?"

I glare at him, and his playfulness vanishes. Tripp continues, this time all business. "Nah, I think he's been talking to Jenny. He invited them both because sometimes there's safety in numbers when it comes to the WAGs." He looks at Matt. "No offense."

Matt agrees with a nod. "None taken. Darcy said some of the women are a little unwelcoming. Mostly the girlfriends. Of course, Darcy is the exception to that rule. The wives seem okay. I get not wanting Jenny to face that alone, especially since they aren't officially dating or anything. I agree. I think Luis is being nice to Jenny's best friend."

Tripp fist bumps Matt after his assessment. "Yeah, no offense, boss, but you practically peed on her at the school project. None of the guys are dumb enough to go there." Tripp and I have been friends since Dad signed him to the Reapers twelve years ago. We started as college pitching rivals, but shoulder and elbow surgery forced me to end my career. I started working with the team, and we became friends since we knew each other casually, had similar back stories, and were the same age. I keep a professional line with the team and, when necessary, with Tripp. He's the only player in my friendship group. But now that looks like it's expanding to Matt by marriage.

"I did not pee," I start.

"Yeah, you kinda did," Matt says. He winces, like it's painful to say to me.

"And then the intern thing," Trevor continues.

"Intern thing?" Chance asks. "What intern thing?"

"Nothing," I grumble.

"Why don't I know about this?" Jules asks.

I groan. How much do I tell them? I decide it's proportionate to the information I want to gain. "I asked Corey to check on her and take care of her refreshments. Instead, she had him treat the WAGs to drinks on me." I smile, thinking about how she managed that situation.

"Cheeky," Jules says.

"That's how she got in my office for the picture," I tell Trevor.

"Picture? What picture?" Jules is practically salivating for the scoop.

"A view of the field from my office during the game. Just letting me know she could." And teasing me in that jersey. I have no doubt she knew I could see it.

"So, where do you stand?" Jules asks.

"I don't know. I haven't heard from her since my last text Saturday night. But I'm open to suggestions." It's Tuesday. It took some work to get everything set up in the penthouse for Trevor, and we drove up here Monday.

"What did your text say?" Chance asks hesitantly.

"I may have let her know I was coming for her." I shake my mouse and act like I have work to do on my computer. I can't look at them.

"Well, that explains her reaction," Tripp says. I look up, and Matt grins and shakes his head like a fucking bobblehead, agreeing with Tripp.

I spin around, giving them my full attention. "What the fuck are you talking about?"

"Whatever you said got a reaction, that's all," Tripp says.

"Good or bad reaction?" My pulse races, waiting for his answer.

"You know what they say?" Trevor interjects. "You're in trouble when you don't get a reaction at all."

I can't believe we're gossiping like a bunch of girls. Have I sunken to that point? Fuck them. I'm doing this my way. Team True Love doesn't know what they're talking about.

"Hey, don't you two have a plane to catch? Go win some

games for me, why don't you?" The team is flying out later this afternoon for the first playoff game in New York.

"Just letting you know I'll be catching a ride with them Thursday night," Jules adds. "Beats flying commercial."

"Of course it does. I suppose you want the owner's tickets too?"

"Nah, I'll be going to the game with Devlin Millbanks. You know we play squash once a week, right? The only thing better than representing Reapers is representing Liberties. His deep pockets don't come with a side dose of guilt." Devlin Millbanks is the owner of the Liberties and friends with Dad. Julian has an insane social circle and networks better than anyone I've ever met.

"Talk about questioning loyalties," I mutter under my breath. "Get out of here and get to work. Am I the only one who earns my paycheck?"

"Hey, we work," Chance says. "We just enjoy it a little more than you grumpy pants."

"See you soon," Jules calls out.

CHAPTER
NINETEEN

DANI

————

It's Wednesday afternoon and I'm at Tyler's T-Ball practice. Sitting on these wooden bleachers is a spiritual experience. I'm praying they don't collapse or give me a splinter requiring surgical removal. I should have learned from last week, but I stood most of the time, excited to watch Tyler. Mental note to get a cushion.

Tyler's coach is Mr. Mayhew, a sweet grandfather who has coached kids for years. He coached his son, Franklin, who was drafted and played in the minors for a few years. Franklin's an insurance agent now in Georgia with a wife and two kids. Mr. Mayhew told me some kids play for fun, some learn about team-work and discipline, and some get to live the dream, at least for a little while. The rare few make it to the show, as he called it.

When Luis came to my class, I taught the students how to use their new computers and the Internet for research. We learned about professional baseball players and their journey to the big leagues. Between that lesson and hearing Franklin's story, I'm more in awe of the guys on the Reapers. They beat the odds and made it to the highest level of a sport that hundreds of thousands of kids strive to reach. I know they're talented, but the years of dedication and practice are humbling.

I watch the kids while poor Mr. Mayhew tries to wrangle them all into one place. It's like herding cats. One boy suddenly falls down while something in the sky captures the attention of two others. The kids throw the balls back and forth, more chasing than catching. These kids don't know the rules or even care about them. They're having fun and not sitting in front of a video screen. It makes my heart smile.

My phone buzzes, and I giggle at the picture in my text. Alexander and I have become texting buddies, sending pictures throughout our day. I love teasing him with a picture and a few words. He acts like he doesn't enjoy the playful teasing, but after the Christmas paper, I think there's a fun side under the gruff and broody armor he wears for the world, and I'm here to help him show it.

His latest text is a view of the Reaper's field from an executive's office, the faint reflection of a certain General Manager in the glass. Seems a little reminiscent of another picture, and I giggle. I snap a quick picture of my view as a reply.

> It's nice, but my view is far more superior. I concede that your seating is better.

AD

How's the little leaguer doing?

> Focused. Well, for him, that is. Think he's ready for the Reapers?

Are you?

> Probably not. It's a big step up from where I am now.

Don't worry. I've got you, sunshine.

I smile at the nickname. I know he thinks I'm always sunny, but I experience the occasional eclipse every now and then.

Practice is almost over when the bleachers groan because someone is brave enough to climb on them. I'm shocked to find Alexander moving up the few rows to join me. The entire structure wobbles under his weight as he sets a large brown paper bag in front of me.

"Hi, sunshine. Hope you don't mind me dropping in like this."

I'm stunned into silence. How did he know where I was? Why is he here? I snap my mouth closed so I don't catch flies.

"I'm not stalking, I promise." His tone conveys he's a little worried about my reaction, but his smirk says he's hoping I won't be mad.

I quirk an eyebrow at him.

"I reverse imaged the picture in Google, and it gave me an address." He responds to my unasked questions.

I finally find my voice. "That is the literal definition of stalking."

He chuckles. "Yeah, maybe. But do stalkers come bearing gifts?"

"Some do, yes." I give a visible shudder.

"Well, in that case, I'll just take this and go." He picks up the bag and begins to walk away, the bleachers swaying with his movement.

"Stop! If you move, it could cause the entire bleacher structure to fall. You should stay in the name of structural integrity." He came all this way, and I'd hate for him to leave. Besides, it was curiosity that killed the proverbial cat.

"You want me to stay for structural integrity?" At this point, he probably thinks I'm insane.

"Yep. Sit." I bite my bottom lip to stop my growing grin. My pulse quickens at his nearness, and I do my best to keep my wits about me.

He reaches into his bag and pulls out two Reaper seat cushions. He places one next to me and gestures for me to stand up.

"Can't stand up, structural integrity." I work hard contain my smile. This banter is silly and makes me laugh at him trying to keep up. It's obvious he's not used to being silly.

His eyes scan me, looking for a solution. He moves behind me, the bleachers sway, and I grip the wooden slat. Before I know it, his hands are at my waist, and he picks me up like I weigh nothing and places me on the cushion. He sits down next to me.

If he weren't the only man here, the pressed shirt, dark dress pants, and expensive shoes would make him stand out in our little crowd. I'm suddenly self-conscious of my ripped jeans, t-shirt, and flip-flops and glance down to make sure my shirt isn't stained.

"You always just take charge and make things happen?" I ponder. I'm a little flustered that I already lost this battle.

"Usually. I'm a busy man, so it's the best way to get things done."

"Then why are you here?"

"Several reasons, actually."

I cock my head to the side, waiting for the reasons. The bleachers sway again as several of the other moms move a little closer to us. Curious minds want to know.

"First, I wanted to bring you this cushion because your comfort is my priority." His deep baritone voice is smooth, serious, and sexy.

"Um, hm." I do my best not to roll my eyes. I'm also trying to keep my smile at bay because his stalking should not be rewarded. "And?"

"Second, it's never too early to start scouting prospects, and I'd be remiss if I didn't start in my own backyard."

"Isn't your backyard Reaper Stadium?"

"A metaphorical backyard, if you will." He clears his throat as if about to make his closing argument. "Third, I brought snacks for the team. Athletes burn a lot of extra calories, and they need to replenish." He rattles the large bag that once housed the cushions. I peek over the edge to look in the bag to find oranges, small Gatorades, and cheese crackers.

"And finally, Ms. Frankin, I wasn't sure if you had dinner plans, but if not, I'd like to take you and Tyler out after practice so I can hear about baseball from the superstar himself. That is, if you're interested."

Am I interested? Of course, I'm interested. However, I protect Tyler by vetting the people I allow close to him. It's probably why I haven't dated much over the years. I don't want him to get attached and feel the pain of losing someone he may care about. At least not this young. I broke that rule with Alexander when we went to the pet store. Tyler has already formed an attachment to Matt, too. I twist my lips while I decide how to respond.

"I'm curious, Mr. Decker. Do you have much experience with children?"

"What do you mean?"

"Have you ever gone to a kid-friendly restaurant?"

He seems to give genuine consideration to my question. I can practically see the gears turning as he contemplates how to answer. "Of course."

I quirk my eyebrow. "I mean, lately?"

He looks at me with a gaze that could melt the polar ice caps. His ocean-blue eyes look deep into mine, attempting to unearth my darkest secrets.

"Dani, tell me what's out of bounds." He lowers his voice, causing me to lean in. "Is it Tyler? I understand if you need to protect him. But I want to assure you, hurting him or hurting you is the last thing I ever want to do." He pauses to make sure I'm listening. His gaze deepens, as if he wants me to believe his words are intentional and authentic. One thing I've discovered about Alexander is that he is always intentional.

He continues. "I want to make sure you two are never hurt again. But if you need me to stay away from Tyler, I will. But make no mistake. I'm interested in getting to know you, Dani Franklin. And I know he's a part of you. And I want to know all of you. Do you understand?"

I'm stunned. All I can do is nod.

"So, tell me the boundaries. I respect the hell out of you, sunshine, and I won't cross them. You're in charge. I'll do anything you tell me."

His eyes never leave mine.

"Mom, Mom, did you see me catch that pop-up?" Tyler is running toward the fence that divides us from the field. His voice and the title Mom break the spell I'm under. Tyler is my number one, always.

I turn my head to give him my full attention, but sitting this close to Alexander, I'm not sure my full attention will be available to anyone again. "Hey, tiger, you're doing amazing. Are you having fun?"

His fingers wrap around the chain link, looking up at me, his eyes shaded by the bill of his hat. "Mom, this is work. If I'm gonna be like Matt, I've gotta work hard."

Alexander's face breaks into a grin. He always looks so severe when I see him, but when he smiles, a dimple pops, and he goes from a ten to a fifteen. I'm a sucker for dimples. And apparently, this incredibly sexy man sitting next to me.

"Tyler, I'm sure Matt would tell you it's work, but it's also fun. And fun comes first. If you don't enjoy playing, then don't do it." Alexander's deep voice carries across the field, and several kids look our way.

Tyler processes who said those wise words, his mouth dropping open as he straightens a bit before responding.

"I'm having fun. Coach said we have to work to get better, and I want to be the best so I can play with Matt when I grow up."

I love the way he dreams with his entire heart. I don't know the retirement age of baseball players, but I'm not sure Matt will be playing when Tyler is old enough to play. The thought of him growing up so fast has me clutching my chest, trying to keep my emotions in check.

"Your coach is right. Work means listening to your coach. You can learn a lot from him. But I bet Matt will tell you his favorite games were when he wasn't much older than you. Mine were. So have fun, okay?"

Tyler nods slowly, like he's processing every word. "You played baseball?"

"Yup." Alexander's attention is on Tyler, but he glances my way. What was that about? Is he checking to see my reaction to this conversation?

"Tiger, why don't you get your stuff? We're going to dinner with Xander. Maybe he can tell us more about baseball?" I don't have to tell Tyler twice. He takes off like a shot, running faster than he has all afternoon. I smile at his enthusiasm and energy.

I stand, and the bleachers sway again as several of us leave to gather our kids. Alexander pops up and reaches out to hold me steady. When he's this close, I don't think I'll ever be steady again.

CHAPTER
TWENTY

ALEXANDER

———

The restaurant is loud and chaotic, the colors bold and overwhelming. When I said Dani calls the shots, I meant it. That includes her choice of restaurants. My feet stick to the floor and surprisingly, I don't even grimace, because the smile on their faces is worth it. I have a fleeting thought that I'd walk across this sticky floor barefoot for them.

Most of the dinner options are fried, but they're still edible. But the company? Intoxicating. Tyler talks a mile a minute, sometimes with his mouth full of chicken fingers. His enthusiasm is award-winning. He peppers me with questions about baseball, my experiences when I was a kid, and my opinion of his budding career. The most surprising realization is I never think about the million other things that need to get done at the office. Because the best part of the dinner? Watching Dani's eyes light up as I answer Tyler's questions like the media are interviewing me after a game. I give him my most heartfelt, age-appropriate answers.

"Mom says I have to do good in school to play baseball. Did you like school?"

"Your mom's very smart. You should listen to her. I did well in school. You need good grades to play sports, but when I got older, I was distracted by pretty girls. They can make it hard to concentrate." I look at Dani and challenge her to jump in. Her eyes sparkle with humor. What's she thinking?

"Mom says I'm too young for girls, and they're bad news. Besides, Katie Parker is pretty, but she drew a purple dog, and I told her dogs weren't purple, and she called me a bad name, and I don't think I like Katie Parker or girls." Tyler seems to think about that for a half a second before his next question comes flying.

"They can make you question things, that's for sure." Dani giggles and focuses on her French fries. Questioning is the best way to describe what's going on with me right now.

"Are you going to marry my mom?" He stops and stares at me, the most still he's been this entire meal.

Dani was drinking her tea and chokes at his question. I want to help her, but I can't help but chuckle at her reaction.

"You ok there?" My tone is laced with a little humor and a whole lot of seriousness.

"Went down wrong," she manages to say. She takes a small sip of water and starts searching for something in her purse. "I think my phone's ringing."

I hand her the non-ringing phone laying on the table, a grin on my face. Watching her squirm is enjoyable, and I want to do it again and again. But I need to answer Tyler's question. Marry Dani? I don't know. I've never thought about marriage. Or a family. But I won't deny it's crossed my mind a few times lately. But we haven't even had a proper date. How can I make this kind of decision? I need information to make decisions. I don't have enough data at this point. My father once told me he knew he was going to marry my mom the first time he saw her at his cousin's wedding. I always thought that was just a story he told, but now I'm not so sure.

"Tyler, your mother is very special, wouldn't you agree?" He nods his head and looks me in the eye. This is a man-to-man conversation. "I would like to get to know her better. Maybe take her on a date. Is that okay with you?"

He screws up his mouth while he thinks. I appreciate that he's not a rash decision maker. My eyes shift a little to Dani to see her reaction. She's acting like she's looking at something on her phone, but I'm willing to bet she's staring at her home screen.

He takes another bite of his chicken tender and keeps looking at me. I'm squirming under the scrutiny of a six-year-old because I desperately want him to say yes. His opinion matters to Dani. And it matters to me.

After what feels like an eternity, he finally responds. "I'm okay with it, but mom decides what we do all the time, so you'll have to ask her, I guess." I appreciate his honest answer, and now hope she says yes.

"That's a very wise answer, young man. Now, can I ask you a secret question?" His eyes bug out, and he leans across the table.

In my best secret-whisper voice, I ask him a very important question. "What are her favorite flowers?" Dani rolls her eyes at my inquiry. She needs to understand, when I want to know something, I'll use all my resources to get the information.

"Um, I dunno." He gives a shrug that uses his entire body. "She gets all happy when those yellow flowers are in the yard when the Easter Bunny comes."

"Good to know." I google something and show it to Tyler. "These?" He nods yes, and I'm doing a mental happy dance with this information.

I send a quick text to Dani since she's still looking at her phone.

Daffodils, huh?

She puts her head in her hand, clearly amused, but defeated.

"You win," she mumbles.

"Not yet, sunshine. But I will." I'm awarded another Dani smile.

I hate to admit it, but now that I've gotten more, I'm not satisfied with a little bit of Dani. I want all of her.

CHAPTER
TWENTY-ONE

ALEXANDER

———

The pure enthusiasm these kids have pulls a core memory of me playing ball when I was their age. Sure, the fields I played on were in better shape, the parents weren't risking life or limb to sit in the stands, and our equipment was better, but I remember it just the same. The excitement of playing a game that was as simple as a ball and a stick and pure adrenaline. Those were the fun days before talent rose and competition grew from within. A time before your teammate became your competitor. A time when the game was just a fun thing to do with your friends on a Saturday morning.

"Mr. Mayhew, thank you for allowing me to join your team." I shake his hand as I meet him for the first time.

"Mr. Decker, appreciate the help. I must say, I'm a little shocked, but I won't say no to extra hands."

"Please, call me Alexander. And I'm happy to help. You tell me what you need, and I'll do it. It's been a long time since I've played T-ball, but it started something pretty big in my life."

"Well, Alexander, prepare yourself to meet the team. We have ten kids, eight boys and two girls, and six of them are rookies. Hope you packed your patience. The goal is to teach some baseball, keep tears and scrapes to a minimum, and give them an hour of fun."

I gulp. Patience isn't my strong suit, but I'll give it my all for something this important. "Got it. I'll follow your lead."

Kids start showing up, and I introduce myself as they arrive. They all come into the dugout and take a seat on the bench. I keep a running headcount and repeat their names, finding ways to remember them. It's almost nine o'clock and no Tyler. I worry, but remind myself I'm here for the team. We go out to third base for our team huddle. I squat down, and the kids circle around me.

"Okay, Coach Mayhew gave you your positions. Go have fun. Everyone put your hands in, and on three, we'll yell, Go, Sluggers. Got it?" I look at their excited faces, several with wide eyes. One kid's hat is bigger than his head. I adjust it so he can see. I'm rewarded with a toothless grin.

"Sorry, sorry," Tyler says as he joins the circle. His eyes go wide when he sees me in the middle of the circle.

"It's okay, Tyler. You'll be in left field, behind third base," Coach Mayhew says. "This is Coach Decker. He'll be helping us."

Tyler's smile fills his face. "Hiya, Coach."

"Okay, on three. One, two, three, Go Sluggers!" The kids yell some variation of the chant, and we send them to their positions. Coach Mayhew put me in charge of the left side of the field. He'll be coaching from the right. In T-ball, the coaches can be in the outfield, giving directions. We can't touch the ball, and it's just another instinct I'll have to curb.

I do my best to focus on the kids, but I admit, I glance at the stands to see Dani's reaction to me being here. Instead of seeing her warm smile, I'm met with the hard stare of her father in the front row. Given the comments from Tyler about my car, I've obviously been the subject of conversation in the Franklin house. While he was polite at the Reapers game, I'm sure my intentions toward his daughter bring a different reaction. Her mother is behind him, a kind smile sent my way. Dani has her eyes on Tyler, actively avoiding me. Interesting.

That's fine. I'm here to share space and time with her. Meet her where she is. During our family dinner last night, the discussion drifted to single mothers. Ashleigh thought she was being subtle, but I caught on pretty quick. Although no one mentioned Dani's name, I knew what they were doing.

She asked Cole and Darcy about being raised by a single mother. They talked about the limited time, which I understand. I had already reached out to Mr. Mayhew before that conversation, but now I'm praying it was the right move.

We've made it through thirty minutes, and so far, no major disasters. A few under thrown balls, which is to be expected. One kid on the other team went from first to third via the mound, cutting out second. The way he bit his lip when he was running showed grit and determination. My patience isn't tested as much as my ability to keep a straight face. Good thing I have a resting grump face.

"Coach Decker, Coach Decker," Cruz calls from third base. "My nose is bleeding." He's trying to catch the blood in his glove, and it's going all over his shirt. I'm not prepared for this. I run to the dugout to grab my gym bag, find a towel, and meet him halfway between the dugout and third base. Tears are filling his eyes, and he's about to lose it.

"It's okay, you're fine. Take a deep breath." I coax him to sit and tell him to tilt his head back. The game stops, and everyone is watching the medical emergency. I use the towel to pinch his nose and hope the bleeding stops quickly. "Is your mom here?" I ask. Please let his mom be here.

He shakes his head no. Great. I heard Coach Mayhew say he would take someone home because his mom had to go to work before the game ends, but I was hopeful she was still here.

"Has this happened before?" He shakes his head yes. Whew. Okay, so not something new. "What did you do to get it stopped before?"

"Twilit pooper," he says from under the towel.

"What?"

"Twilit pooper," he repeats.

I'm at a loss. I look up into the stands, searching for help. Dani's gone. Surely she wouldn't leave Tyler's game because I'm here. I begin to panic. Between the nosebleed and Dani avoiding me, I'm unsure of myself, my typical confidence gone. I look around for help from anyone.

"Here, let me." Dani comes to my rescue, appearing out of nowhere with a roll of toilet paper in her hand.

I release the breath I'm holding and assess the scene. Dani takes the toilet paper and creates a makeshift nose stopper with it. She works methodically and calmly. I don't know if it's her mom or teacher's superpower, but I'll take it. Does she always carry a roll of toilet paper? So many questions. She's a mystery.

"Better?" she asks Cruz.

"Yup. Twilit pooper," he says, like it was obvious to everyone but me.

She swats him gently on the butt and sends him on his way.

"Um, thanks for the save," I manage. We both stand up, and even though we're on an open ball field, I feel there isn't enough air to breathe.

"In over your head, boss?" Not sure what's up with her calling me boss, but I'm turned on by it. Her sassy mouth makes me chuckle.

"Not at all. I'll have a better first-aid kit next time. I don't normally carry toilet paper with me." I'm mesmerized by the flecks of gold floating in her eyes, the way they crinkle when she smiles. Damn, her eyes have some magical hold on me. We don't break eye contact. Our eyes are playing a game of chicken. Whoever looks away loses. But loses what?

She blinks and steps back. "Yeah, well, you were obviously

not a Boy Scout." She laughs at me, leaving me more confused than ever.

"Boy Scouts carry toilet paper?" I'm still baffled.

"No, silly, always prepared. Come on, boss. You can do better than that. Get your head in the game." She pops the bill of my hat and turns around to head back to the stands. If I didn't know better, I'd say there's a little extra sway in those hips as she walks away.

The coach from the other team steps beside me because I'm in the third base coach's box, which is his space. "She's a looker, isn't she?" I glance at him to see his eyes are watching her walk away, and I want to punch him for looking at her like that. His beer belly jiggles a little while he silently laughs. "Down boy, happily married," he says as he wiggles his wedding ring at me. "But doesn't keep me from appreciating the fairer sex."

I feel a low grumble in my chest. Getting into it with another coach is not the impression to make if I want to keep this volunteer gig. Besides, the Reapers don't need another PR nightmare. I put on my boardroom stare and prepare to address the coach.

I remind myself why I'm here. "Thank you for investing in these kids," I say as I shake his hand. I walk back to my place behind the shortstop and make eye contact with my side of the field. "Let's focus, Sluggers!" A loud clap is their signal to watch the ball.

I sneak a glance at the stands to see Dani watching me, too. I wonder what's happened that made her more open to flirting with me. Not sure of the catalyst, but I'm here for it. And when she called me boss? I'd like to show her who's boss. I shake my head to clear those thoughts because popping a boner around a bunch of kids wouldn't be prudent.

After the game, we huddle with the team, hand out snacks, and send them to their parents. Tyler hangs back with me until he's the last kid in the dugout. I'm packing my gym bag and the remnants of the nosebleed incident, trying to think what I should be carrying here. Apparently, toilet paper.

"Hey, Coach Xander?" Tyler is standing near me, a crooked smile on his face.

"Hey bud, you played a good game. You made a few great throws to keep the other team from scoring." I tap the bill of his hat, just like Dani did to me.

He did well. His throws were pretty accurate. Unfortunately, his teammates weren't prepared to catch the ball. They have a few weeks to improve, and we'll work on drills. Tyler's a natural.

"Thanks. You wanna go to lunch with us? Mom said if I played good, she'd take me to lunch at the place they throw shrimp at you. Then I get to spend the night with Grandma, and she'll make me cookies."

"Throw shrimp at you?" I'm not sure I've ever been to a restaurant where they throw food at the customers. It's becoming obvious I don't speak six-year-old.

"Yeah, and they make fire, and it's really good. Wanna come?"

This kid is bold and spunky, like his mom. I like him, even if I have no idea what he's talking about.

"Sounds great, but I've got to get to the stadium. We have a big game tonight." If he's going to his grandparents, that means Dani may be alone. Or maybe she has a date. That thought irritates me. I need to ask what she's doing tonight without coming on too strong. Julian's voice echoes in my head about being subtle.

I could invite her to the game. I tick off the names of the people in my suite tonight and sigh. It's the entire Decker clan. After our evening last night, they stayed for the game. Well, Tripp and Matt were already obligated, but the rest? She hasn't met Trevor, Cole, Emma, or Chance, but hopefully, she'll feel comfortable around the group. I'm inserting myself into her world, whether or not she asked me to. Is she ready for mine?

Like my thoughts materialized her, she peeks into the dugout. "Everything okay in here?"

"Mom, I invited Xander to lunch, but he has to go help the Reapers win, but can we still go to the flying shrimp place?" Tyler is bouncing, all the energy in his body manifesting in his feet.

"Sure, tiger. Go with Grandma, and put your stuff in the car. I'll be there in a minute."

Tyler takes off, leaving us alone in the dugout, and I can feel the electricity in the air. There's a tension there, and I'm not sure if I'm the only one feeling it.

"What are you doing?" Her tone is flat, not playful.

I usually pride myself on my communication skills, but today I'm clueless about what she's asking.

"Packing my ill-prepared gym bag?"

"No," she whispers. "What are you doing here?"

"Coaching?"

"But why?"

Okay. I prepared a response to this question. "Well, several reasons, really. One, I want to be a part of the community. I realized the need for volunteers, and I want to step up."

"That's pretty nice of you, Mr. Decker." She gives me a look that calls bullshit, puts her hands on her hips, and shifts her weight to the side, ready for the next line I'm about to throw. She's letting me continue to dig myself deeper into a hole. "Lots of things you could do. Soup kitchens, clothing drives, homeless shelters. Why here?"

"True. All true. But this is what I know. I know baseball. Me serving in a soup kitchen would be disastrous. Me helping coach the future of baseball? Just makes sense." I hope I sold it because it's true. It may not be my motivation, but I believe everything I said.

I get a slight nod. She bites her bottom lip to contain the smile trying to escape, her hard, inquisitive stare breaking.

"Do all your explanations come in several points? I'm practically waiting for the PowerPoint."

"They do. My decisions are sound, reasonable. I don't do

things without thinking them through. You need to know that about me, Dani. I don't do things on a whim. Now, if you'll allow me to finish," I say with a pause. "I know a lot about baseball. I have information that could make a difference in these kids' lives. You teach in a classroom. I teach on a diamond."

"Those are all excellent reasons, but why here? Why this team?" She crosses her arms under her chest, and her boobs are lifted in my direction. I can't help but notice the distraction. "Eyes up here, Decker."

"Yeah, sorry."

"I told you, no more apologies." Her tough facade cracks a little more. "Answer my question, please."

I clear my throat and look into those magical eyes. "Why here? Isn't it obvious? Because you're here. I want to be in your world, to see you. I know you're busy with work and Tyler, and I respect the hell out of you for that. So I thought I could do some good for the community, help poor Mr. Mayhew, get to know Tyler better, but mostly, see you. Meet you where you are. Is that okay?"

I search her face for a tell, some sign it's okay. I hope she doesn't think I'm using her kid to get to her. If she didn't have a kid, I'd approach it differently. She and Tyler are a package deal, and I'm good with that.

"Good enough. Sounds like a sound decision." She drops her arms and gives me a half smile.

Whew. I wasn't sure how she would react, but I'm glad it's all good. I breathe a little easier when she gives me a full-on Dani smile that lights up her eyes and brightens my world. I give myself a mental celebratory fist-pump. I did it! I made Dani Franklin smile.

"So, I have this thing tonight," I start.

Her smile beams. "You mean the game that could decide if your team wins the division and goes to the World Series?"

"Have you become a baseball fan, Ms. Franklin?"

She gives a slight shrug. "Meh. I might know these people, and baseball is important to them."

"Well, yeah." I clear my throat. This dusty field is getting to me. "I would like to invite you to attend tonight's game. As my guest. That is, if you're interested." I can't explain why being there because I asked is important to me, but it is. It's like she's saying yes to me.

"Won't you be working?"

"Not much tonight. My friends and family are in town." I adjust my hat, turning it backward to see her better. "So I should warn you about that. You need to make an informed decision. If you decide to attend, you might be of more interest to them than the game."

"And why would I be of interest, Mr. Decker?" She knows, but she's making me say it, anyway. And I swear, when she calls me Mr. Decker with that sassy mouth, I have images that are inappropriate for this dugout with her kid and parents a few feet away.

I clear my throat again. "Trust me, you will be. If you would like to invite Jenny to feel more comfortable, she's invited too."

"Do you think I'll be uncomfortable?"

"That wouldn't be my intention, but I like to plan for all scenarios."

"And are you always thinking of all scenarios and planning for them? Or do you just ever go with the flow?" She gives me a devious smile. Where is she going with this?

"I don't like to be caught unprepared," I answer honestly. "Like the nosebleed. But I'll be ready next time."

"Good to know." She's nodding like she's having a private conversation, and I'm definitely the topic.

"Moooooommmmmm," Tyler calls from somewhere outside of the dugout.

"Um, wow. Yeah. I've gotta go."

"So, tonight?" I've never been more unsure of a response. Usually, I can tell which way people are leaning when asked for a decision, but with her? She's unpredictable. I don't know what she'll say next, but I want her to say yes.

She shrugs. "Maybe? I guess you'll see. Gotta keep you on your toes." She gives a wink.

"Okay. I'll leave credentials for you and Jenny at the VIP window."

"Planning for all scenarios?" She's teasing me, and I'm unsteady. Is she flirting?

"Planning for the best scenario." I smile at her. It pains me to say goodbye, but she has obligations, and I won't get in the way of them. "Go. You promised Tyler flying shrimp or something?"

"Yep. Something like that." I'm not sure what that is, but I'll be asking around to find out. If it's something they like, I'll try it too. "See ya' around, Coach." She gives me a wink and walks out of the dugout, most definitely putting some extra swing in her hips.

What the hell am I doing? I'm used to being the one in charge, but this woman? She's one hundred percent calling the shots.

CHAPTER
TWENTY-TWO

DANI

––––––

"So you left it with a maybe?" Jenny's looking at me like I'm crazy. Maybe I am.

"Yeah. It's a big night for him. I don't want to be a distraction. Besides, he said all his family and friends would be there. He seemed to think that was a big deal." Although I'm curious about his inner circle, I'm not sure I'm ready for that. Or would getting to know him in a group setting be better? Because alone? He's intense. Every time it's just been the two of us, I feel like I'm on the verge of bursting into flames. Maybe the group setting is better. But I'll make sure there's a fire extinguisher nearby, just in case.

"Girl, it is a big deal. To introduce you to his people? That's huge."

"But I've already met his brother and sister." I shrug.

"And they were great, right? I think you should go."

"Do you want to come? He said he'd leave credentials for both of us." Why am I nervous about this?

"I'll go if you want me there. You know I'm always your ride or die. I won't hover, but I can be your escape plan."

"Do you think I'll need an escape plan?" It's a baseball game. There will be other people. He'll be busy. Maybe I need to prepare for all scenarios, just like him.

"No, but I'll be there anyway. Besides, I'd love to see Luis play, so see, win-win." She acts nonchalant, but that's a dead giveaway. Jenny is usually all in with guys, and she falls hard and fast. I'm not sure why she's keeping Luis at arm's length.

"Okay. So do I let him know I'm coming?" I know he'd like to be prepared. It's what's best for him, but suddenly, I think he might need a little spontaneity to keep him on his toes. Besides, plans are more of a wish list if he'll be part of my world. I guess it's time to see how he does.

"Up to you. My initial thought? No. Surprise him. Although, I'd bet he has surveillance and will know as soon as you step onto the premises." The thought of him waiting, wondering, gives me butterflies. It's a new, scary feeling, but I like it.

Parking is insane, so after a long drive getting nowhere, we return to my place and take the light rail in. Unfortunately, that means we're late, and the pregame has started. We spot the VIP window, and Corey greets us right away. He breaks into a huge smile.

"Hi, Corey. Can you do me a favor and not announce my arrival? I want it to be a surprise." Corey and I became friends when we did a little breaking and entering on my last visit to Reaper Stadium.

He looks a little conflicted, but agrees. "Yes, ma'am. Is this Ms. Atkins?" He reaches out to shake Jenny's hand.

"Hi, just call me Jenny," she says as she takes his hand. Corey's smile widens as he checks her out. She's wearing Luis's jersey tied into a crop top with leggings that fit her like a glove. Her long dark hair is down in soft, sexy waves. Her eyes are bejeweled with red rhinestones, and she looks hot. Luis is going to flip when he sees her.

I went with a more subtle look of jeans that make my ass look good and a red sweater set, rocking the Reaper's colors without looking like a super fan. I left my hair down and tried to tame my curls, but my hair usually has a mind of its own. My sandals have a slight heel, giving me a little extra height.

He hands us both lanyards with personalized badges that say *All Access*. Wow. So many questions.

"I need to ask, were you going to stand here all night if I didn't show up?"

"Yes, ma'am. I'm under strict orders not to leave until I deliver you to the owner's suite." Did he assume I'd come tonight?

"And if I didn't come?"

He gives me a friendly wink. "I was prepared to wait, but knew you'd show."

"Am I that predictable?" How could he be so sure?

"No, ma'am. There's just something," he starts. "Never mind. If you're ready, I'll take you through the back entrance to avoid the crowds."

"It's really packed, isn't it?" Jenny asks.

"They have a chance to take it all this year. It's exciting." When Corey and I were hanging out last time, I learned he's a lifelong Reapers fan who hopes to work with the organization after graduation.

The crowd is electric, and the concourse is wall to wall people making their way to their seats, buying food, and shopping. I hear the announcer say, "Play ball," and realize the game is starting. Being late is going to drive him crazy, but our tardiness was unintentional. I didn't account for traffic at all.

"You think we can make a slight detour before we head to the suite?" Corey cringes a little, but agrees.

"Your wish is my command," he says as he offers his arm to both of us.

Corey is a gem and helps me with my errand. True to his word, he doesn't let anyone know I've arrived. When we open the door to the suite, all conversations cease, and silence fills the space.

All eyes turn to me. I swallow and smile as I scan the room, looking for my host. Each person greets me with a welcoming expression. It's Ashleigh who breaks the awkward stares and comes to give me a warm embrace.

"We were afraid you wouldn't come," she whispers, so only I can hear. "I'm so glad you did."

"Thanks." I'm grateful Jenny is by my side to give me strength.

She hugs Jenny, and everyone pretends their attention is anywhere but on us. A tall, handsome, dark-haired guy comes up and puts his arm around Ashleigh.

"Hi, I'm Cole Davidson. I'm Leigh's fiancé." He extends his hand, and I shake it. He's wearing a Liberties hat with a Matt Hartman Reaper jersey. Regardless of the score today, he can't lose.

"Leigh?"

"Long story," Ashleigh says. "You can call me Ash."

"It's nice to meet you. This is my friend, Jenny." Cole shakes her hand.

"Rodriquez, huh?" he comments.

"Yeah, he's a friend," she says, blushing slightly.

"That's not what I hear," Darcy says as she joins us. She gives Jenny a teasing wink. "I hear he might be crushing on a certain teacher."

"When did that happen?" Julian says as he greets us. He gives me a light kiss on the cheek and a wink. He reaches over to hold Jenny's hand and steps back. "Damn, girl." He gives a low whistle. "I'm a fan."

Jenny giggles and bats her eyelashes at Julian. He holds out his arm to her, and she takes it. "Come on, let me get you a drink." Their locker room escapades clearly bonded them for life.

They approach another gorgeous guy sitting at the bar. I

think that's Chance Fuller. "Is this the girl that helped you prank Tripp?" His deep, throaty laugh fills the suite.

"This is Jenny," Julian says as he introduces her to Chance. So much for my ride or die. I look around the suite and see the rest of the people from the picture on Xander's desk. I don't know the couple sitting on the couch, but the cast gives me a hint that it must be Trevor, Xander's best friend. He's next to a petite, cute girl, and both are smiling at me.

And then I see him. He's standing by the railing at the back of the suite. His eyes smolder as he gives me a slight smirk. It's not one of his full smiles, but a new look I've yet to see. I'm not sure what it means, but I think he's happy to see me.

He's wearing a white button-down that looks tailor made. His dark pants accentuate his lean torso and trim waist. His usually coiffed hair is slightly disheveled, like he's been running his hands through it. This is becoming my favorite version of Alexander.

He saunters toward me like a lion stalking his prey. All eyes are now focused on him.

Ash, Cole, and Darcy fade away until I'm standing alone near the suite's entrance. The butterflies are going crazy in my stomach as he approaches, and I consider bolting because I'm so nervous.

"Hey." His voice covers me, making me feel warm despite my body shivering. Treacherous body.

"Hey." Well, this is going well.

"I was worried you wouldn't come."

"Parking was an issue, so we took the light rail. I wasn't thinking I'd be walking that far when I picked out these shoes."

"You walked from the rail station?" His smile is gone.

"Yeah, it's not a bad walk."

I'm learning his scowls, and this one says he's not happy. Maybe I should leave? "I could have made arrangements," he starts.

"And ruin my grand entrance?" I tease and give him a

playful punch in the arm. I shake out my hand. I feel like I just punched a wall. "I'm fine."

"Is he misbehaving already?" the guy from the couch calls to me.

As if the comment flips a switch, his scowl is erased, and a slight smirk appears. "Come on, let me introduce you to everyone," Xander says. He puts his hand on the small of my back and guides me toward the couch.

"This asshole is Trevor, my best friend and temporary roommate. Trevor, this is Dani." He glares at him. "Behave."

The tall, dark, and handsome man gives me a charming smile. His dark skin accentuates his white smile, and his scruff further ups his hotness factor. Shamar Moore has nothing on this guy. Damn.

"My apologies, Dani. I'd get up to greet you." He waves his hand down his body. "But it's a production. It's great to meet you." His eyes are warm, and his smile is disarming. I relax and give him a full smile in return, immediately put at ease.

"I heard about your accident. I'm glad you're on the mend."

"He would be if he followed the doctor's orders. But you can't tell T anything," the girl says as she hits him with a throw pillow.

"And this scary girl is Emma. She's Ash's best friend and a fellow teacher." The adoration in Xander's voice is evident as he introduces her. He may call her scary, but it's obvious he loves her.

She waves from the couch and places another pillow under Trevor's leg. "Hi, Dani! It's nice to meet you. Are you enjoying your class this year?"

"Absolutely. Exhausting but worth it."

"One hundred percent. Got your Erin Condren planner stickered out?"

"Absolutely! Was that you?" Another teacher understands the importance of a good planner and stickers.

She covers her face, realizing she might have spilled the

beans. "Well, I love my room and can't tell you how this team has impacted the students. It's been an epic start to the year."

"Can I get you anything? A drink, food, a foot massage?" Xander interrupts.

"Foot massage?" Where did that come from?

He looks at my feet, and I remember the walking comment.

"I'm fine. Really." Everyone is watching me, even Jenny. "What? Do I have a wardrobe malfunction or something?" Everyone quickly looks away, avoiding my confused look. They all go back to their conversations. A crack of the bat and the crowd's roar fills the suite.

"There it is," Cole yells. "Great play!"

I'm not sure who did what, but Darcy is hugging Cole, so I assume Matt did something good.

"What happened?" I ask the room.

"Double play," Xander says.

I quirk my eyebrow. I'm not ignorant about baseball, but it's not really my thing.

"Two outs on one at bat," Xander explains. "Now we're up." He seems to relax a little. I wasn't thinking about how stressful this game would be for him. Maybe my presence is just adding to his stress.

"Hey, I know this game is important to you. If I'm in the way or something," I start.

His scowl returns. Yep. I said the wrong thing.

"I'm sorry," Xander says. "It's important, but it's my job to ensure the fans have a good time. That includes you. So how can I make this a memorable experience for you?"

Wow. The way he shifts from not so grumpy to grumpy. I look around at the fancy suite with all his friends and realize he needs to relax and enjoy the game. A spark of an idea forms.

"Let's go for a walk." I take his hand and tug on his arm to move back toward the door.

"But your feet?" He looks down at my shoes and scowls again.

"I'm good. I promise." He looks skeptical. "We aren't going for a run, just a leisurely stroll through the concourse. That is, if you can leave?"

"He's the boss," Trevor says. "He can do whatever he damn well pleases. So take your guest on a walk, Xan." Emma pinches Trevor and he grimaces. Trevor looks at me and winks.

I blush. I'm so caught up in Alexander that I wasn't aware anyone was paying us attention. My mistake. Several sets of eyes still watch us. All the more reason to leave the suite.

I take two steps toward the door, turn, and hold my hand out. He puts his hand in mine, and my heart speeds up. I take another step, and he quickly moves to open the door for me, dropping my hand.

"Where do you want to go? Something particular you're looking for?"

That's a loaded question. I wasn't looking for anything but may have found an unexpected treasure. "Let's walk the concourse, and I'll let you know." I shrug a little and walk to the elevators.

Alexander is a man that does everything with purpose. His intentionality and focus are defining personality traits. My wanting to wander must be driving him crazy. He reaches for my hand and takes it, his palm connecting with mine, sending a shiver down my spine.

We enter the elevator, and neither says a word. The announcer calling the game fills the gap in conversation. When the doors open, we're assaulted by the sounds of the stadium. The crowd, the concession stands, the beer guy walking up and down the aisles. Now that the game is underway, the concourse isn't as crowded as when I arrived. People are still walking about, but it's not shoulder-to-shoulder anymore.

I head right and walk counterclockwise. If I'm going to push his buttons, I might as well push them all. He hesitates for a split second and joins me on my walkabout. My heels click on the concrete as we stroll. He slows his pace so that I'm not taking two steps for every one of his.

We walk in silence for a few minutes as I take in the sights and sounds. We come out from the covered concourse and are near the outfield. To our left is a hot dog vendor watching the game, probably grateful he doesn't have any customers at the moment.

"Oh, a hot dog," I exclaim. "Let's get one." I pull to the left, and Alexander dutifully follows. I reach for my purse with my free hand, and Alexander scowls at me. Was this not a good idea?

"Hi, Franco," Alexander says as we approach the vendor. At the sound of his name, the vendor turns around and sees us standing there.

"Hi, Mr. Decker." The boss catching him watching the game doesn't surprise him at all. I wouldn't be surprised if Alexander makes the rounds during games.

"What's your prediction for the night?" Alexander asks. There's no reproach for his game watching.

"Well, Stevenson is off to a good start, but he needs to watch his slider with Kurtz. It won't be a shutout, but it should be a win," Franco responds.

I'm fascinated by this man beside me. He runs this entire operation and still knows the concession stand employees. He's involved. All in. Is that how he operates?

"What can I get you two?" Franco asks.

Alexander looks at me, waiting for a response. "Two dogs, please. And two Reaper beers." I smile up at him and squeeze his hand.

Franco looks at Alexander for confirmation, and he gives a slight nod. Franco reaches into the steamer for the two hot dogs and the cooler for two beers on ice. He wipes down the side of the cans and sets them on the small counter in a carrier. Alexander releases my hand to grab the food, and I reach for my purse.

"No, ma'am," Franco says. "The boss has a tab and is good for it." He gives me a wink. "Enjoy the game." He turns his back to us and continues watching the game.

"Where to now?" Alexander asks.

"Come on," I say as I walk toward the grassy corner between the outfield stands and the first baseline. This is the family section, where people can buy a cheap ticket, bring a blanket, sit on the hill, and watch the game while the kids run around. I asked Casey about it last time I was here, and I'm curious to see it up close.

I find us a spot and sit down, grateful I didn't wear a dress tonight. My shoes might have been the wrong choice, but my jeans are perfect for this.

He looks down at me, sighs, and sits on the ground beside me. "What, will we get in trouble for sitting here without a ticket? I assumed this," I wave my lanyard at him, "all access means I can sit here, can't I?"

"Of course. I'm just wondering," he starts.

"Wondering what?"

"Why here?"

"You mean instead of the suite, where everyone was watching me, and we were waited on hand and foot? Because this is more my speed. And you, Mr. Decker, need to see that you're doing a darn good job. Look at all these fans having a great time." I lean in and bump shoulders. "So relax." I grab a hot dog from the carrier on his lap.

I can't believe I'm lecturing him, but it's probably because I'm a nervous wreck. My false bravado comes on strong when I'm nervous. If I'm not careful, I'll double down and kiss him. To stop myself from doing that, I take a big bite of the hot dog and let out a moan. Damn, this is good.

CHAPTER
TWENTY-THREE

ALEXANDER

––––––

She lets out a low moan as she bites the hot dog, and holy fuck, my dick takes notice. Calm down, Decker. The woman is sitting on the grass in the family section, watching a baseball game, and eating a hot dog. It is not an invitation to jump her bones. Shit, one asshole has already assaulted her. I won't be another one.

The statistics shared by the self-defense instructor were devastating. Almost eighty percent of women experience sexual harassment. I get sick when I think about Ash and her response when I asked her about it. Women shouldn't have to worry about how a man will react to everything they do. Like Dani eating a fucking hot dog. But damn, I'm attracted to her.

I don't know which is more sexy, her hot as fuck ass in those jeans or her desire to watch the game from the cheapest seats in the house. Honestly, they both turn me on.

I rarely find a woman who wants to spend time with me and not spend my money. Although, technically speaking, I did spring for the hot dog. When she reached for her purse, I almost snapped. Like I would let her spend a penny of her hard-earned money when I have more than I'll spend in this lifetime. And at my ballpark too? No way. But I also appreciate the gesture. It wasn't an expectation that I'd pay. It's not about the money. Could it be about me?

"How did you know this is one of my favorite spots to watch a game?"

She reaches over, takes a beer, and washes down her hot dog. No dainty sip. It's a turn-on, watching her swallow. My mind goes to places it shouldn't.

She grins and leans into me so that our shoulders touch. She gives a slight shrug. "Just a hunch. You seemed kind of wound up in the suite. I thought getting out and being part of this would help." She looks up at me. Her long eyelashes frame her mesmerizing eyes, her lips part, and she licks her bottom lip. "Did it?"

I'm stunned by her beauty. "Did what?"

"Did it help to get out? Look around you, Xander. People are having the time of their lives." She takes another bite of her hot dog and settles in to watch the game.

I do as she says and scan the crowd. People are having fun. Smiles abound. Everyone around is wearing Reaper's colors, even the kids sitting in front of us. A little boy looks up at his dad while his father explains the game to him. His glove is ready to catch a home run ball. The Liberties are up to bat, so I hope there isn't a ball heading in this direction right now.

Dani's right. I'm relaxing. Although, to be honest, my tension wasn't because of the game. We're in the playoffs, and this is a big game, but we've been here before. The team is good this year, and they've had a great season. The stadium team is outstanding and practically runs itself. They don't need me on game day. My nerves? I wasn't sure she would show up. When it comes to Dani, she's unpredictable, and she leaves me unsure, unsteady.

"I'm more interested to know if you're having a good time?"

I know she's not a huge sports fan, so I don't know if this is fun for her or not.

She finishes her hot dog and takes another big sip of her beer. "I am. This is fun, just being out here, soaking up the excitement. It's a gorgeous evening. And I'm hanging out with you." She looks at the carrier in my lap. "Hot dogs and beer not your speed? Or has Costco spoiled you for all hot dogs?" She indicates the hot dog and beer still in the carrier. I'm so captivated by her I forgot about them.

I give her a little chuckle at the memory. "I'll put my dogs up against any on the market. While I'll concede on their price point, I'm willing to pay for quality over quantity every day." I give her a little wink. "I'm soaking it all in like you suggested." I open the hot dog and take a bite. It's a perfect, high quality, plain hot dog. I finish it in a few bites. I take our trash and tell her I'll be right back.

I get another round of beers, go to guest services, and pick up two blankets. The ground is cool, and I don't want her to get cold. When I return to Dani, she's made friends with the family sitting beside her. She's tossing a ball back and forth with the little boy.

"Looks like you made a friend." She smiles up at me and takes the beers. I spread out one blanket, and she moves to it while I place the other blanket over her lap. She goes back to tossing the ball to the kid, leaning into my side.

"Hayden, this is my friend Mr. Decker. He knows a lot more about baseball than I do." The little boy looks at me with a sense of wonderment.

"Hi, Hayden. How old are you?" He holds up four fingers. "Wow. Four, huh? Practically ready to sign with the big guys."

His parents smile at me, probably glad I'm not being an asshole to their kid. This section is supposed to be family-friendly, but sometimes a guy will have one too many and move this from a PG to R rated section pretty fast. That's why I have adequate security constantly watching this area.

I note his oversized glove. "You look like you're ready to catch a ball. Let's hope the other team doesn't hit one out here, or we'll be in trouble." I give him a wink and a pat on the head, and he runs to his mother's lap.

I look at Dani, and she's in her element around kids. It's like they flock to her. She's the kid whisperer or something. When she's with Tyler, she practically glows. I've never given serious thought to kids. Probably because I've never been around anyone who I could envision myself having a family with. Until now.

"Is Tyler mad you didn't bring him tonight?"

"A little, but I promised to bring him to another game. And he was tired after his big win today. Sitting out here would be something he'd love, but being closer to the players has spoiled him. I don't think this would fly with him again." She gives me a full-on smile so bright it practically blinds me.

"Any time you want to bring him, let me know. He can sit anywhere he wants. Hell, Matt would love to have him on the bench if he could. He's a great kid." Tyler is funny, full of spunk, and well-behaved. He has an outgoing personality but is balanced with a dose of respect and manners. He has a kind heart, just like his mom. I'm still curious about his father and hopeful she'll share the story.

"Thanks. I appreciate it. I try to keep him grounded, you know. Teaching gratitude is difficult these days."

"Well, I think you do a damn good job. Building up a child's character isn't easy, I'm sure. What about his father? Is he in the picture?"

She leans away, losing contact, making my body cold, instantly missing her touch. "He died before Tyler was born." Her smile dims, and I can feel a cloud of sadness surround her. Probably not the time for this discussion, but curiosity was getting the better of me.

"Oh, I'm sorry to hear that. Really." I can't imagine the grief she must have felt losing Tyler's father. Grief while pregnant has to be extremely devastating and heartbreaking.

"Thanks. It's a messed-up story." She wrings her hands. I reach over and take hers in mine.

"When and if you want to tell me, I'll listen. I know what it's like to lose someone you love. My mom died way too early. I know it's not the same, but grief is grief where love is concerned." Did she lose the love of her life? Is that why she's unattached?

"Thanks. It's not quite like that." She takes a deep breath and watches the game for a minute. For the first time in a long time, I couldn't care less what's going on out on the field. I'm more concerned about the woman next to me. We sit in silence, her watching the field. Me watching her.

She talks, still looking at the field. "I was young, graduated from college, finishing my Masters. Out on my own for the first time. Just got my first teaching job in D.C. I met Riley at a bar." She pauses, recalling each sentence like a distinct memory. "He was stationed at the Pentagon. He was fun, a nice guy. We had chemistry but never had the same goals, you know?" She gives a little shoulder shrug.

She takes a swig of her beer, and the heavy subject sits between us. After another pause, she continues speaking. "We dated for a few months on and off. We were both busy, and dating or a relationship wasn't a priority for either of us. A drunken night, a round of antibiotics for a sinus infection, and a forgotten condom, I had a positive pregnancy test a few weeks later. This was about the same time he was being deployed over-seas. We got married at the courthouse, just us. He wanted me to have his benefits for the baby. We both knew what it was, but were trying to do the right thing. We weren't in love. But like I said, nice guy." She has a slight smile as she says that. "Anyway, six weeks later, his helicopter was shot down. Then I'm sitting at a gravesite surrounded by his family I'd never met." A small tear slides down her face, and she quickly wipes it away. I want to wrap her in my arms and take her away to keep her safe.

She needs to tell her story, in her own way, and in her own time. But if this is too much for her, she doesn't need to continue for me. Watching her is breaking my heart. "You don't have to," I say, but she interrupts me to continue.

Her voice is a little stronger now, but still a hushed tone, so no one else can hear. "There was a scene at his funeral. His sister went ballistic when they gave me the flag that covered his coffin. I immediately gave it to his mother, not wanting something I didn't deserve. Then it got worse when they realized I would get his life insurance and widow benefits. They wanted the money, but nothing to do with me and the baby. So, I gave it all to them and haven't heard from them since. There I was, alone, pregnant, and ashamed. Not one of my best days, that's for sure." She gives a weak chuckle. "I got the best part of the deal. Tyler's my world."

Fuck. That's not the story I was expecting. She was in a tough situation, and she tried to make the best of it. I put my arm around her and pull her into my side. She's not alone now.

"Agreed. He's awesome. I'm sorry you had to go through it all alone. That must have been hard." Her protectiveness and determination to parent right makes more sense. She's compensating for his lack of a father, too.

"My parents have been great. At first, my dad was angry at my irresponsibility, but then he held Tyler in his arms and immediately became wrapped around his finger. They make up for the shitty grandparents he lost in the deal too." She pauses. "If I'm realistic, if he hadn't died, we probably wouldn't have lasted, anyway. We had to put in a lot of effort to make it work. You can't build a relationship on chemistry alone."

My heart's heavy at her story. She's a strong, single mom doing it all by herself while dealing with the ghost of Tyler's father. I can hear the guilt in her voice as she talks about him. They were never in love. I can't imagine what kind of guy wouldn't fall head over heels for Dani, but I appreciate his attempt to care for her. This woman deserves to be loved and worshipped. The chemistry I get. But there's just so much more to her than that.

"Hey, look at me." I put my finger below her chin and turn her face to mine. "Thanks for sharing your story. You're amazing."

Her smile lights up her face, any trace of sadness erased.

The little boy hits me with his gloved hand.

"Kiss her," he says.

His voice breaks the spell she has over me. "What?" He points to the Jumbotron behind us, where we're on the kiss cam.

I look back at Dani, and she giggles. Fucking giggles. She leans in and gives me a chaste kiss. Her soft lips feel like heaven against mine. A blush fills her cheeks, and I want to run my fingers through her curls. I lean in, about to kiss her like I want, when everyone around us cheers. I almost forgot where I was. Who I am. The camera moves on to some other unsuspecting couple.

My phone buzzes in my pocket like a beehive in my pants. I'm sure the group chat is blowing up right now. Bastards.

"Sorry," she says shyly. "I shouldn't have done that."

"What?" I'm still stunned at the course of events this evening.

"I'm sorry I kissed you. I shouldn't have been that forward."

Wordlessly, I stand up and offer her my hand. When I pull her up, she falls into my chest. She feels good there.

"Come on," I growl as I take her hand. "Let's take another walk."

"Don't you want to watch the game?" she asks innocently.

"I'll catch the highlights on ESPN," I mumble. I take her hand in mine and walk with purpose.

"Are we going back to the suite?"

"Absolutely not."

She stops walking, and I take a step before I feel her resistance. I turn and look at her, her hand on her hip.

"Where are we going, Mr. Decker?"

"Somewhere a little more private." I'll be damned if our first kiss will be some kind of middle school peck on a fucking Jumbotron for all the world to see.

"And where would that be?"

Where is this sass coming from? Any other time, I'd like it. Right now? It's not my favorite thing about her.

"My office." Hell, I'll take a dark corridor at this point. I need to taste her.

She grimaces. "Yeah, been there done that. Are you taking me to the principal's office?" Now I picture her bent over my knee, getting spanked. Not helping.

"You aren't in trouble, I promise." Well, not that kind of trouble, anyway.

"I'd rather not go up there if that's okay with you." She looks guilty. Of what, I have no idea.

I stop and turn toward her. It's between innings, and the crowd is growing, everyone making their way to the bathrooms and concession stands.

I stop myself. Fuck, am I forcing myself on her and making her uncomfortable? I'm no better than Pauly. I clear my throat. "Fuck," I mumble. "I'm sorry. I can't believe I'm putting you in an uncomfortable position." I run my hand down my face. "I'm so sorry."

She gives me a little smirk. "First, I'm not uncomfortable. Nervous, maybe, but not uncomfortable. And second, I told you no more apologies." She takes my other hand, and her look is sincere. She's okay being with me. Thank fuck.

"Why don't you give me the private tour of all the forbidden places that mere mortals like me never get to see?"

"Are you sure?" I quirk my eyebrow at her.

"Positive."

CHAPTER
TWENTY-FOUR

DANI

———

I'm playing with fire. Xander looks like he wants to devour me, and I'm here for it. I almost suggested we leave and go to his place, but I couldn't ask him to leave during an important game. Surprisingly, he doesn't seem too interested in what's going on down on the field. That gives me the confidence to suggest finding some place a little more discrete. Would his office be the perfect place? Sure, if I hadn't already been up there today before meeting him in the suite. I left him a little surprise and prefer he find my note tomorrow.

He intertwines his fingers with mine and gives a slight squeeze, silently acknowledging what's coming. He moves us through the crowd with an obvious destination in mind. He uses his badge to open an unmarked door. The security guard nods slightly. "Mr. Decker."

"Carlos," he acknowledges. He doesn't slow down as we enter a dimly lit, nondescript corridor. The game is piped in through the speakers, echoing down the hall.

"Where are we going?" I bite my bottom lip in anticipation of our destination.

"This is the behind-the-scenes tour you asked for. This leads to the clubhouse, workout center, indoor batting cages, and offices for the players to meet with agents, lawyers, that sort of thing."

"Oh wow. There's a lot under here, isn't there?"

"Yep." We continue to walk down the corridor until he opens the door to our left and pulls me in. The lights must be automatic because the dark room immediately lights up to an office with a small couch, desk, computer, and a few chairs. Large, framed pictures are on the wall, all Reapers promotional posters.

He leads me into the room, and the door closes behind us. I automatically step back until I'm against the cool, painted brick wall, and he stalks toward me. His forehead barely touches mine. His blue eyes are dark, his pupils wide, and they search my face.

"I want to taste you so bad I can't think straight," he says, his voice so low, I question if that's what he actually said. His hand reaches up and cups my cheek, his thumb lightly tracing my bottom lip. He hesitates.

He's controlling himself, no doubt still worried about me being a victim. I take matters into my own hands.

I stand on my tiptoes and reach around his neck, pulling him down to me. When his lips hover over mine, I pull him down the last inch and stretch to kiss him. His lips mold to mine, and the butterflies take flight in my belly. His tongue sweeps out, gently seeking entrance. I open for him, and what started as sweet quickly morphs into a sultry, passionate kiss, our tongues wrapping around each other, dancing, tasting, devouring.

His hands embrace my head, his fingers threading through my curls until he tilts my head back further for a new angle. I've never been so thoroughly kissed. He moans into my mouth, and I gobble it up, his presence all-consuming. My core heats, and if we don't stop, this will be more than our first kiss.

My nails drag across his scalp and neck until I trace his shoulders, and my hands come to rest on his pecs. I gently push him away, breaking our kiss.

His forehead rests against mine, his eyes searching for a reaction.

"I knew you'd taste like heaven," he says, more to himself than to me.

"Um, wow. I don't think I have words, Mr. Decker. You've taken them all away."

A smile fills his face, reaching his eyes. "I'll give you a few words, Ms. Franklin. Fucking amazing, delicious, erotic, sensual, life-changing."

Life-changing? I felt that too. It was like the Earth shifted on its axis, finally where it's supposed to be.

"Yeah, those will work." His hands slide back to my face, holding me in place. He gives me another chaste kiss, which makes my toes curl.

His hands slide down my shoulders and arms until his fingers wrap around mine.

"I'm sorry I couldn't wait a minute longer. I'm usually more in control of myself, but something about you makes me want to lose control. I promise I'm not an animal."

"This sounds like an apology, and I told you no more of those." His smirk returns. Yeah, I've got your number, Alexander Decker. "I'm just afraid if we don't stop, we'll start something we can't finish."

"Oh, I assure you, sunshine, I can finish you, but you're right. This isn't the time or place. But I promise you, when the time is right, prepare to be worshipped like you deserve." He gives me a smoldering look and seals it with a wink.

Worshipped? Is he for real? Yes, please.

He pulls me away from the wall and toward the door. "I need to get you back into public view, or I can't be held responsible for my actions."

"Why, Mr. Decker, are you saying you might end up in detention for being a naughty boy?" I laugh at him as his face gives away his thoughts.

"Come on, before Jenny sends out a search party." We exit the room, walk past the locker room door, and await an elevator, the sexual tension thick between us.

"Trust me, she won't be looking for me." I laugh at his assumption Jenny would worry. She'll be disappointed if I don't get thoroughly fucked soon.

We step into the empty elevator, and I catch my reflection on the shiny walls. My lips are swollen from the kiss, my unruly curls untamed. I lick my lips, and I notice Xander watching me.

"You okay?" His voice has a hint of concern.

"Yeah, I just look like I've had the best kiss of my life, that's all. Not sure I want to advertise that to your friends and family."

"Best of your life, huh?" His smug smirk returns. His hands run through my hair, attempting to smooth the wild curls down, but he doesn't know that makes them even worse.

"Don't let it go to your head, Mr. Decker." He leans down and kisses me again. This one is just as hot but more controlled. The doors open, and he breaks our kiss.

"Come on. You can freshen up before we go in." We take a few steps, and he stops in front of a ladies' room. He leans down and whispers in my ear, "But for the record, I like the thoroughly kissed look on you. It's hot as hell."

I reach up on my toes and give him a quick peck. "You're cute."

I turn around and enter the ladies' room. As soon as I see the padded bench, I sit down and take a deep breath. The smile practically hurts my face. My fingers trace my lips, remembering every detail of the most amazing kiss of my life. I can't stop the sigh that escapes. There is no doubt this man is going to rock my world. I hope he doesn't break my heart in the process.

CHAPTER
TWENTY-FIVE

DANI

———

We walk back into the suite, and everyone has settled into the game. The friendly banter is flying, and everyone is comfortable. Jenny sits between Cole and Chance, watching the game and cheering when Luis catches a fly ball, ending the inning.

Xander leans down and whispers in my ear, causing goosebumps to cover my arms. "What can I get for you, sunshine?"

I shake my head, not trusting myself to speak just yet. I'm still keyed up from our kiss.

"You'll tell me when you want something, right?" I give a slight nod.

"Well, well, well, look who decided to join us," Trevor says from the couch. He shoots us a devious grin. At that statement, all eyes turn to us.

Xander runs his hand down my arm, letting me know he's still with me. His smile is another new one for me, directed at his friend. "Fuck off." He chuckles, and I can feel his chest against my back. He does a quick sweep of the suite. "Where are Ash and Jules?"

I look around and notice they're missing from the suite. Alexander keeps tabs on everyone. He's the shepherd watching over the flock. That can't be a simple job with this group. No wonder he's stressed.

"They went to see your dad," Cole offers. "I wasn't sure he'd think I was dressed appropriately, so I stayed." He tips his hat as a reminder.

"Nah, your jersey speaks volumes, and you know he wouldn't care. Admit you just wanted to watch the game," Chance says.

"How are my boys doing?" Xander asks as he guides me down to the stadium seats where most everyone is sitting.

We take a seat behind Jenny. I can't see a thing sitting behind Chance's broad shoulders. How tall is he, anyway? I stand back up. "I'm going to get water. Can I get anyone anything?" Xander stands, and I place my hand on his shoulder, signaling him to stay put.

"I'll come with." Jenny pops up from her seat. She squeezes past Chance, her ass in his face, and he diverts his eyes and is greeted by a snickering Cole.

Jenny reaches her hand to me, and we take the few steps up to the bar away from everyone.

"So?" she asks, her eyes wide as saucers.

"So what?" I whisper back. We're shoulder to shoulder, doing our best to keep this discussion between us. Jenny gives me a skeptical look. She's not buying my innocent look.

The bartender puts two bottles of water in front of us, gives a wink and knowing smile, and steps to the other end of the bar to give us privacy and watches the game on the TV.

I gulp water to buy time before responding. What do I tell her? That I had the most sensual, soul-crushing kiss I've ever had in my life? That I'm scared I might be in over my head. That I want to see more underneath that grumpy facade. This totally out-of-my-league guy rocked my world with a kiss.

I don't want to share those details. "I told him about Riley."

"Shit." Jenny takes a drink of her water. "And?"

"I don't know. He was understanding." I'm not sure what Xander thinks about me marrying someone I didn't love for his military benefits. I'm not sure how I feel about it seven years later. It happened so fast and seemed like a quick solution to an uncertain situation. My father was furious and felt it was dishonest. We didn't expect it to happen the way it did. Riley wanted to provide for his kid, and his life insurance would have done that. It's the thought that counts, I guess. I still have moments of sadness that he's missing out on Tyler.

"Well, it was a messed-up situation, and you did nothing wrong. If he wasn't understanding, that says more about him than you, right?"

"Yeah, but it is what it is. At least he knows." I know that kiss was judgment free. Xander doesn't hold my past over me.

"And the kiss?" She wiggles her eyebrows at me.

"Unforgettable." I sigh and touch my lips, still feeling his scorching kiss.

"Um, there must be more to the story than what I saw, or you are in worse shape than I thought." She's glaring at me. She senses I'm not telling her the whole story.

"Oh girl, so much more to the story." I giggle as the suite and stadium burst into cheers.

"That's my boy!" Cole yells, hugging Darcy.

I watch on TV as Matt casually runs the bases, rounding third. He must have hit a home run.

"World Series bound, boys!" Cole shouts, hugging everyone. He reaches for Alexander, and there's a pause. Alexander gives a slight nod and hugs Cole. I suspect there's a story there too.

He looks at me over Cole's shoulder and gives me a new look. This man has a thousand different expressions, and I vow to learn them all. I'm not sure about this one, but I'll label it as a promise. His eyes sparkle and smolder as they lock onto me. A slight smile peeks from his lips. He gives Cole a hard slap on the back and focuses back on his friends.

"You think we should leave them to celebrate?" I ask Jenny. "I don't want to be a distraction."

"Girl, I think you're beyond that. And if you think he's letting you walk out of here, you are sorely mistaken. He's locked on you, so you best buckle up."

I think she's right but also wrong. I don't think he'll ever do anything I don't want because he still sees me as a victim. I notice it in his hesitancy before he touches me. Being a young, pregnant widow adds to my narrative, but it's part of my story I can't change. The most important thing to me is he doesn't see me that way. There's only one way to erase those images from his mind, and I devise a plan to start a new chapter with Alexander Decker. He may see me as a victim, but I need this man to see me differently. But first, he needs to celebrate and enjoy this moment with his team.

CHAPTER
TWENTY-SIX

ALEXANDER

―――――

My team is headed to the World Series. Regardless of talent, hard work, and sheer determination, you still need a heavy dose of luck to make it to this point. And this year must be my lucky year. The stadium is alive with celebration, everyone on their feet cheering for the Reapers. The team is celebrating at home plate. It's a sight to see, and I've never been more proud or conflicted. I know I need to go to the clubhouse and celebrate with my team, but I look over at Dani, the smile on her face, those curls begging me to run my fingers through them, and I don't want to leave this spot.

For years, my life has been the Reapers. But now? For the first time, I have someone competing for my time and attention, and I'm not mad about it. I go to the bar where Dani and Jenny are taking it all in.

"Hey," she says shyly. Where did my sassy girl go? Did I spook her? I told her I was coming for her. Now I'm questioning my approach.

"Sunshine," I say, somewhat disapproving. I don't like her retreating from me.

"I'm thrilled for you and the team. I'm sure you have some celebrating to do, so I'll leave you to it." She leans in for a hug, thinking this is goodbye. Yeah, not happening.

I let her hug me, but then I don't let go, keeping my arm around her waist.

"You aren't going anywhere." I look at Jenny for backup. She's smiling like the cat that ate the canary. "Come on. We're all headed to the clubhouse. I'm sure Luis would love to see Jenny, and I promised you behind-the-scenes all-access. That starts now."

She looks unsure. "Unless you don't want to." I put my knuckle under her chin to make her look at me. "I'll never make you do something you don't want. Ever. If you're uncomfortable, say the word, and I'll move heaven and earth to fix it. Understand? You call the shots. Always. Okay?"

I say those words like an oath. I mean every word.

"Well, as long as I'm not a distraction."

"Sunshine, I can assure you, you are most definitely a distraction. A very, very pleasant distraction. I don't want our time to end, but I have obligations. You can either come with me, or someone will escort you home. Always your call." I'm already planning for both scenarios.

"I don't want this to end either, but I want you to celebrate and enjoy the moment with your team." Her smile lights up the room.

"Let's enjoy the moment together," I whisper as I lean down and capture her lips with mine.

When we catch our breath, I notice the suite has cleared, except for Trevor. "I drew the short straw to wrangle you to the clubhouse." He looks at Dani and winks. "Go ahead, Xander. Take the stairs. Dani and I will be right behind you. Go have your moment with your team."

I'm conflicted. "You okay? He's harmless, mostly. I promise."

She giggles as she looks at Trevor with his cast and blinged out scooter. "I think I can take him."

The Reapers are going to the World Series. Dani is waiting for me. Life can't get any better than this.

CHAPTER
TWENTY-SEVEN

DANI

―――――

Trevor never lets me out of his sight. He leaves his scooter outside the locker room and grabs a pair of crutches from the training room. He's just as comfortable here as Alexander.

The clubhouse is absolute pandemonium. The room is full of players and families, and shouts of congratulations ring throughout the room.

Chance and Julian surround Tripp, and when Trevor and I step up, he pulls us both in for a hug. I'm pulled away by Luis, who swings me around.

Trevor hits him with his crutch, and he puts me down. I give Trevor a disapproving look, and he laughs. I can't have Trevor breaking the players with the biggest series of their lives coming up soon. Luis hugs Jenny, and his eyes eat her up as he takes in her cropped jersey top.

The celebration in the locker room is controlled chaos. Baseball players are in various stages of undress but at least have their pants on. Alexander is drenched, and his shirt clings to his chest, teasing me with what lies beneath. I'm not disappointed. He holds a bottle of champagne by the neck and takes a swig. And it's got to be the hottest thing I've ever seen. He's off to the side of the room, talking to the coaches and other non-uniformed people. I wonder who they all are when I notice a distinguished man who looks like an older version of Alexander and assume it's his father. If that's how he'll look in twenty years or so, all I can say is, damn. That family has seriously fantastic genetics.

After a few minutes, I step back out of the way and watch the friends and family celebrate. Joey has Archie on his shoulders, and Casey is taking pictures. Cole is beaming at Matt and just randomly slaps his back in congratulations. It's all surreal. I can't believe I'm a witness to this moment in history.

"I'm headed over to Luis's after he cleans up. Are you okay if I leave you?" Jenny looks at me, a conflict warring on her face.

"I'm great." She watches Luis do a victory dance. "This is different, isn't it?"

"Yeah, who would have thought we'd hang out in a baseball locker room after the big game?"

I was talking about this thing between her and Luis. She's not as head-first with him as when she first dates someone. I hope he doesn't break her heart, but when I catch him looking at her from across the room, I may have to worry more about his heart.

"We can get you home." She's still worrying about me.

"Do you think Alexander would let that happen?" I suspect he has other plans, and frankly, so do I. After that kiss, I'm open to round two.

"Let what happen?" Trevor asks. How did he show up over here in our corner? I'd hate to see him operating at full strength if he moves that fast with crutches.

"Jenny is going home with Luis. She's my light rail buddy. You're stuck with me until I can call an Uber." Trevor's face scrunches up and he looks at me like I've gone insane.

"Yeah, that's not going to happen. Like it or not, you will not be getting in cars with strangers ever again. No ma'am. Not on our watch." He gives an exaggerated shudder.

I arch an eyebrow and challenge his words. Our watch?

"Hey man, we're headed out," Chance and Julian say to Trevor. "What's your deal?"

"Dani and I are going to wait for Xan. I'll see you at home."

Chance and Julian give me smiles that could make any girl melt. "We'll see you soon," Julian says. I'm not sure if he's talking to me or Trevor because I'm distracted by Alexander's father making his way over to us.

His blonde hair is slightly gray, giving him an extremely distinguished appearance. His blue eyes are the same shade as Alexander's, and they study me like Alexander does, like I'm a puzzle he's trying to solve. He's dressed in slacks and a red Reaper's golf shirt, casual but all business.

"Boys," he says, greeting the group, clamping his hand on Julian's shoulder. I look at these three hulking guys, and boys is the last word I would use to describe them. I can't help it when a giggle slips through my lips.

"I don't think I've had the pleasure of meeting these charming women. I'm Sully Decker. If these boys give you one ounce of trouble, you let me know. I may only claim one by birth, but the others answer to me, too." He extends his hand to me, and when I put mine out, he embraces it with both hands instead of shaking it. He smiles, and I am immediately under his spell.

"Dad, this is Dani Franklin and her friend Jenny Atkins," Julian says. "They're Alexander's guests tonight."

"Is that so?" His smile widens. "Dani Franklin? Why does your name sound familiar?"

My smile falters. Of course, he's heard of me, but in a different context. I pull my hand away and drop my eyes. His smile dims, and he looks at me like he's trying to place how he knows me. I'm the victim, I almost say.

"We met Dani and Jenny through a mutual acquaintance," Trevor says. He puts his hand on my shoulder and squeezes. I peek up at Trevor to see his usual charming smile is gone, and he's challenging Alexander's father to drop it.

Mr. Decker takes the hint, and his smile is back. "Well, any friend of Alexander's is always welcome here. I hope to see you both again in a more conversational setting." He looks around the locker room slowly, shakes his head, and smiles. The chaos is slowing down to frat party level.

"That would be nice," I say.

"Chance, glad you could be here tonight. Good luck this season." He reaches up and grips Chance's bicep.

"Thank you, sir. I'm ready." Chance gives him a look that speaks of admiration and respect. The closeness of the relationships isn't hard to see. The love they all have for one another speaks to family. Alexander's family.

"We'll walk out with you, Dad," Julian says. "Make sure Luis behaves," he says to Jenny as he gives her a light kiss on the cheek. He hugs me, and I'm caught a little off guard. "Be patient with him," he whispers so only I can hear. I blush at his words. "See you around, Dani."

"Bye, Dani," Chance says. "Hope to see you soon."

They walk out, and I wonder what Julian meant.

"Come on, ladies. This room is about to turn into a true locker room, and you aren't ready for that. Hell, who am I kidding? I'm not ready for it. Jenny, I'll show you where you can wait for Luis. Dani and I will wait for Xander. You okay?" Trevor looks at me, and his funny guy persona is gone. He's in full bodyguard mode, and it's very alpha-hot.

What will Alexander's father say when he figures out I'm the victim his family needed to quiet for PR purposes? What will he think of me then?

"Fine," I respond, lost in my spiraling thoughts.

"You sure?" he questions.

"Yeah, I'm just tired. It's been a long day."

"Come on. I've got you."

He takes me to a large room that looks like a private movie theater but with couches and recliners. This is how the other half lives, I guess. It's beyond nice, but I'm too tired to give it much thought. I get comfortable in a recliner and yawn.

"Can we talk for a minute before Xander storms in here and accuses me of moving in on you?"

"He wouldn't do that, would he?" Would he? Is Trevor letting me know about red flags I should pay attention to?

"Probably, but then he'd come to his senses, realize it's me, and break my other leg as a warning." I look at him in shock. I need to leave.

"Kidding, just kidding. I promise you're safe with me. And him, for that matter." He takes a seat next to me and wraps his hand around mine. He takes a deep breath and closes his eyes. "I've known him all my adult life, and I just want you to know he's a stand-up guy. A little grumpy and uptight, but that man has a heart of gold. And he's a protector. He thinks I was out of it, but I heard him in my hospital room. He was a guard dog, making sure I got the best care. He was relentless, demanding updates, and getting second and third opinions. I'm sure the medical team thought he was an ass, but I also heard him crying and talking to me while in my drug-induced coma. He doesn't love many, but when he does, it's fierce." He presses a button, and we both recline back.

"Why are you telling me this?" This is personal, and I just met him. Why is he confiding in me like this?

"Because Xander has a lot on his plate. The team. His family. Me, even though I tell him to quit mother henning me. But you see, that's what he does. He protects us. It's a huge burden none of us asked him to take on, but he does it anyway. I see the way he looks at you. I just, well, I wanted you to know. He may come on strong, and it's intense. But I promise, he's one of the good guys."

"I know." I yawn again, and my eyes get heavy. It's a lot to take in. I can see how the responsibility weighs on him. Why does he feel so responsible? I let my mind wander. Trevor says something, but it sounds far away.

I think he says, "Please don't break him," as I drift off. I just need a few minutes to rest my eyes.

CHAPTER
TWENTY-EIGHT

ALEXANDER

———

I burst into the media room and am shushed by Trevor. He has his finger over his mouth and points to the recliner beside him. Dani is lying on her side, facing him, her eyes closed like a sleeping angel.

Trevor grins at me as I approach them. "She's had a long day."

It's well past midnight. I shouldn't have kept her here this late, but I didn't want to let her go. She looks so peaceful, and I don't want to disturb her.

"Why don't you head home? Tripp's still here, and he can walk with you. I've got her from here. Thanks for keeping her safe."

"It was my pleasure. I can see why you like her. She's got a spark." He wiggles his eyebrows at me.

I nod my head. That's one way to put it.

I hold out my hand, pull him up, and hug him. "Thanks, man."

"I won't wait up," Trevor says and gives me a wink. He gets on his scooter and leaves me alone with a sleeping beauty.

Do I wake her and take her home? Her place or mine? My place is at capacity with testosterone, so that's out. She looks so content. What is it about this woman that shakes my confidence and makes me indecisive and unsure of myself?

The closet in the back has blankets, because this room is a favorite place for a few guys to take pregame naps. I grab two, gently cover her, and take Trevor's place in the chair beside her. I brush her hair off her cheek, and a slight smile graces her face.

"This isn't how I pictured our first night together, but sunshine, I'll take every moment you can give me," I whisper.

I watch her sleep for longer than is considered proper and finally surrender to my tiredness. I close my eyes and drift off, dreaming of my sunshine.

Her hushed panic wakes me and puts me on high alert.

"Oh my god, oh my god," she mutters to herself.

I open my eyes to find a blanket and an empty chair beside me. I turn to the sound of her voice and see her pacing, too close to the door and too far away from me for my liking.

"Good morning, sunshine." My morning voice is rough and deep.

She jumps with a start. "Oh! I didn't mean to wake you." She's looking around like a scared animal, unsure what to do or where to go. It's adorable.

I get up slowly and move toward her, not wanting to spook her. I don't break my eye contact and as I get close, I open my arms, inviting her in. She hesitates, and I drop my arms.

"I'm sorry, I should have taken you home last night, but you looked so peaceful. I didn't want to disturb you." I glance at the clock and see that it's almost seven o'clock. I can't remember the last time I slept this late.

She steps closer, still hesitant. She covers her face with her hands. "No more apologies, remember? I'm so embarrassed. I can't believe I fell asleep. I swear, I can't even do grown-up hours anymore." She's shaking her head in disbelief and embarrassment.

I take a step closer, closing the gap. I take her hands away from her beautiful eyes and put her hands in mine. "It was a late night, and you had a busy day. After a long week of busy. You needed to rest." I tilt her face to mine. "It's okay. Hear me?" I give her a quick wink, bringing a slight smile to her gorgeous face.

She gives me a little nod. "Now, what do we do? I'm not exactly practiced in the walk of shame."

I can't control my joy at that statement. I didn't get the impression she dated much, but hearing no other man is getting to see her in the morning does something to my chest that I can't quite describe.

"Breakfast?" I'm unsure what her plans are for today, but I'd like to be part of them.

She looks hesitant.

"No pressure. If you want me to take you home, say the word. Never ever do I want you to feel uncomfortable, especially around me. Got it, sunshine?"

She wraps her arms around my waist, and my heart melts. Her curls are unruly this morning, and they tickle my nose. I could get used to this.

I kiss the top of her head, and she relaxes in the embrace. Her breasts rub against my chest, and my morning wood begs for attention. But this is neither the time and definitely not the place.

"Why don't you freshen up, and I'll take you to breakfast? I know a great place near your house that will hit the spot. Sound good?"

"Okay." She steps back, and the separation makes me feel cold, my sunshine pulling away. She gives me a questioning look. "How do you know where I live?"

Shit. I don't want to confess I've done a background check on her. What will she think of me then? "You said you live in

Southend. Take the light rail? Which we won't be doing, by the way."

"You a public transportation snob, Mr. Decker?" She challenges me. And fuck if it doesn't turn me on a little more.

"Not at all, Ms. Franklin. It's just, well, I want you to be safe."

"Got it. Can you direct me to the nearest ladies' room before we start today's adventure?" She runs her fingers through her hair, and I wish that were me.

"Absolutely." She's giving me the gift of her time. I'm going to cherish every second. "Right this way, sunshine."

CHAPTER
TWENTY-NINE

DANI

————

I can't believe I fell asleep next to Xander, and all I have to show for it is messy hair, raccoon eyes, and a little drool at the corner of my mouth. Nice. I'm sure he's not used to this kind of classy. I do my best to make myself somewhat presentable and will take care of the rest when we go home.

He must have changed at some point last night because the last time I saw him, he was doused in champagne, the wet shirt clinging to his body like Rose to the damn door at the Titanic sinking. And did it look good? I had to step away to get myself together, or I was going to lick the champagne from his body in front of everyone. Now in the florescent lighting of the morning after, he's showered and wearing the most delectable pair of joggers, which aren't doing a damn thing to hide his morning erection.

Well, Jenny is right on several counts. I'm attracted to Alexander Decker, and it's been a very long time since I've slept with a man. My lady parts are waking up from a long slumber and are starving for some attention. I'm sure Xander knows how to show attention in all the right ways, and I'm ready to test my theory.

I sigh as I look in the mirror at the mess that is my hair, face, and everything. I square my shoulders and resolve to own this. He might as well get used to my authentic self if he wants me. Because honestly, that's all I know how to be, anyway. If he wants me, he gets this version, drool and all.

I wipe my face with a wet paper towel. Well, maybe not drool and all. I need to hang on to a shred of dignity. I pop in a piece of gum to tackle the morning breath until I make it home. Welp, it is what it is. I am what I am.

Alexander brought me a Reapers Division Champions t-shirt, which I change into, so I look less wrinkled and rumpled. I throw my sweater across my shoulders and shove the tank top into my bag.

I check my phone and don't see any texts from Mom. Tyler will be fine until lunch or so. I have a few missed texts from Jenny. It's amusing how she assumes I'm too busy getting busy to respond. And a little sad. No, Jenny, I was sleeping. In a recliner at the stadium. Gah. I'm not good at this dating thing, if that's what this is.

I take a last look, determine it's the best I'll be, and step out to find Xander leaning against the wall, looking down at his phone, scowling at something. The line between his brows creases his handsome face, and I want nothing more than replace his scowl with a smile.

"Something wrong? I can head home and…."

"What?" He looks at me and shakes his head like he's physically pushing whatever it was away in his mind. "No, it's fine." He forces a smile. "Ready?" He holds out his hand to me, and I take it.

His big hand engulfs mine, and the warmth spreads through my veins like a warm IV. I like it, but I don't want to ignore his cause of distress.

"Sure. If you need to take care of something, we can reschedule." Something's going on.

"No, I'm right where I need to be. Well, not quite." He pulls me in and gives me a toe-curling kiss that rivals the one last night. Somehow, this one is even hotter than I remember. His hands run through my hair and fist at the nape, holding me tight. His moan into my mouth practically brings me to climax from a kiss. Is that even possible?

A door slams in the distance, reminding me we're in a public place. I pull back because it's the right thing despite my body strongly disagreeing.

"Um, let's get out of here."

He looks at me like a starving man, and I'm even more turned on. His fingers run through my hair before he releases me.

"I love these curls," he whispers. "It takes a lot of effort to keep my hands to myself. Just thought you should know."

I blush. I've always been self-conscious of my hair, and now this incredibly hot man tells me he loves my curls. I'm not sure how to process that statement.

"Thanks. You sure know how to make me speechless," I confess.

He chuckles. "Somehow, I doubt that. You okay walking to my place to get my car, or do you want to wait here, and I'll get someone to bring it to us?"

I remember how upset he was about my footwear comment and walking. "Yeah, I'm fine. Let's go."

I let him lead me through the maze of tunnels until we find ourselves outside in the warm morning fog. It's still an early Sunday morning in the city, and I guess most people are tucked in bed, sleeping off the excitement of yesterday. We walk hand in hand to his building.

"Do you mind coming up to my place for just a minute?"

I arch my eyebrow at him. I don't mind, but I'm also a little excited of what might happen if left alone with him and a bed is anywhere in the vicinity.

"I want to say goodbye to Chance. He's headed out shortly. I should warn you, my place looks like a frat house right now with Jules, Chance, Trevor, and Emma crashing there."

Well, there was the mental ice bucket my body needed. Nothing going to happen there.

"Sure, no problem."

Obviously, Xander has never been in a frat house. His enormous penthouse has floor-to-ceiling windows and a sizeable second-story loft overlooking the sunken main room. The open-concept kitchen flows into a dining area and den with the biggest sectional I've ever seen. The place is neat, clean, and spotless.

We walk in, and I'm so taken aback by the luxury condo it takes me a few moments to notice what's going on in the den. Julian is sitting on the couch, his t-shirt soaking wet, a smirk on his face, while Ashleigh is beating him with a pillow.

"Seriously, Jules? Glitter?" She shouts as she takes another swing at him.

Xander groans beside me, and I flash back to our kiss. He takes a few quick strides in, reaches down, picks Ashleigh up at the waist, and swings her away from Julian.

"Oh, for fuck's sake," Xander says. He's holding her back but trying to touch her as little as possible. That's when I notice Ashleigh is a little sparkly. Well, maybe more than a little.

"I don't know what you're talking about," Julian says. I may not know him well, but I can tell he's lying.

"Well, your place is covered in glitter now, thanks to you. I'll be washing it off for weeks," she growls. "How do I interview new assistants looking like a stripper after a three-day shift?"

"I told you not to stir up stuff with my assistant, or I'd get you back. I warned you," Julian says, trying not to laugh.

"I did no such thing. I merely suggested she go out with someone. It's not my fault she's in love and moving."

"Mary Kate's leaving?" Xander asks.

"Yeah, now what am I going to do?" Julian says, his smile long gone.

"I'll help you hire someone else," Ashleigh offers, her anger morphing to sympathy so quickly that I'm not sure it's possible to shift gears that fast.

I don't know what's happening, but this sibling dynamic is fascinating. It's another layer of Xander that many people don't get to see. I'm trying to piece together the drama when I'm wrapped in massive arms and pulled into a hug, my body a foot off the ground.

"Morning Dani!" Chance says. "Sleep well?" He gives me a suggestive wink that would make most girls melt. Instead, I cringe, thinking that my answer is I slept well.

"Too well," I mumble. "Is this normal?" I motion to the scene unfolding in the den.

"Sometimes," he says, nonchalantly. "Coffee?" He guides me into the kitchen, which seems to be the neutral zone. He's dressed in gray sweatpants and a worn, faded Renegades T-shirt. Wow. Seeing both Alexander and this morning version of Chance is proving to be too overwhelming for me, especially before I've had my coffee.

He pulls a cup down from the cabinet and pours me a coffee, clearly comfortable in this setting. He sets it next to a tray with flavored syrups, cream, and sugar. This is a better setup than Starbucks.

"Thanks." I make my coffee, turn around, and lean against the counter, watching the sibling drama play out.

"Sorry, Xan walked into this. Jules was sleeping on the couch, and I woke up to Ashleigh screaming at him. A hell of a good morning, if you ask me," Chance says to catch me up to speed. For the record, it doesn't.

"I didn't expect him back this early," he continues.

"He wanted to say goodbye to you," I say.

"Figures. He may act like a grumpus, but he's a thoughtful

grumpus. You guys crash at your place?" Chance is so relaxed with everything around him, and he goes with the flow. I always thought hockey players were tough guys with all the fighting and everything. I need to reexamine my assumptions. I watch the Deckers huddle up and work together to solve this problem.

"I'm about to complain to management about the ruckus at this establishment," Trevor says in greeting. He hobbles into the kitchen, and Chance pulls out a stool, ordering him to sit without saying a word, and Trevor complies. Chance makes Trevor's coffee and puts it in front of him, slides a muffin and pill bottle over, and gestures with his eyes. Trevor nods, takes his medicine, and picks at his muffin. Not a word said. They all work as a group, stepping up when someone needs a hand.

"You should," Alexander says from across the room, acknowledging Trevor. The fact he's following conversations in both rooms is impressive.

"You guys just getting back from the stadium?" Trevor asks.

"You slept at the stadium?" Chance asks.

Now is when I die of embarrassment. The walk of shame might be less embarrassing.

"Yeah," I say and take a sip of my coffee. The rich, bold flavor is a jolt of lightning to my brain. This is delicious coffee. A rich person's luxury I shouldn't get used to.

Chance shakes his head and looks at the clump of siblings. Emma shuffles into the kitchen wearing a cute pink pajama set covered in donuts. "Hey Em," Trevor says. "Sorry, they woke you."

"All good. Gotta head out shortly anyway," she mumbles. "What happened?" She gestures to the Deckers.

"Well, best I can tell, Mary Kate fell in love, quit her job, and is moving. I think Ash had something to do with it. So Jules did something with glitter to Ash, Ash dumped water on Jules, and now they're figuring out how to solve the Julian assistant problem." Chance did a good job summarizing it all, but I'm still lost.

"That's not good," Emma comments.

I take another sip of coffee. I feel awkward watching this family drama play out, but also strangely comfortable. For all the money and fabulous condos, they're still human, with everyday issues and relationships. I mean, sort of normal. Do regular people have executive assistants?

Every defense around my heart is falling, crumbling brick by brick. And this morning, standing in his kitchen, watching him care for his brother and sister, I start falling hard for Alexander Decker.

CHAPTER
THIRTY

ALEXANDER

———

I said goodbye to Emma and Chance. I tried to send Julian home, but he said he's staying a few more days, so I kicked him, Ashleigh, and Trevor out of my house for the day. No one is allowed back in until the sun goes down.

Just thinking about my sunshine going down gives me a semi. Fuck, this woman is killing me. Whenever I think I'll have a minute alone, something or someone happens. And the unfortunate part? It's my friends and family getting in the way, not her son, who should always get top billing.

"Alone at last," I say, pulling her into my arms.

She wraps her arms around my neck and puts her lips to mine. I like this Dani, taking what she wants from me. It's such a fucking turn-on. I've never been a fan of kissing, it's usually just a precursor to the good stuff. But with this woman? I could die a happy man just kissing her. Her mouth is sensual, turning me on in ways I've never felt before. Each kiss is better than the last, and I can't wait for the next one.

"Still want to go out for breakfast?" I say this as my lips skim down her neck, her head leaning away, giving me more access.

"No," she says, breathless. "I want to see your bed."

"Tired? Want to take a nap?" I tease as I nibble on her earlobe.

"Not exactly," she says, her hands roaming, finding the hem of my shirt and pulling it up, her hands exploring my chest and abs.

"Well, in that case, let me show you the way." I scoop her up, my hand going behind her knees, sweeping her off her feet and into my arms. I carry her down the hall to my bedroom, kicking the door closed on my way to the king-sized bed.

I lay her down gently on the bed. I kiss her again, our tongues doing a passionate dance, exploring, tasting. My hands caress her face, my thumb rubbing against her soft cheek. Her face warms, her body heating with excitement. I let my hands move her curls from her face, my eyes searching hers for a sign. Is she feeling what I'm feeling?

"Tell me what you want."

"You," she says, breathless.

"You've got me." I chuckle. "Need you to be more specific, sunshine." I know what I want to do to her. Hell, I have a list, a very long list. But I won't push her or do anything she doesn't want. She's been through enough. I won't be that asshole who makes her feel uncomfortable. But I will be glad to volunteer to make her feel lots of other things.

"I want all of you, Xander. Use me," she whispers.

I can't stop my smile. I was hoping she'd say that. But hearing her pant that she wants me makes my cock so hard I may come in my pants if I don't slow down. That's what this woman does to me. And I want to take my time with her. I want to take all the time she can give me.

"How much time do we have?"

"What?" She seems taken aback by my question.

"What time do you need to get Tyler?"

At the mention of Tyler, she returns to her senses for a minute. "I need to get him around two."

"That works," I say as I take her mouth to mine, reaching down to lift her shirt over her body, leaving her in a red, lacy bra.

"Oh, these are perfect," I say as I take her tits in my hand, marveling at how they fill my palm. My thumb rubs over her nipple, and her peaks harden under my touch. Her body responds and her sounds encourage me to explore and learn all her sensitive spots. I want to know what makes her moan, what makes her breathing stutter, and what makes her scream my name. I have to know everything about her body and make it my personal challenge to make her come over and over again.

My mouth trails down her jaw and neck, licking and sucking at her collarbone, savoring the taste of her skin. Goosebumps cover her arms as I gently kiss behind her ear. Ah, that's a spot she likes.

I unhook her bra, slide it off her shoulders, exposing her perfectly rose-colored nipple, and my tongue worships at her breast. I can appreciate the wrapping, but I'll always enjoy the gift more.

My fingertips gently caress her body, hips, and stomach until my fingers tease at the waistband of her jeans. I make eye contact with her to make sure we're still on the same page. She's been touched at least once without consent, and I'll be damned if she has that experience with me. Her hands move away from my body to hers, unbuttoning her pants for me. Okay then. She's still giving me the green light.

"Good girl," I growl, giving her a wicked smile. My mouth waters with the anticipation of tasting her pussy with my tongue. I'm ready to unwrap her and gobble her up. I slide her jeans down, and she lifts her ass to help me out. Yes, she's still good. I'm spurred on by the fact that she wants this as much as I do.

I'm rewarded with matching red lace panties with a fucking

bow right above her entrance. It reminds me of that damn yellow ribbon and how horrified she was when I cut it, her chastising me for not taking time to untie the bow. I'm debating about which way to go with this gift. My first inclination is to rip these panties off her body with my teeth. But there's something fun about playing and teasing, too. Decisions, decisions.

"Something wrong?" she asks shyly.

"Just the opposite," I say. "Do I go slow and savor you like the goddess you are, or do I ravage you like the savage I am?"

She looks at me, her eyes growing wide with excitement. "Wow, I, um, don't know." She bites her bottom lip. "Your choice." She gasps as I slide her panties to the side to feel her wetness. She's fucking soaked. I slide my finger along her slit and bring my fingers to my mouth for a taste.

"Just like I thought, pure sunshine and happiness," I say as I lick my fingers clean. Decision made, I slide her panties down and feast on her, my tongue playing with her clit, giving her an orgasm that comes on fast.

"Oh. My. God," she pants. "Xander, your mouth is magical." That praise makes me want to hear more from her. I want to make her come on my face, on my hand, on my cock. I want to squeeze so much pleasure out of her body that she'll feel me on her for days. I can't get enough of her. I'm insatiable where Dani is concerned.

I finger her slit, sliding one, then two fingers in, finding that spot that will send her over the edge again. I pepper her with kisses, exploring, still discovering her sensitive spots. Her pussy clenches around my hand as she comes again. Her sounds are music to my ears. When she comes, her angelic face is the most beautiful sight I've ever seen, and I crave to see it again and again.

I stroke her until the last of her orgasm leaves her sated, and she sinks into the pillow with her eyes closed. I'll let her have her moment while I work my mouth back up her body, worshiping her tits, each getting special attention. My tongue roves up her neck until my mouth finds hers. She takes the lead with our kiss, and it's slow and tender. It's full of feeling and emotion and something I haven't experienced before.

She reaches for my cock through my pants and finds it hard as steel. "My turn," she says with a dirty grin. "But you have way too many clothes on." She pushes my pants down, and I help her along. My pants hit the floor and with a quick tug, my shirt is on the floor too. My cock peeks out from my boxer briefs, wanting some attention. Her hands reach behind me and grab my ass.

"God, you have a great ass," she says as she sinks her nails under my briefs and into my flesh. She finishes undressing me and strokes my stiff cock with her soft hand. I'm filled with satisfaction that my body turns her on because Dani's body is a fucking work of art. She's got curves, hips to hold on to, and even faint stretch marks that I appreciated with kisses and words like "incredible" and "so hot." Her body created a human, and it's the sexiest thing I've ever seen.

I reach into my nightstand and find a condom, sheath myself, and kiss her like my life depends on it. My tip seeks her entrance, and she raises her hips, her hands guiding me in. So that's the way it's going to be, huh? I fucking love it.

It's like we're made for each other, two halves of a whole. She takes all of me, inch by inch, and when I'm buried to the hilt, she makes a sound that practically makes me come on the spot. I want to hold on to this memory forever.

"You feel so good, sunshine." I barely touch her clit again, and she falls over the edge, her thighs holding me tight, while her walls pulse around my cock. "Good girl," I growl.

I pump harder, faster, getting lost in this woman. I'm almost there when she nips at my shoulder and my balls tighten. Dani's pure ecstasy, and she's mine. I brush her curls back from her face, loving how they're spread across my pillow. I force my brain to memorize everything about this moment. Her expression, her scent, her touch. This needs to be a forever memory.

Her eyes lock on mine, and she's more beautiful than ever. This woman is amazing, and I need more of this, us, in my future.

I tilt her hips to go deeper and come so hard I see stars. Fucking stars. Her back arches, and she wraps her legs around me, ankles locked together, holding me close as another orgasm pulses through her. I roll over so she's on top of me, keeping our connection. My arms wrap around her, holding her close. I've never been a smash and dash kind of guy, but I'm not a cuddler either. Until now.

CHAPTER
THIRTY-ONE

DANI

———

Oh, wow. I know it's been a long time, but even in my best fantasy, sex isn't that amazing. Xander has ruined me for other men, not that I want to think about other men at this minute. This man is consuming my every thought, breath, cell. He's ingrained himself into my molecular make up with those orgasms.

And now he's lying under me, still hard inside me, or hard again, I'm not sure, just looking at me like I'm, well, something. His hand caresses my face as he twirls a curl around his finger.

"What's that look for?" I ask.

"It's a look of absolute adoration," he says, not an ounce of hesitancy in his voice. He must still be coming down from orgasm heaven, like me.

"Hmmmm."

"What? You don't believe me?" He almost looks hurt.

"It's not that," I hesitate.

"Then what?" He sounds genuinely curious.

I shake my head, sit up, and pull away. This isn't a conversation I can have in post-orgasmic bliss while he's still physically connected to me. He reaches for me, but I stop him, and true to his word, he doesn't push.

I gather my clothes, go into his bathroom, and close the door. I need a minute or ten. What am I doing? Was that the best sex I've ever had in my life? Absolutely. Do I like Xander? Again, absolutely. But it's complicated. So complicated. I'm a school teacher, barely making ends meet, a single mother, and I'm in a bathroom bigger than my bedroom. He's used to glamorous, classy, and expensive. I'm none of those things.

I freshen up and get myself together. When I open the door, Xander's dressed, sitting on the side of the bed, his head in his hands. His serene smile long gone. A shot of guilt hits me. I did that to him. I took that rare, easy smile away, and he's reverted to stoic and worried in a blink of an eye. The pang of guilt sits heavy in my stomach that I did this to him.

"Hey," he says, looking at me, concern filling his eyes.

I need to fix this. At least fix it the best way I can.

I make my way to him and sit beside him on the bed. I lean into his side, and he relaxes. Well, barely. I reach out and take his hand, weaving our fingers together. They were just like that when he had my hands pinned above my head, and the memory makes me think we should get undressed and go again.

"You okay?" I ask.

"I feel like I should be asking you that. I crossed a line, and I'm sorry." He's looking at our hands but not making eye contact with me.

"An apology, Alexander. Really?" His withdrawing and punishing himself makes me feel like the worst person on the planet. "Which line did you cross exactly?" I'm a little irritated with him, and he knows it.

He looks at me, pain and regret filling his face.

"Did you cross a line when we had very consensual sex, giving me the best orgasms, and yes, multiple orgasms of my life? I don't think so, mister." The corners of his mouth turn up a little. "So which line, because I'd like to know where the lines are?"

He finally looks at me and sees that I'm not freaking out. His shoulders relax, and he leans in to kiss me. I meet him halfway, and it's a sweet kiss. It has more feeling, less passion, and scares me more than anything we've done. It feels different.

"I'm new at this," he says.

"Wow. For a newbie, you've got moves. I wonder how you'll improve with practice." I boop his nose with my finger. My teasing must push a button because the next thing I know, he pulls me into him, straddling his lap, our hands never letting go.

I press my forehead against his and breathe him in. This man is complex, which may be my favorite thing about him. He has so many facets, and he's multidimensional.

I'm complicated. I haven't dated much in the past few years because of Tyler. I don't want to be two different people: a mom and a girlfriend. I don't want to divide my time and focus. Life is already overwhelming as it is. Besides, I need to protect Tyler from the loss of broken relationships. That's my job. But what if this relationship doesn't break?

Unfortunately, complex and complicated can be a recipe for disaster.

But this feeling right now? It's exciting and a little bit scary. Something I'm willing to explore. But I'm afraid the more I explore, the more addicted I'll get. It's confusing, so I need to sort it all out in my head and heart.

"Still hungry?" For him or food? The answer is both.

"Yep. You promised me breakfast." I glance at his phone lying on the bedside table. He has multiple missed calls and texts, validating he's a busy and popular man. But another significant observation is that he hasn't looked at his phone once. He's solely focused on me and not preoccupied with anything else. Just that thought makes my heart flutter all over again. "Although I think we've crossed into brunch at this point."

"We have." He gives a rare laugh, and I'll cherish it forever. "Tell me the parameters of time and food cravings, and I'll make it the best brunch you've ever had." He lifts our joined hands and boops my nose with his finger, mimicking me, but still not letting me go.

"Wow. That's quite a claim, Mr. Decker." I give him a quick kiss and stand up, going to find my purse and phone. He's trailing behind me. Good news. No missed calls or texts.

I spin around and find him so close we bump chests and I giggle. "We have an hour and a half before I need to get Tyler. And I want waffles." I give him a quick peck that seals the deal.

He seems to like my decision, if his grin is any sign. "Great! Give me five minutes to make a quick call, and I'll be ready to go. Make yourself at home for a few minutes." He quickly kisses me, walks back into the bedroom, and shuts the door. I hate it when he walks away, but damn, he's got a great ass. His walking away almost makes up for it.

I look around the massive penthouse and wander over to the glass door that opens to a huge balcony. Like the rest of his place, the furniture looks expensive, but comfortable, like he uses the space to live, not just for show. Like him, his home has layers. But it's neat, orderly. Everything seems to have its place.

I slide the door open and step out to take in the view. The city skyline is spectacular from this vantage point. The stadium below is empty except for a few grounds crew tending to the grass, a stark contrast to the crowds and celebration of last night.

I'm lost in my thoughts when arms wrap around my waist, pulling me away from the rail. "What are you thinking about?" he whispers in my ear, and chills go down my spine.

"Just how different it is from yesterday to today. Quite the contrast." So much has changed since yesterday. Not just at the stadium, but with me. With us. I catch the double meaning in my thoughts and wonder if he's thinking the same thing.

"Yep. They can seem like opposites, but it's more like balance. Both need the other." We stand there for a minute, while

I think about balance. Is he talking about the stadium or us. Before I can ask, he takes my hand and pulls me back inside. "Ready to go?"

"Absolutely. I'm starving."

"Well, Ms. Franklin, get ready to have your world rocked. I'll introduce you to waffles that will ruin you for all other waffles." He kisses me on the cheek and leads me out.

The waffles did not disappoint. I'm not sure there's much Alexander Decker does that is disappointing.

CHAPTER
THIRTY-TWO

ALEXANDER

———

Preparing for and hosting the World Series means travel, long days, and nights in the office for me, which is limited time with Dani. We had a quick rendezvous Tuesday at her house while Tyler was at her parents, and it was hot. And now I have a constant craving for Dani Franklin.

But then I had to miss T-ball practice and dinner on Wednesday with them because of work. She's more under-standing than I am. She grounds me, calms me, and with these extra work activities, I need calm. I need her.

Tonight is our first home game, and we're coming into the series tied one game each from the road trip. Being on a national stage is a lot of added pressure and extra obligations. I've got a championship team in the front office and on the field, and everyone is working extra hard. While I'm accustomed to red carpets and media, they aren't usually at my stadium. Keeping the press wrangled might be the most challenging part of the week, and it's draining. Although, the list of VIPs to manage and pacify is exhausting too. But my team in the World Series? Priceless.

While A-list celebrities are clamoring for the hottest tickets in town, I've made it clear to our Reapers team that we don't forget who we are as an organization. We represent family and community. So tonight, in my suite, I'll host the most important people in the stadium; ten kids and their parents, known as the Southend Sluggers. While the other suites are serving steak and lobster tails, I asked Tyler to help me create the menu for our suite. We'll be having unlimited hot dogs, chicken fingers, mac and cheese bites, quesadillas, and sodas. The bar was converted into an ice cream sundae station with the most decadent toppings and milkshakes in town, prepared by Brady. Tonight, we're going alcohol-free, and I'm not even phased by it. Dani insisted we have some healthy items thrown in for good measure and limit the sugar and caffeine, but when Tyler and I explained this could be a once in a lifetime event, she gave in and let us have our way. Sure, I'll have a veggie tray and adult food in the corner, but tonight, it's about the kids.

Since I've been with Dani, she's chastised me about my language, especially around the kids. Dani made a swear jar, and it travels with me. Every violation by anyone is one hundred dollars. The first day or so, it filled up fast, but I've been getting better. The first day or two, I filled it up and wondered if we needed a bigger jar. But her laughter and encouragement are all I need to work on my lifestyle change. The swearing penalty fees will go to a charity of her choice. If changing my language makes her happy, then I'll do everything I can to make it happen. She's worth it.

This might be the most fun I've ever had watching a game. The kid's excitement feeds my soul more than attendance numbers and the score at the end of the game. They are eating their weight in hot dogs, playing with Scoville, and dancing between innings. I think they're even giving Trevor ideas for his antics-filled baseball games. He's enjoying the night as much as the kids.

The worst part? Keeping my hands off Dani. My appetite for her is insatiable, but she asked for us to keep it quiet, and I've agreed. For now. Hell, I mean, heck, I'll agree to anything she wants as long as she's giving me the time of day. It's the bottom of the fourth inning, and I've reached my breaking point. We've only been passing glances for the past hour.

"Hey T, mind being in charge for a bit?"

"That's a big ask." He looks around at the chaos of the Sluggers.

"They've gotta crash eventually, right?" Admittedly, I don't know much about kids, but I'm learning.

Emma doubles over in a full-on belly laugh. "Y'all are so clueless. It's cute."

"What?" we both ask at once.

"Where are you going?" Trevor asks.

"Um, I need to show Dani something in my office," I say. I track her movement as she flits around the suite, taking care of the kids, wiping faces, and constantly laughing. I haven't been able to keep my eyes off her.

"Is that what we're calling it these days?" Emma asks, elbowing me in the ribs.

"Don't push me, Em," I say gruffly. Her response? She hugs me around the waist and kisses me on the cheek. Dynasty, one of my Slugger girls, sees her and lets out a loud, "ohhhhh." This encourages Emma to be even more playful. Dani looks our way, and her face goes through multiple expressions in less than two seconds. Confusion. Jealousy, or at least I hope that's what it is. And then happiness, my favorite. I'm figuring out how to read her, and I'll have to ask if I'm right.

I make my way over to Dani and put my chin on her shoulder, whispering in her ear. "Hey sunshine, how you doing?"

Her eyes light up even more, if that's possible. "Good. You?"

"I'm okay. But I have a problem that I need your help with."

"Oh, what's that?" Her question is full of concern. She's always ready to jump in for the rescue. She'll help anyone, even if they don't know they need it.

"Think we can go to my office to discuss it?"

She looks around the room. She's conflicted. "Trevor and Emma will watch him. He's in good hands." I've learned when she's hesitant, it's usually because of Tyler, and I find it endearing. Her devotion to her son is very attractive.

"Okay." She looks at me with apprehension until I give her a quiet "good girl." Now her wicked smile appears, and that's my favorite expression.

She tells Tyler she'll be back and heads to the door at the rear of the suite. I'm two steps behind her when Jules gives a slow clap. "Subtle."

"Fuck off," I mumble.

"At-ah," he says and wags his finger at me. He points to the swear jar on the counter. I reach in my wallet and begrudgingly add a bill, and Trevor laughs from across the room.

"I don't have time for this." Dani's already out of the suite.

I meet her in the hall and we quietly walk to the elevators, the sexual tension between us thick. I'm a little surprised actual electric sparks aren't bouncing off of us. We get to the elevator, and Kylie is inside, making sure people get where they should be. On game day, and especially during this series, we have too many people who wander where they shouldn't, so we have actual elevator operators. Right now, I'm hating it.

"Mr. Decker," she says in greeting. "Where to?"

"My office, please." I swipe my badge to override the system since we locked down access to that area for tonight. It should be empty. Perfect for when Dani screams my name.

We stand at the back of the elevator, looking ahead, acting like total strangers, when the back of her hand brushes against mine. I link our pinkies, just that small connection giving me a taste of what I'm craving. I'm getting hard just thinking about her.

"Thank you, Kylie," I say as we exit the elevator. Her smile lets me know she's on to us, but honestly, I don't care.

We walk off the elevator, my hand at the small of Dani's back, guiding her. Without saying a word to each other, we walk past empty cubicles and offices. Why is my office so far away from the elevator? I'm wound tighter than a spring about to explode. We get inside, and the automatic lights come on. Fuck. I fumble to turn them off. The lights from the game give me enough light to see her silhouette, and it's driving me insane. The reflection film on the windows should keep us private, as long as we don't have the backlighting of the overhead lights.

Dani giggles as I hit several switches, trying to turn them off. Once I have the privacy situation taken care of, I stalk toward her, a lion eyeing his prey. Her giggle stops, and she bites her bottom lip. I can't take it anymore, and I kiss her roughly, my tongue demanding entrance. I need to relieve this tension between us before I spontaneously combust. My fingers are into her curls, and they serve as my personal stress ball. Having her in my arms relaxes me, while also winding me up. It's a paradox. I can't get enough of this woman. She's burrowed under my skin and become part of me.

As I kiss down her jaw to her neck, I'm encouraged by her moan. "Sunshine, I've dreamt of the day I could bend you over my desk and sink into your luscious pussy. Is tonight when my dreams come true?"

"We won't be seen?" That's not the yes I was hoping for.

"Not with the lights off." My hands caress her curves as they explore her body. She's wearing a denim skirt, making my objective easy access. Her lips give a wicked smile. She knows exactly what she's doing to me. I slide her skirt up around her hips and palm her center.

"Always so wet for me." My nose skims her neck, taking in her scent of sunshine and something tropical. All my blood flow is south of the beltline, so not much going to my thinking head. Words elude me.

Her giggle sends me to the edge. If I don't bury myself in her soon, I'll come in my pants like a teenaged boy. "Sunshine, I'm waiting for you to tell me the rules here so we can play." I always want her to have control. My greatest fear is she has regrets about me or anything we do. Whether or not she knows it, this woman owns me.

She turns around and bends over my desk, her ass in the air. Well, I guess I have my answer. I slide her panties down and unzip my pants. My dick strains at the zipper. Reaching into my pocket, I pull out a condom. Now that I'm around Dani, I don't leave home without one. When did I become such a horn dog that I keep a condom on me at all times? Oh, that's right. When my dick met her pussy for the first time. And now it's waiting to be reunited with his best friend.

"I'm not sure I can be gentle," I warn as I slide into her slowly, savoring the feeling of her tightness.

"I'd certainly hope not," she says, turning her head over her shoulder to give me a wicked smile. Holy hell, what she does to me.

I pound into her, balls deep, one hand on her hip, the other massaging her clit. Her seductive smile is gone, her reflection in my computer monitor telling me she's close. "Come for me, sunshine. That's my good girl." A few more strokes and she clenches around me, and I come with her. It was quick and dirty, but oh so satisfying. "Incredible," I whisper. I pull her up and turn her head to mine for a kiss. I'm still inside her and am already dreading our separation.

The crowd goes wild. My sentiments exactly. I forgot there were forty-thousand people watching a baseball game because at this moment, it's just me and her. When I'm with her, it's more than the physical ecstasy, it's just, I don't know, something special. I think about telling her those three words I've never said to a woman, but don't want it to be in the afterglow of sex. I want her to know I mean it. I love her, not for the off-the-charts orgasms, but because of her heart, her kindness, her patience, her sunshine.

"I think they just scored," she says.

"Or they're cheering for us scoring," I chuckle. "Because baby, that was the most magnificent grand slam I've ever seen." I pull away and step into my bathroom to clean up. When I come back to my office, she's sitting on the desk, watching the game.

"It's incredible, isn't it?"

I'm next to her, my arm around her shoulders. "You're incredible," I say as I nibble at her ear.

She swats at my chest, playfully pushing me away.

"Everyone's so happy," she says sweetly. "The team, the fans, me. There's so much positive energy here, can't you feel it?"

All I can feel is her, and that's more than enough for me.

"I can. And you magnify it all." We take it all in and bask in the happiness. I feel a piece of my heart shift and come to life. She's done it. She's changed me. As we leave my office, I'll never look at it the same way again. Not because of what we did in here tonight, which was phenomenal, but because this is no longer the center of my universe. No, my universe now revolves around Dani, my personal sunshine.

CHAPTER
THIRTY-THREE

DANI

———

It's Friday afternoon and Xander said to call him as soon as I get home and am out of Tyler's super powerful hearing range. He got home two days ago after the Reapers lost the World Series. I'm sure he's upset, probably figuring out all the things he could have done better to come to a different outcome. That's what he does. He plans for every scenario, analyzes the details, looks for changes or improvements. It's such a contrast to my enjoy the moment outlook. Somehow, I think we're good for one another in an opposites attract kind of way. But I try not to get carried away. We're still complicated and complex.

Tyler is playing video games, so I sneak into my bedroom to call Xander.

"Hey, sunshine. How was your day?" I'm still amazed he cares about my mundane world.

"Good. It was a small class because a couple of kids were out sick with a stomach bug. The rest of the kids were wired because it's Friday, but, you know, a typical Friday. They were still buzzing about you and Tripp coming to class yesterday and sharing the division trophy. They were all decked out in the Reapers gear you guys gave them yesterday. You're spoiling them."

"I'm glad they had fun. Just trying to match their teacher's brightness." I roll my eyes at his ridiculousness. Even over the phone, he makes me blush. I'm not nearly as saintly as he treats me, and once he realizes that, I'm afraid this entire fantasy will crash down around us.

"How are you doing? How was the team dinner last night? Everyone bummed?"

"Yeah, a little, but we had a good time. They played with heart. That's all I can ask for. Just wasn't our year." He doesn't sound as sad as I would have thought. As a matter of fact, he's pretty upbeat, and I'm pleasantly surprised by his response. He doesn't seem as intense and focused as he's been these last few weeks. He sounds relaxed, which is a word I'd never use to describe Alexander.

"Listen, I've made plans for tonight with multiple options. You pick. It's like a choose your own adventure."

"Oh, like a why choose romance?" I love teasing him. He's picked up a few of my romance novels to see what all the fuss is about. When he started a why choose book, we had a long discussion about why I would like something like that and his expectation of faithfulness when in a committed relationship. One thing I'll say about Alexander, he's loyal. When I googled him, a few women appeared in multiple pictures, and while he looked incredibly hot in those shots, his expressions were hard, not the grinning man I know. No rumors of cheating appeared tied to him at all. He's a one-woman man, or at least one at a time.

"Absolutely NOT like a why choose romance. The only guy I'm willing to share you with is Tyler, and not in that way. Fuck, sunshine, why do you do that to me?"

I laugh out loud. "That's one hundred for the swear jar, Mr. Decker."

"Nope, that's only around little ears, and if Tyler heard me, that's on you." He's trying to watch his swearing around Tyler, and it's adorable. I've never heard more variations of fudge, funk, frick, fug, and shitake mushrooms in my life. Lucky for me, I gave up the F word six years ago, so I'm not contributing to the jar, especially since he declared it's one hundred dollars an infraction.

"That's fair. So what do I get to pick?"

"I'd like to spend the next twenty-four hours with you, if you want, of course."

Of course I want to, but I don't want Tyler to be exposed to a man in my bed. Call me old-fashioned that way, but it's just not something I'm comfortable with. And calling my parents to keep him last minute will raise questions I'm not prepared to answer. My father makes too many comments under his breath and I don't need Tyler repeating any more conversations.

"Of course I'd love to Xander, but…"

"Tyler. Yep. Here's where the choices come in." He sounds almost giddy. Well for Xander, giddy. There's an actual lilt to his voice, an excitement I've never heard before.

"Option one: we go to dinner with Joey, Casey, and Archie. Then Tyler spends the night at their house after dinner. I've fully vetted them. Archie is seven and has no emergency room visits, so that's something. Hell, I had stitches twice by the time I was his age." There's a brief pause to let that soak in. He continues without allowing me to respond or ask why he got stitches as a kid.

"Option two: we have dinner at my place. Tyler and Trevor go downstairs to Matt and Darcy's for game night afterward, and they both spend the night there. This option means Tyler is technically under the same roof since he'd be in the same building. While none of them are parents, Matt is CPR certified, and Darcy is very mature for her age. I wish I could say the same about Trevor, but it is what it is. Tyler hero worships Matt, and the likelihood of him missing you will probably be zero."

"That hurts a little."

"Didn't mean to hurt, just stating the facts, sunshine. Option three: the three of us have dinner, do our own game night, and we all go our separate ways at an appropriate time. And option four is you don't want to see me tonight, and Trevor gets absolutely hammered because he has to listen to me cry into my bourbon. But just know that Trevor's liver is still sensitive, so it could be harmful to his health. So which option is it, sunshine?" He whispers, "Please don't say four."

He's gone to a lot of trouble to arrange this evening. And every single option includes Tyler. He focused all the scenarios on Tyler having fun, not just getting rid of him. My heart flutters thinking about this guy calling in favors to ensure Tyler is taken care of.

"They all sound great," I start.

"Even option four?" He says it with a pout, and I can practically see his lip poked out.

"No, that's not even an option. But are you sure? The guys just came off a devastating loss, and I'm sure the last thing they want is…"

Alexander interrupts. "Is to get rooted back into normal life. I've talked to them all. They really don't mind. But your choice. Or Tyler's. That's your choice too. I need you to both be okay with any situation. Always. I'll never make you do something where you don't feel comfortable, Dani. Never. You're always in charge." He's said this before, and I know he means it. He says it with conviction. It's fact. An oath. He doesn't know what his consideration of Tyler means to me. His inclusion is everything.

"Let me see which Tyler wants to do, and I'll get back to you in a few minutes. Is that okay?"

"Absolutely, sunshine. As long as it's not option four."

"Nope. He only gets two choices." I can't wait to spend an entire night with Xander. Granted, we spent the night together once before, but that involved a lot of sleeping and not even in a bed. I'm hoping tonight will be different. I'd better up my lingerie game.

———

Well, tonight is different. We had dinner with Matt, Darcy, and Trevor before they took Tyler for a sleepover. I'm not sure who was more excited. They were delighted to hang out with my kid tonight. They prepared a lineup of games, a Mario Cart challenge bracket, and a ton of junk food. Xander was right. Tyler won't miss me one bit. It may be hard to get him back to our reality after this weekend.

I started feeling queasy during dinner. Xander tucked me in on the couch and called a doctor friend of his, which was totally unnecessary. I'm afraid I may be the latest victim of the stomach bug.

"Xander, I don't want to get you sick. I'll just go home and see you in twenty-four hours once it passes." I try to throw the blanket off, but he isn't having it.

The look he gives me is the opposite of caring and compassionate. It's fierce, determined and absolutely terrifying. If I didn't know him, I'd be cowering in a corner. "Fuck no. You'll stay here, and I'll take care of you. I know I told you that you'd always have a choice, but I'm changing the rules to say as long as you're healthy. When you're sick, I make the decisions."

I can't keep the little smile away. I bet he caused absolute havoc at the hospital when Trevor was hurt. "Yes, sir."

He gives me his sexy smirk. "I like it when you say that, sunshine." He kneels next to the couch and gently brushes the hair away from my face. His touch is tender, comforting. "You feel a little warm. Let me get you some Tylenol, and I'm going to run downstairs to talk to Matt, so they keep an eye on Tyler in case he gets sick. They can send him back up here if he does."

"You don't," I say. And then I quickly and forcibly push him out of the way, run to the bathroom, and throw up my dinner. I didn't bother to close the door, and Xander's beside me, holding my hair and rubbing my back. So much for sexy time. I can think of nothing, and I mean nothing, less sexy than putting your head in a toilet and throwing up the contents of your stomach.

"It's okay, baby, I've got you. I've got you." He's rubbing circles on my back, just like I do for Tyler. Tears threaten to fall as it hits me. I love this man.

CHAPTER
THIRTY-FOUR

ALEXANDER

———

She was sick for two days, and I never left her side. I Door Dashed half a pharmacy the first night, so she had everything she needed to get better while the rest of my team rallied to help. Trevor, Matt, and Darcy kept Tyler and watched for signs of illness. Dani Face Timed him between naps, and Darcy sent periodic pictures of him having fun. Kate made Dani soup and bland foods her stomach could tolerate. I count my blessing that I have such a strong support system.

When she was awake and had the strength, she introduced me to her favorite television show and teased me about wearing a kilt. She underestimates my level of commitment. If it would make her happy, I'll have one flown in from Scotland. Hell, I considered reaching out and having Jamie Fraser himself show up. Her historical romances aren't really my thing, but with her tucked into my side, it's something I'll watch for hours.

She got sick several times over the next forty-eight hours, and I never flinched. When her clothes were in the laundry, she borrowed some of mine. It was hotter than the sexy lingerie she had on. She's so fucking sexy, no matter what she wears, but I gave her accolades for the effort.

Once her fever broke, she finally let me snuggle with her. Waking up with her in my arms was the most content I've ever been. She makes me feel whole. Settled. And it's obviously not just about sex. I mean, hell, that's amazing, but even this weekend where we barely kissed was great. It was real. Is this what it means in sickness and in health?

Thankfully, Tyler didn't get sick. She convinced me to let her go home Sunday evening so they could be ready for school Monday morning. It damn near killed me, but I can't keep her prisoner forever. Although I'd like to.

While the weekend didn't go as planned, I wasn't disappointed. Tyler had fun. I think Trevor, Matt, and Darcy did too. They took him to the park, worked with him on baseball skills, and Trevor let him design a jersey for the Pajamas next summer. The kid had the time of his life.

I won't deny I was a little worried and hated seeing her sick and weak. It triggered a few flashbacks of my mom, but a stomach bug is different than cancer. My mother died ten years ago, and there were moments this weekend that had me thinking about those days. There wasn't anything I could do but be by her side and watch her sleep. Make sure she was breathing. I spent some time reminiscing about my mom, and I'm convinced she'd chastise me for not settling down with a family by now. I also think she'd like Dani. Mom was a half-full perspective person, too. Like my Dani. I hated seeing Dani sick, but my sunshine was just knocked down for a few days. She's strong. She'll be fine.

This week she's busy with school and Tyler, but we make time to text and talk in the evenings. Now that the season's ended, I have more time to devote to her and Tyler, and they are my priority.

It's Wednesday, so it's practice for the Sluggers. I can't wait to surprise the kids with a few special guests. Most players go home for the off-season, but a few haven't left yet or make Charlotte home. Matt, Tripp, and Luis are meeting me at the field this afternoon. When I pull up, I smile at the sight of the new bleachers that were installed this week. At least those wooden deathtrap things are gone.

"Hiya, coach." I see Tyler walking to my car with a beaming Dani behind him. She's wearing an oversized Reapers sweatshirt she must have "borrowed" from my closet when she was over yesterday for our afternoon delight. It was the highlight of my day.

I crouch down to meet him at eye level. "Hey, Tyler. How was school today?" He shrugs. "Nope. I need words. Didn't you work on sight words today?"

"Y.E.S." I suppress my laugh at his smart-ass response. This kid is funny.

I arch my eyebrow at him. Why is he in a mood? Or is this just typical six-year-old behavior? I'm learning a lot about kids here, and surprisingly, I'm enjoying it. "And how did you do?"

"Fine. I got them all right." He looks in my car and sees the bucket with balls and a bag with other supplies. "Want help with the balls?"

"Sure." I reach in, get a small bucket, and set it between us. He puts his glove on top, carries it toward the field, and joins a few of the other kids that beat us here.

I give Dani an appraising look up and down. "Nice shirt."

"This old thing? It was just lying around, nothing special." Her smile lets me know she's not ashamed to be a clothes thief. My return grin lets her know I'm not mad about it either. It's a total turn-on to see her in my clothes.

We're still keeping our relationship on the down-low for now, especially from Tyler, so PDA is out. I respect that boundary, even though I want to stand at the top of those new bleachers and claim this woman as mine. She's calling the shots here.

"Hey, boss," Tripp says as he walks up to me and Dani. Luis

and Matt are with him. "Glad you're feeling better," he says to Dani.

"Much."

"*Chica*," Luis says as he goes in for a hug with Dani. I clench my fists as he kisses her on the cheek.

"Down, boy," Tripp says under his breath.

"I didn't know you guys were coming," Dani says, her smile lighting up the parking lot. "Tyler's going to be ecstatic!"

"Y'all mind getting the equipment out of my car? Coach Mayhew isn't here tonight, so start with playing catch with the kids, will you? I need to talk to Dani for a minute."

"Sure, no problem, boss," Matt snickers.

I reach for her and pull her behind my car, out of view of the field. My mouth descends on hers, and I do my best to keep our kiss PG. Well, maybe PG-13. "Do you know how fucking sexy you are?" I say against her lips.

"Hi to you too." She touches my cheek, grounding me and reminding me where I am.

"Can I take you and Tyler to dinner tonight?" I've been good about meeting her where she is, not pushing, but now that I have a little more downtime, I can only think about how I want to be with her. Them. All the time.

"Sure, but nothing too late. It's a school night, you know." She gives me a little wink. She reminds me about her early bedtime on school nights because she's not a morning person, and school starts way too early for her liking.

"How about I bring takeout to your place? I'll cut practice a little short. I brought reinforcements to help."

"I see that. Where's Trevor?"

"Therapy kicked his butt. I think he's home crying in his beer." Trevor is doing great and got a walking cast last week. I expect him to go home soon now that he's more mobile. A few months ago, I was a content bachelor, happy to live alone and according to my schedule. Between having Trevor as a roommate and Dani and Tyler in my life, the thought of living alone isn't as appealing as it used to be. Another thought I've been pondering more often than not these days.

"Oh, his poor liver," she teases. She boops me on the nose. "You better go, Coach. Those guys need help."

"Hey, I've seen some improvements." They're doing better. In our last game, almost all the balls thrown were in the right vicinity.

"I meant the Reapers, not the Sluggers." Her laugh fills my heart, and I give her one of my smiles that is only for her. She stands on her tip-toes and gives me a chaste kiss, and as she walks away, I swat at her ass. It's such a nice ass.

As predicted, the kids hang on every word the guys share. They listen and work hard to do what they say. Tyler's enamored with Matt and couldn't pick a better baseball role model. Matt's a stand-up guy, a hard worker, and keeps his life clean. He's in love with a sweet girl, and I can see that relationship staying solid. Pro athletes have a lot to juggle, and given Matt's age and how he was thrust into the national spotlight so quickly, I would typically worry about him, but he's handling it like a champ. Jules is stepping up as more than an agent for him, guiding him with finances, his work-life balance, and even his relationship. He'll be a hell of a franchise player for us for years to come. His future is bright, and with that realization, I'm wondering if Dani has changed me into a half-full kind of guy.

"All right, let's huddle up," I yell. The kids come running. Some are out of balance from the oversized gloves and practically fall, and I flinch and chuckle at the same time. "Take a knee." I smile as even my Reapers do it. "Good practice. I'm seeing lots of improvement." I'm greeted with smiles, a few missing teeth here or there, and they almost look like hockey players. "Now, who had fun?" Hands shoot up quickly, especially my Reapers. Luis puts his hand on Cruz's head, and he turns and looks up at him in awe. Luis turns the kid's head back to me. "Good job. Everyone pick up all the balls and put them back in the buckets. Snacks in the dugout. I'll see you all on

Saturday, okay? It's our last game. Let's end this season strong." Heads nod, and Dynasty's hand goes up.

"Yes, Dynasty?"

"Will Mr. Tripp be back Saturday?" She looks at him like he hung the moon. I think Tripp has an admirer.

Tripp chuckles. "I'll see what I can do." I think he's blushing from the attention of a seven-year-old girl. It's adorable. I thought he was headed to Cancun, but maybe he'll wait a few days. Our annual guy's trip was pushed back because of the World Series, and now, looking at these faces, we can't miss this game. What's another few days before vacation?

It's time to focus on my evening. Tyler is sitting in the dugout, talking Matt's ear off. Matt laughs and seems to enjoy the conversation. I enter the dugout and hear Tyler talking about Joe and Mickey.

"But don't tell Mom, okay? I'm not supposed to let them sleep with me," Tyler says as I walk up.

Matt looks up to me for help in how to respond. I shrug. I'm not sure what the proper protocol is when kids confess something they aren't supposed to do. Do I tell Dani? Is it my place to step in?

I squat down in front of Tyler. "You know, bud, maybe don't do that. What if you roll over on them or they fall off the bed? They could get hurt. You wouldn't want that, would you?"

Tyler looks shocked. The thought of them getting injured never crossed his mind. "No! I don't want them to get hurt. I love them so much."

Matt taps the bill of Tyler's hat. "Yeah, Coach is right. Probably not best for them. Besides, they have their own bed to sleep in. We all need to sleep in our own beds, you know."

I look at Matt and smirk. Look at us figuring out this parenting thing. Of course, I'd give anything to sleep in Dani's bed. Waking up with her would be the best part of my day. But it's not best for her and Tyler, so we haven't managed any more overnights. Yet.

"Hey Tyler, instead of going out, I thought I'd bring dinner to your house. What would you like to eat tonight? You did so great in practice, so you name it." I'm still learning kid cuisine but I've learned chicken fingers are on every menu in town.

He twists his mouth while he thinks. "Mcdonald's cheeseburger?"

"Done." I guess I'll be swinging by two places because I can't remember the last time I ate a fast-food burger, and I'd prefer to keep it that way.

"Oh, that sounds good," Matt says. "This week is a cheat week before I start bulking up for next season." He looks at me, letting me know he's still focused on his career, even in the offseason. "I'm headed out. See ya' around, Tyler."

"Bye, Matt," Tyler says, holding his hand out for a fist bump. Matt obliges. He's Captain America, all-around nice kid.

"Come on, buddy. Let's go find your mom, and I'll be by soon with your dinner." Who knew I'd be a Door Dash driver in the offseason?

CHAPTER
THIRTY-FIVE

DANI

———

"I'll get it," Tyler yells as he runs to the door.

"What have I told you about answering the door?" I call out, but it's too late. Tyler swings the door open to find Alexander on the porch with bags of food. I'm not sure who he's planning on feeding, but he's loaded down.

"Here, let me help." I take the Mcdonald's bag and drink carrier holding a shake and Sprite. He remembered Tyler isn't allowed to have caffeine after school, or he'll never sleep. His thoughtfulness touches me. It also looks like he and I won't be eating McDonalds.

"Come on in." I close the door and take a moment to appreciate his ass as he walks past, making his way to the kitchen. I love that he's comfortable in my house, even though it's not as fancy as his penthouse. He spent a few hours here once when Tyler was at my parents, but he didn't see much of the house outside my bedroom. I blush, thinking about how he took me against the wall and again in my bed. Our sexcapades are things of fantasy novels or porno movies. I think there's a fine line between the two, and we're walking it. I went from born-again virgin to sex addict quickly, thanks to Alexander, and I'm not mad about it one bit.

"I got us Thai. I wasn't sure what you'd like, so I got several options." He unpacks the bag.

"Smells delicious, but it's just us. There's enough food here to feed an army." I get Tyler settled at the table and tell him to eat. He devours his fries, and I steal one to his protest.

"Figured you could take some for lunch tomorrow if you want," Xander continues from the kitchen.

He's considerate and does things like this to care for me. It's sweet. That's not what I expected from the grumpy, brooding guy I met a few months ago. One of his most admirable qualities is his thoughtfulness to the details in our lives. I appreciate his attempts to keep money from affecting our relationship because I'm more than aware for both of us.

We fill our plates with pad Thai and curry chicken and settle at the table next to Tyler. We chat about school and baseball. Tyler challenges Alexander to a round of Mario Cart after dinner. To my surprise, he accepts the challenge and even talks smack about his skills.

"Trevor thinks he's the video game champion, but don't underestimate me on Mario Cart. I've got a decent score on Rainbow Road." This is another side of Alexander's private persona that's endearing. When coaching the kids, he's focused, letting them have fun while teaching them the skills. He's also always on high alert, watching all the kids to ensure they're safe. He's in protector mode on the field, and I worry he's not having fun. I asked him about it once because he preaches fun to the kids, but I want it to be fun for him too. He assures me it is.

But this Alexander? His shoulders are relaxed, and he's laughing with Tyler, enjoying the smack talk. Here's another layer of this complex man, and I'm enjoying each new glimpse he shares. It's fascinating to see his complexity in action and understand who he truly is. Watching them together makes me rethink my views about complex and complicated.

After dinner, true to his word, he plays Mario Cart with Tyler. For all the smack talk, Tyler beats him. Mr. Tough Guy is a big softie. He asks if he can stay while I put Tyler to bed and I agree, but cryptically let him know there will be no sexy time. Not with Tyler home. First, I don't want to explain it, and I can't save enough money for his future therapy. Second, I can't keep quiet when Xander is inside me. I've never been loud or vocal during sex before, but something about this man and his constant praise makes me lose my mind. Not complaining, but just setting boundaries. Third, I've got to get some sleep because I'm up at six-thirty on school days to get us ready and at school by eight. Who thought kids needed to be at school that early? I'm exhausted most days and feel much older than my thirty-two years.

"Mom, is Xander your boyfriend?" Tyler asks as I tuck him into bed after reading a quick bedtime story.

"What? No, um," I stutter.

"I know you like him. I like him too. But I wish Matt was your boyfriend because he's gonna help me be a ballplayer like him." He gives a little shrug, and I can't help but smile. I love the way this kid thinks.

"Well, first, Matt has a girlfriend. You know he loves Darcy, right? And I'm way too old for him." Matt's a good kid, but he's, what, twenty-three or so? I'm pushing thirty-three. "But Xander isn't my boyfriend." I think about our evening, a smile filling my face. Is it time to tell Tyler the truth? Xander is more than my boyfriend. He's worked his way into my heart. He could be our future if I allow it. It would be nice to have evenings like this be our normal routine. I can almost picture it. Us. A family.

"It's okay if he is, that's all." He rolls over and tucks his stuffed Scoville under his arm. He's been sleeping with the base-ball-playing pepper since his first game a few months ago. Has it already been a few months? It's hard to stop and think about. Time moves so fast these days.

"Sleep tight, tiger. Love you." I kiss him on his head and quietly close his door.

Tyler accepts Xander. I let his acceptance sit with me. I didn't realize how important it was to me. I need to get a few things wrapped up and put behind me so I can look forward.

"Hey, sorry, that took so long." I join Xander in the kitchen. He's cleaned up dinner, put dishes in the dishwasher, leftovers in the fridge. Wow. Who knew he would develop domestic skills too?

I wrap my arms around his waist. That's when I notice his body is rigid and tense, his content demeanor a thing of the past. He's not pulling me in like he always does. Oh no. Did he hear my conversation with Tyler? What would that have sounded like from his perspective?

I pull back and look up to see his brows furrowed. "What's wrong?" I'm on heightened alert.

"Why didn't you tell me?" His tone is flat like he's holding back anger. It's that hardened boardroom Alexander I first met, one of restrained emotion. The one that is sexy as hell but a little frightening and a lot standoffish.

"Tell you what?" Oh no. He heard me.

"About the summons."

My stomach drops to my feet. Shit. I'm immediately angry and embarrassed, and my emotions swirl like a cyclone of disaster. I thought we had moved past the victim thing. I didn't tell him about the summons and deposition because I want to put everything behind me. Become less complicated. But I'll never be less complicated. Not to him.

But wait? How does he know about the deposition?

"Did you go through my things?" I snap.

"No, but you left it out. It caught my eye." There's no apology this time.

"I can't believe you went through my mail." I don't want to

talk about this, so I direct all my anger toward his keen eye of observation. I wasn't even thinking about it being out on the kitchen counter. My house is not the neat and orderly living space he's used to, that's for sure.

I'm overcome with the memory of the brutal interview last week. An attorney accused the Deckers of using me to lead Pauly Jackson on and set up the incident. He grilled me for two hours, twisting my words, making it sound intentional and sordid. The entire experience was worse than the assault itself. If I wasn't a victim before, I was after that deposition.

Jackson sat there and smirked at me the entire time. I was asked about my involvement with the Deckers, which became uncomfortable when they showed pictures of us on the kiss cam. I tried not to answer their questions, but that made it worse. I didn't lie, but it's none of their business. This was about what Jackson did, not the Deckers.

All I could think of during the barrage of horrible accusations was to protect this family. They're nothing but kind, generous, and loving. They don't deserve to have their reputations slung through the mud.

Maybe I should have told Alexander about it, but what could he do? It's my complication. Besides, he had enough on his plate with the team and others depending on him. I'm used to facing life on my own, and I thought I could handle this. They were just going to ask me about the incident, right? Boy, was I wrong. It ranked up there with Riley's funeral as one of the worst experiences of my life. Or maybe worse, because they were threatening Alexander. It was confusing, humiliating, and terrifying, and I want to put it behind me. Like Riley's family.

Unfortunately, the trial is in a few weeks, and I'll have to go through it all again. This is precisely why I didn't want to press charges. And looking at Xander's reaction now, why I didn't want to tell him about it. I'm filled with anxiety and dread.

"Why didn't you tell me?" His voice is strained.

"Because it's none of your business!" I raise my voice, which is very out of character. My outburst shocks him, and he reaches out, but I pull away. I put my hands to my face to keep him from seeing me broken.

"Dani," he says softly. "I'm sorry, sunshine." His hand touches my arm, and I flinch away. His face goes through multiple reactions in a split second. He settles on hurt, and my heart breaks a little looking at him.

I can't handle the pain I'm inflicting and need to do something, anything, to make it end. "No! Stop. I hate this."

"Hate us?"

"No, this!" I point at him. "How you always see me as a victim. Someone you have to care for. I'm not a victim! I can take care of myself. I don't need you to swoop in and fight my battles. I've done it before you, and I'll do it after. I'm not your charity case!"

The lawyer's questions fed my fears and bore into my insecurities, where they took up residency in my mind. He implied the Deckers were using me. I don't believe it, but suddenly all my fears and frustrations manifest into words, and my filter has left the building. I've always felt it a little, especially at first, but I'd convinced myself he liked me for me and that I might be more than his PR problem. Why did I lash out at him? Say those things? I don't know, but they hang between us, the damage done.

"Wow." He turns around and runs his hands through his hair, pulling at it. When he speaks, it's a quiet shout, keeping his restraint in check. This is the Alexander I don't like. His walls are up, and I built them myself.

He turns back to look at me. "Is that what you think of me? That I'm here because you're a charity case? That I feel sorry for you? Or that I'm using you? That's the kind of man you think I am?" I'm surprised by his words.

"Mom, are you okay?" Tyler stands in the doorway looking at me, then Alexander, concern filling his face. The last thing I want my kid to do is worry about me. I flash back to the assault.

I need to protect him, keep him safe. He's never heard me raise my voice to anyone, so I'm sure my shouting frightened him. I need to fix this for him.

I hold my hand out to Tyler, and he comes and stands beside me, snuggling into my side. I cradle his head into my hip. Yeah, Alexander may be complex, but I'm complicated. This legal stuff is so complicated I hope I can get through it and keep the Deckers from having another PR problem. I need to free him of this complication. It's the merciful thing to do.

"I'm fine, tiger. Alexander was just leaving." I look at Alexander and will my tears to hold until he's gone and I'm alone.

"Dani," he starts.

"I can't," I whisper. "You said you'd never make me uncomfortable, so please leave."

His eyes plead with me, but when a tear escapes, he gives me a curt nod and leaves. The front door closes, and my focus turns to Tyler.

"Come on, let's get you back to bed."

I look down into his big brown eyes, seeking reassurance. I dig deep and muster a smile. "We're fine. Come on, we both have school tomorrow. Let's go."

I lead him back to his room, tuck him back in bed, and go to my room. My phone is lying on the nightstand, tempting me to call him, apologize, and explain. Instead, I turn it off, get ready for bed, and cry myself to sleep. It's best for him.

God, I hate complicated.

CHAPTER
THIRTY-SIX

ALEXANDER

———

I drive home in shock and disbelief. What the fuck just happened?

We'd had a good evening. A great evening. It was different, so domesticated, and I can't deny I liked it. Dinner and hanging out with Tyler, the secret touches under the table, the anticipation of watching TV just to spend time with Dani. Hoping for a goodnight kiss or even a hot make-out session, knowing there wasn't more tonight, but this isn't about sex. It's about her. Them. Us. I was anticipating our next evening like this. Maybe a lifetime of evenings like this. Tonight was the first time I ever had that thought in my life. I thought I'd be single forever until she made me rethink everything just by trusting me. Until she didn't. She didn't tell me. Trust me.

FUCK!

I play it all back in my head. I cleaned the kitchen, trying to help her in little ways. Give her one less thing to worry about. She has so much to do, and I don't know how she does it all.

Then I saw a stack of legal-looking papers, and my curiosity got the better of me. I've fallen under her spell that I practically forgot how we met. Why we met. Fucking Pauly Jackson.

I shut him down on my end. How did I forget about his ongoing impact on Dani? Because her sunshine made me forget. Her happiness, kindness, forgiveness. She made me forget there was a scumbag still walking the streets. She made me forget she was assaulted.

But she had a deposition last week. Why didn't she tell me about it? I would have been there for her, World Series be damned. How was it? Was it difficult to relive the incident? I can't imagine having to answer all those questions. Was Jackson there? And they've set a court date for December? Why did she close me out? I don't understand why she didn't tell me.

Because she thinks you're using her, that's why. Because she thinks you see her as a charity case. A victim. That label never described Dani Franklin. She's so many things, but a victim isn't one of them. Strong. Confident. Protective. Loving. Caring. Yes, she was a victim in the legal sense, but she's not someone who cowers or hides. She's brave. She's so many things, but never a victim.

Does it boil my blood thinking about that bruise and someone hurting her? Absolutely. If I were ever to see him again, I'm not confident I wouldn't kill him. But he's not worth it. He's not worth us. I can't believe Pauly Jackson is between us right now. Another reason to hate him.

I walk into my place and find Trevor stretched out on the couch playing video games. I hear the familiar music of Mario Cart and almost lose it. I pour a large glass of bourbon and gulp it down. I refill the glass and snap at Trevor, "Can you fucking grow up and stop acting like a six-year-old?!" I storm past, drink in hand, and head to my bedroom.

"Whoa, whoa, there, Xan, what happened?" Trevor hits pause on the TV, and the silence surrounds us. I freeze, realizing I don't want to go into my bedroom, maybe ever again. I'll still smell Dani on my sheets and picture her perfect body with mine. I also don't want to talk this out with Trevor. I want to fix this if that's possible.

"Fucking Pauly Jackson." I grind my teeth so hard I might break a molar.

"What? Did something happen?"

Trevor's on his feet and limps to get in front of me. He looks at the glass in my hand and quirks his eyebrow at me. I give him the same look back and down the amber liquid in one gulp. The burning doesn't match the burning in my veins.

"What happened?" he bites out, his mood changing to mirror mine.

I run my hand down my face, trying to erase the past hour. Shaking my head, I quietly say, "I don't know." I feel defeated, the fight leaving my body. She doesn't want me.

"Okay, let's start from the beginning."

Instead of responding, I walk back to fill my glass up and head for the balcony. The cool evening air might help me think. Trevor joins me with a beer, turns on the fire, and sits silently with me.

Silence is not his strong suit, and he holds out as long as he can. Finally, he speaks. "Is Dani okay? Tyler?" I can hear the fear in his voice. Yeah, I'm scared too, buddy.

"I guess." That's part of the problem. I don't know if she's okay. She didn't tell me about what she's been going through. And she's not with me, so no, she's not okay. We're not okay.

"You guess? Come on, man, talk to me." Trevor is one of the few people who can accept my grumpiness and let me be. Apparently, there's a limit to his tolerance, because he's pushing me to open up.

I gulp the rest of my drink down. I know it's not the answer, but it eases the pain in my chest. Something to numb the loss I feel. I sigh.

"She had to give a deposition last week." I need to shut off these emotions and think about the facts. These fucking emotions have me losing my shit and unable to think about what happened. All I want to do is bang on her door, take her in my arms, and protect her from the world. But I can't do that now because I make her uncomfortable. How did we get here?

"Okay. So it didn't go well?"

"I don't know."

"Come on, man. You're losing me here. Why don't you know?"

"Because she didn't fucking tell me!" So the cork's out of the bottle. I stand and pace, the energy coursing through my veins. "She had to face lawyers and an abuser alone, and she didn't fucking tell me. I found the paperwork in her kitchen, and she got pissed." I go to take another gulp of my drink, but the glass is empty. I slam it on the floor, the crystal shattering into a million pieces, just like my heart.

I turn back to Trevor, tears filling my eyes. "She thinks I'm using her. That she's a fucking charity case. How? How can she even think that? What does that say about how she sees me?" How does she not know she has rearranged my DNA? I'm a different man with her, a better man because of her.

Trevor's thoughtful when he quietly asks the question I don't have an answer for. "Why would she think that? What's happened that would make her believe that?"

I sit back down in my chair, defeated. "I don't know. I fucking don't know." I let the tears fall.

Is that how she feels? What have I done to make her feel that way? I try to think back on conversations, but it hurts too much.

After a few minutes, I give in to the whiskey, allowing it to numb my mind.

"Maybe it was something from the deposition?" Trevor often thinks out loud. Most creative people do. Where I keep everything in, he lets everything out. We are an opposites attract friendship. Like me and Dani, her sunshine to my, well, not sunshine.

"Is it too late to call Jack?" I mumble. I check my watch, still unsure about the time.

"Yeah. Let's not do that now. And is he even in town?" After the Series, we shut down operations for a few weeks for everyone. It's normal for the players to scatter for the offseason, but we wanted to reward the entire organization. It was a total team effort. We don't report back until after Thanksgiving.

"I don't know." I start to get up for another drink. "But if anyone can help, it's him."

"Hold tight," Trevor says, touching my shoulder to keep me down. He hobbles back inside while I begin to formulate a strategy. It's what I do. Tackle a problem head-on. This is too important to play nice and take the subtle route.

Trevor places the fresh glass in front of me, half a pour compared to my last two, but I hold it, watching the amber liquid swirl in the glass.

"What are you thinking?" Trevor's hand creeps toward my phone. He's taking it from me to prevent me from drunk texting anyone. It's probably for the best.

"I'm thinking I need to round up my lawyers and bury Pauly Jackson. And if they can't do it legally, I'll hire someone who can do it literally." With that decision made, I get up and head to the guest room. My bed is off-limits until I have Dani back. The thought of her scent on my pillow makes me feral.

A good night's sleep will clear my head when I head into battle. People think I'm a hard ass. They haven't seen anything yet.

CHAPTER
THIRTY-SEVEN

DANI

———

I made it through two days without totally breaking down. As a single, working mom, I don't have the luxury of a breakdown. I have to put one foot in front of the other. The sun will come up each morning, giving me a fresh day, a clean slate, to start over. I dig deep down for my eternal optimism. Unfortunately, it's buried deep.

Today, though, I don't want to start over. I want to turn back time to when a certain man was beside me. Too bad that won't be happening. It's what's best for him. I always knew we had an expiration date because we didn't make sense. Except we did.

"Mom?" Tyler peeks into my bedroom, trying to be considerate, his attempt at letting me sleep in. We do this sometimes. If he finds cereal on the counter on a Saturday, he knows he can watch TV and eat until I join him. It's rare, but we've done it a few times. Today I'm in bed longer than usual.

"Hey, tiger. Come here." I pat the bed, and he scurries over, snuggling under the comforter, his cold feet hitting my legs, making me reflexively pull away. "Brrr. Where are your socks?" I pull him in tighter, wrapping him in my warm embrace.

"It's our last game today, but you don't feel good." He looks at me, worry lining his face. He's been extra clingy for the past few days. He knows something's wrong but doesn't know what. Kids have that sixth sense. But it's not his job to worry about me, so I need to step up my game.

"I wouldn't miss it for the world." I pull him close and hold on to him with everything I have. This kid is my reason for getting out of bed every day. I don't know how I'd be managing without him. "Let's get ready. Put a long sleeve shirt under your uniform today. It might be a little cold."

His smile lights up his face. Did he think I'd miss his game? How could he think that about me?

Xander's words echo in my head. *Is that what you think of me? That I'm here because I think you're a charity case? That I feel sorry for you? Or that I'm using you? That's the kind of man you think I am?* The hurt in his eyes haunts my dreams. How could I think that about him? I don't. But I fear the lawyer could certainly persuade a jury to believe that, and I won't let that happen.

We get ready and head to the ball field. The new, sturdy stands are full of supporters for the Slugger's last game. I think the word has leaked out that there might be some Reapers here, explaining the larger-than-expected crowd. I'm surprised to see Darcy sitting beside Jenny, both with a blanket over their legs. It's almost Thanksgiving, and the fall chill is upon us.

I put on my best smile, greet my parents, and join the girls with a hug. "Darcy, this is a pleasant surprise."

"Yeah, Matt wanted to be in the dugout. You can't keep that guy away from the field. Is it okay I tagged along?" She's sporting a gorgeous camel-hair coat and scarf and looks so put together. Jenny looks adorable, as usual. Me? I'm more than my usual mess.

Jenny keeps up the small talk as we cheer on the kids. Alexander is coaching the Sluggers with the Reapers' players staying on the field for both teams. They're giving back. Taking care of the community.

I wasn't sure he'd show, but he's a man that keeps his word. He told the kids he'd be here, and he is. But this game feels different to me. He hasn't looked in the stands once. The realization hits me, and the cold washes over me. I asked him to leave me alone. And he's a man of his word.

"Luis said you found a house?" Jenny and Darcy are still chatting, but I'm lost in my own thoughts.

"We did, and I love it. It's close enough to the stadium for Matt and has tons of charm for me. I'll have my work cut out, but I'm excited. We'll have a housewarming once we're settled, and I expect you both to come. Promise?" Darcy reaches over and squeezes my hand. How can I say no to her? She's just the sweetest.

"Of course we will," Jenny replies. "Won't we, Dani?"

I nod and give her a forced smile. "Umhum."

Jenny leans in and whispers. "Everything okay? You seem off."

"Yeah, fine. Just got a lot going on." I mentioned the court date to her but didn't share anything about the deposition. It was hellacious, and I want to put it behind me.

"I know. Everything okay with Alexander?" She looks at me anxiously, dreading the inevitable answer. I've shared my hesitation and concerns about us. She knows how guarded I am. I haven't told her I've asked him to step away.

"It's as it should be," I respond. I reach for the positive. "Luis looks like he's having fun. He's a keeper." I bump into her shoulder.

"Yeah, things are good. He's going home for a while over the holidays. I might miss the goof." I'm happy to see her with a guy that deserves her.

The game wraps up, the kids gather around their coaches, and someone suggests a group photo. I see Mom down there and know she'll get one. I'll stay where I am. It's his team now. I asked for space, so I need to abide by it. Alexander never looks my way. Good job, girl. You sold it.

The kids say goodbye to their coaches. Jenny and Darcy go to join their guys while Tyler skips over to me. "Mom, Mom, did you see me? I made three outs. I told you I'm a good third baseman like Matt."

"You were awesome. You ready to head home?"

"Yeah, I'm going to miss baseball." His excitement escapes like a deflating balloon.

"Me too, tiger. Me too."

Alexander heads to his car. He never looks back. As he walks away, he takes a piece of my heart with him.

CHAPTER
THIRTY-EIGHT

ALEXANDER

———

I've waited days for this meeting. Jack reached out to his friend in the District Attorney's office and agreed to share what he could regarding Pauly's case.

Trevor's still with me, and I'm not sure when he'll head back to Savannah. He's keeping a watchful eye on me. It's an interesting role reversal. The inmate is now the warden.

After that first night, he hasn't asked a lot of questions. I still sleep in my spare bedroom. I'm not sure if he knows why, but he doesn't ask. My friends and family are supportive in their own way. No doubt there's a group chat where I'm the main subject. That's what we Deckers do. We rally. I know these people all too well. But so far, they've all stayed radio silent with me because they know me too. That's how I operate. It's not often I'm in this situation, but when I am, I'm thoughtful and strategic. I need quiet to think, to function. But that was before them. Dani and Tyler are anything but quiet. Now the silence is a reminder of what I've lost. I miss the chaos.

But I can't talk about this. Her. This is the time for action.

Seeing her at that ballgame, sitting in the stands, pretending to smile. It damn near killed me not to storm over there, throw her over my shoulder, and lock her in a room with me until she knows how much I love her. Yep. There it is. I love her, and she doesn't even know. No. She thinks I'm using her.

But she asked for space, so I give it to her. I'll give her anything she asks for, even things she doesn't. Like help.

"Thanks for coming in on your off time. I appreciate it."

"Of course." Jack looks at Trevor. "You look good, T."

"Almost one hundred percent," Trevor grins. He pops his cast on the table for inspection. He's expecting to get it off next week.

"So, what did you find out?" Anxiety consumes me. Once I know what I'm dealing with, I can solve this problem. But I need information.

"First, I'll share what I can, but you aren't going to like it."

I nod. "I don't like a fucking thing about this, Jack. That monster attacks an innocent woman, and now she has to relive it in a courtroom. Believe me, there isn't a fucking thing I like about any of this right now." I get up and start pacing. I've kept my anger at bay by damming it up, staying focused on the issue, working out the problem. But the dam is about to crack, and I pity anyone in the way when that happens.

Since she told me to leave that fateful night, I've been like a caged animal, ready to fight. Fight for her. For us. I've contained it, but Trevor knows I'm a ticking time bomb. Totally explains the watchful eye.

"So, we have two things going on simultaneously. First, the criminal charges. They set the court date for the first Monday in December. The DA's office thinks it should be cut and dry. The video footage speaks for itself. Regardless of motive, it was assault." Jack looks at Trevor for support when he says the words.

"What do you mean, regardless of motive?" I say each word

with slow precision. Motive? What reason would he have to hit her other than being a worthless human being?

"That's the second part. The request for deposition wasn't for the criminal case." Jack's letting it sink in. Going slow. Letting me process what he's saying.

"He's suing her," Trevor whispers. He's fucking thinking out loud.

"What?!" I roar. "How can that be?" I throw my water bottle against the wall. It doesn't have the same satisfaction as a whiskey glass, but it's all I have.

"I don't have much information on the details," Jack starts. "But here's my educated guess. Based on what I've gathered, he's suing her, naming her as the reason he lost his job. He's alleging that you hired her to set him up so you would have an excuse to fire him and void his contract. He knows you were in talks to trade him, and no one wanted his hefty contract. He's claiming he was set up."

I knock over a chair, fury running through me. I don't think I've ever been this angry and frustrated. Jack and Trevor let me simmer for a few minutes, both frozen in place.

When I get control of my temper, Trevor asks the obvious question. "Why sue her and not Xander or the Reapers? They're the ones who fired him and have the deep pockets." All of this is true. I nod, agreeing with Trevor.

"Why is he going after her?" I ask.

"I don't know, but I suspect he's not actually going after her." I give him a quizzical look. After a long sigh, he says, "He's going after you."

"Me? What kind of fucked up logic is that?" Is this my fault? She's going through this because of me? I keep coming back to the question that hurts every time I ask it. Why didn't she tell me? Does she blame me?

"Again, I don't know. He won't have a case coming after you or the Reapers if convicted. But if he goes after her, he figures you'll hear about it and settle something with him off the books and out of court."

"What makes him think I'd do that?" Of course, I will. I'll do anything to protect her. Pauly Jackson doesn't know that, though. What is that slimy bastard up to?

Jack holds up his phone, and a picture fills the screen. It's me kissing Dani behind my car at Tyler's practice. My hand is fisted in her curls, her hands around my neck, pulling me in. He swipes at the picture, and there's another one of us getting ice cream and another one of me with her and Tyler eating dinner at a restaurant.

My stomach rolls, and I feel like I could vomit. "He had someone following her?" I pace again. "I need to get her security and find someone to get this fucking peeping tom off her immediately. Tell me how to do that, Jack. How do I keep them safe?" I'm begging him for help. I've never felt so desperate in my life. This helpless feeling is foreign and I don't know what to do.

"We can arrange something, but they probably followed you and stumbled onto this. You aren't going to like this, but I think if you stay away, she'll be okay. You absolutely cannot be near her or that courtroom. Don't fight me on it, please. It's what's best for her." Jack winces.

I'm grateful for my friend. He's shooting it to me straight. I'm not sure how he got those pictures, but I've no doubt he's called in more than a few favors for me.

Meanwhile, he's told me she has to go through this alone.

"What does she know?" Trevor asks.

Jack shakes his head. "I don't know. She's aware she's being sued, but she didn't have a lawyer present during the deposition. Or if she did, they did a piss-poor job of representing her. I'm not sure she gets the full picture." My brave, strong, trusting sunshine. I can't imagine what they put her through. The thoughts and images they put in her head. Charity case? Makes a little more sense now. I don't need to think about us or me at the moment. This is all about her.

I sit down and put my head in my hands. I need to help get her out of my mess, and knowing how we left things, I need to do it with as little direct interaction as possible. She'll refuse my help. Our focus, MY focus, needs to be on her. I'm getting her out of this nightmare with as much dignity and positivity as possible.

"So what do I need to do, Jack?"

"I've got a few ideas, but you've gotta let me handle it." Putting someone else in control of this is hard, but if I can trust anyone, it's Jack. It looks like I don't have much of a choice.

"Do it."

CHAPTER
THIRTY-NINE

DANI

————

The last bell rang fifteen minutes ago, signaling the end of school. My Dad picked up Tyler to work on some secret Thanksgiving day surprise. I'm not sure what it is, but I'm grateful for the extra time to get my life in order. Or at least just have a quiet moment to mentally rehash the mess I'm in.

There's a knock at my classroom door. I look up to see Mr. Davis escorting a stunning woman in her mid-forties, dressed very professionally for this setting. I'd bet her shoes have red bottoms. She's rocking a flawless chignon, with not a hair out of place.

She's a stark contrast to me today. I'm wearing chocolate milk from a lunch mishap, and what little makeup I had on this morning washed away with my afternoon tears.

"Hey Mr. Davis. What can I do for you?"

"This lovely woman was asking to see you, but wasn't on the visitor list. I hope it's okay that I brought her to you."

"It's fine. Thanks Mr. Davis." He gives an appreciative look at our visitor and smiles.

"It was nice meeting you," he says to her. "Dani, let me know if you need anything."

"I will, thanks." I haven't shared any of my legal issues with him, or frankly, anyone. It's too much. It's embarrassing. I turn my attention to the woman at my door.

"Hi Dani. May I come in?" I nod at her as my stomach rolls. I have a bad feeling about this.

She steps into the room and closes the door. Her heels click as she makes her way to me. While Mickey enjoys his exercise ball on the floor, I'm petting Joe at my desk. Her expression morphs from power suit to childlike wonder almost instantly. These hedgehogs have a way of doing that to people. It makes me think of Xander, and I give her a weak smile.

"He's adorable. May I?" She's reaching out to pet him.

"Of course. His name is Joe. You can hold him if you'd like, but I don't want him to mess up your clothes." The moment I say yes, her eyes light up.

"Oh, I don't care. He's the cutest thing I've ever seen." She takes him from me and snuggles, cooing at him like a baby.

"I'm sorry, I didn't catch your name," I say to get us back on task. I don't know what she wants, but I doubt it's good. I might as well address it head-on. Another wave of Xander's memories washes over me. He's rubbed off on me.

"Oh my gosh, I'm so sorry. How unprofessional of me." She shifts Joe to one hand and offers me her other. "I'm Courtney Brown, an attorney with Hargrove and Associates."

I shake her hand as my smile falters. An attorney. Now what am I being served with?

"How can I help you, Ms. Brown?"

"Courtney, please. And I'm here to help you. Our firm handles celebrity cases, especially assault cases against women. I was part of the team that got Taylor Swift her victory in court after that horrible man groped her. I'm tired of women being victimized by men and then again in the courtroom. It's not fair, and I'm sick of it. I help women fight back. Do you have counsel for your case involving Pauly Jackson?"

Mickey rolls his ball to my feet, and I reach down to pick him up. I open it up and hold him in my hands. Now each of us has a hedgehog. At least we should stay civil at this point. We both cuddle our therapy animals while she waits for my response.

"I'm sorry if I'm a bit confused. First of all, I'm certainly no celebrity, and second, I can't afford a lawyer."

"Do you have a dollar?" she asks, holding Joe and rubbing his fur on her face.

"A dollar?"

"Yes, one dollar will retain my services. The rest is pro bono." She holds Joe up and looks at him eye to eye. She whispers, "That's free." She gives him a wink and focuses her attention back on me. "Then, anything you say to me will be attorney-client privilege. Do you have a dollar?" She's staring me down, challenging me to say no.

I look at her like she's got two heads. She's a high-powered, or at least expensive, lawyer, cuddling with a hedgehog, asking me if I have a dollar. I rummage in my pen drawer, find enough change to make a dollar and place it on the desk. I give her a shrug.

"Perfect. Now let's begin." She quickly moves Joe to one hand while she pulls out a notebook and a pen.

"Are you aware of exactly what's going on? Legally, that is?"

"Not really. I have a court date about the assault. The Assistant DA assured me I need to answer the questions directly and honestly, and everything will be fine."

"I bet he did," she mumbles. "Continue."

"Then a guy shows up at my house serving me with papers that say Pauly Jackson is suing me because he lost his job. He's suing me for a million dollars," I scoff. "I'm a teacher and a single mother. I'll never see a million dollars in my life. The entire thing is ridiculous. During this deposition thing, they accused me of working with Xan, I mean, Alexander Decker, to set him up. Since the video doesn't have sound, they said I was blackmailing him or something. It was all lies." Thinking about that day makes me angry. Thinking about Alexander's face when I sent him away makes me physically ill.

She looks at me with a harshness that would make me buckle on the stand. I'm not made to deal with lawyers. The deposition proved that.

"Anything else?"

"No, not really."

"What about your romantic relationship with Alexander Decker?"

"What relationship?" I'm not lying. It's over.

"Are you romantically involved with him?"

"I was." My heart clenches. What would I give to change my answer to I am?

"Before or after the assault?"

"After. I'd never met him until we attended a Reapers game in his suite." I remember that day like it was yesterday. The man with the hard exterior but a heart of pure gold.

"Are you in love with him?"

Why is she asking me this? Is it relevant to the case? I don't know, but I can't deny it any longer. I can't deny it to myself or her.

"Yes, I love him. But we aren't together anymore."

"Why not?"

"Because," I swallow. Why aren't we together? "I broke his heart."

She screws her mouth as she thinks.

"I can work with that."

CHAPTER
FORTY

ALEXANDER

"You know I can't tell you anything," Jack booms through my car's speakers. "Anything she says to Courtney is privileged. They met a few days ago, and she agreed to work with her. You have to trust me. She's in good hands."

"Can you at least tell me how she's doing?" It's been two weeks and three days since I've seen or talked to her. Jack says I can't even text because phone records can be pulled up in court, and given the accusations, it's a strong possibility.

"Damnit, Xander, I can't believe I have to tell you this. Use your fucking Decker Connection. Have someone else reach out and ask her friends. But don't ask me and don't ask her. At least not until this gets resolved. Wheels are in motion here, and I cannot have you fucking this up. Be patient. You're not great at that, so it's a stretch. I need you to do this."

I run my hand through my hair, pulling at the strands. I'm not used to feeling so helpless. "I appreciate you, Jack. You're right. I know you're right. It's just." I can't finish the sentence.

"I know, man, I know. We all know. Just hang in there. It should be over soon."

I take a deep breath and focus on what he said. As much as I hate to admit it, he's right. "Enjoy your Thanksgiving. Tell Lucy I said hi. I'll make it up to her for all the overtime."

Jack and I are going in different directions for Thanksgiving. He's driving to the mountains to see his family, and I'm on my way to Charleston to see mine. It's been five months since my friends and family gathered at Chance's beach house to celebrate Darcy's new business. That was the night that changed everything. The night I got the call Pauly Jackson was involved in an assault. The night that sent me on a trajectory to meet my sunshine.

Everyone's gathering at the beach house for the holiday weekend. Chance said we're forgoing the traditional turkey and dressing for a more coastal-themed feast. I'm not sure what that entails, but since he's the only one in season, I'm sure it will include lots of alcohol and desserts for the rest of us. That's all I know about the weekend. I'm sure there were more details in the group chat, but the one I'm in has been pretty quiet. Not normal.

I almost canceled. I'm prepared for this weekend to be some sort of inquisition or intervention. Either way, I'm sure I'll be the center of it, and I'm not in the mood. Frankly, I'm never in the mood for that shit, but definitely not now. Not when it feels like my heart is getting stabbed with a hot poker. It sucks.

Trevor went home for a few days last week, so I've had peace and quiet. Usually, I like solitude. But this week? It's been hell. I don't want to be alone anymore.

I've spent more hours in the office than I should, especially since I've closed down everything for another week. I've even made up work to do to keep me there. I sit at my desk for hours and stare at the card Tyler made. *Thank you for giving us a family.* I know he was talking about Joe and Mickey, but that word. Family. That's what I want with them.

The other item that occupies too much of my attention is the piece of Reaper's stationery I found on my desk the day after our first kiss. Her lipstick signature forever captured on paper. She didn't want to come up to my office because she'd snuck up before the playoff game. When I asked her favorite intern, he just shrugged. Proves everyone loves her and will risk their jobs and anything else important for her. I have both valuable items tucked into my suitcase. They go everywhere with me.

As I drive onto the quiet coastal island, I know it's time to surrender and ask Team True Love for help. Maybe Jack's right. I've got the connections, and they're all in one place. If this gathering is about me, I might as well use it to my advantage.

Opening the front door, there are people sprawled out everywhere, and I do a quick headcount. Matt, Darcy, Jules, Chance, and Emma are playing a game at the dining room table with two of Darcy's friends. Samantha and Jay, I think? Trevor's asleep in the recliner. Tripp is reading a book by the fireplace. It looks like Cole is on the deck talking on the phone. That must mean Ash is here somewhere.

"There's my favorite big brother," she says as she comes down the stairs, wrapping me in a tight hug. A hug I desperately need.

I laugh. "I thought Jules was your favorite?" He is, and I'm okay with that. We both serve a role. I'm the protector, and Jules is the confidant. We Deckers play to our strengths.

"I just tell him that because he has a bigger ego." She stretches up on her toes and kisses me on the cheek. "I've missed you."

"It's good to see you too. You still plan on marrying that boy?" Playing my role.

"Yep." She follows my line of sight and smiles. "Something's going on, but he won't tell me what it is. That's his third call today." She slaps my arm and shakes her head. "Boys." She sighs and walks into the den. "Hey everyone, look who decided to finally show up." Everyone turns their heads toward me and shouts various greetings.

Well, now that everyone knows I've arrived, the fun can begin.

I get caught up with everyone. Tripp went to Mexico for a week and invited me to go back with him after this weekend. I politely decline.

Matt and Darcy found a house, and it sounds perfect for them. When they talk about the big backyard, I think of Tyler having a place to play and maybe even have a dog. He really wants a dog.

It's still early in the season, but the Renegades have a decent shot at the cup this year. They have a lot of young talent that's been in development for the last two years. It's time to see the payoff. But that means a lot of extra work for Chance. As the captain, wrangling and mentoring a bunch of twenty-year-olds with unlimited money and tons of puck bunnies is no easy task. That's why he makes the big bucks. But here in this setting, he's the most laid-back host I've ever seen. He only has two days before he's back to work for his next game in Charleston, so this gathering worked out perfectly with his schedule.

Emma loves teaching and is thriving in Savannah. She and Trevor spend a lot of time together, and maybe she even missed him while he was with me. He finally got his cast off and has a removable walking boot, a considerable improvement. I can't believe I almost lost him this year. I still get emotional thinking about it.

Later, I track Cole down in the upstairs living room where he's watching Sportscenter and preoccupied with his phone.

"Hear she still wants to marry you." I grab a beer from the bar fridge and sit in a chair facing the beach. We get along fine after our rocky start, but I don't know if I'll ever be one hundred percent with him. Maybe ninety-nine percent because she's still my little sister, but that's the best he can ask for.

"Shocking, huh?" He gives me a goofy, in-love grin.

"A little. So what's going on with you? Nothing work related, I hope." I glance at his phone, which he keeps checking. Baseball is a business, and no one knows that better than me. The offseason is a busy time to review contracts and make moves, trades, and cuts. It's the time to strategize for the year. The young guys like Cole are literal pawns on a playing field. One phone call and their lives can change instantly. New city, team, division, or maybe it's the end of the dream. I've never taken that lightly, but it's business. I doubt New York would do anything drastic with Cole after one year, and if they were thinking about it, Jules would have the inside track. It's unlikely his distraction is baseball related, but you never know.

"No, not really. I expect a full year in Nashville and am okay with that. I like it there."

"So what's got Ash anxious?" I give him my big brother look. He may be her fiancé, but I'll kick his ass if the situation demands it. Won't be the first time.

"Promise not to tell her?"

"No." Depending on what it is, I won't make that promise.

He laughs. "Figures." He runs his hand through his shaggy, curly hair. "I've been approached to cowrite an album with Pineapple Sunset. I never knew music would involve more lawyers than baseball, but there are."

"Pineapple Sunset, the boy band?" Dani loves their music. I'm not much of a pop music fan, but their name invokes a memory of watching her sway to their songs in my living room and me fucking her on the counter in my kitchen.

"Yeah, they're pretty cool, really. Down to earth, you know. Almost normal. Just a bunch of guys chasing a dream. And apparently a girl or two." He grins like the smug bastard that caught the girl he was chasing.

"So why keep it a secret from Ash? You guys don't do secrets well." Secrets can kill a relationship. Exhibit A sitting right here. Fuck, I miss her.

"I know, I know. I'm not keeping a secret, not really. I want to tell her once I know what it'll look like. Right now, it's just a lot of what ifs and maybes."

"Well, she's a little nervous, not knowing. If there's one thing I know about us Deckers is that we like to know what we're faced with. We have pretty active imaginations and can go pretty dark. Don't let her do that. She knows something's up."

First-hand experience, right here. I've been in some dark places wondering about Dani. "Tell her. Let her support you. For some reason I'll never understand, she loves you. Let her." I give him a genuine smile. Despite my tough bravado, he's a good man for Ash.

He twists the phone in his hand, thinking. "Yeah, you're probably right. I didn't want to worry her. She's got a lot going on." Now I'm on heightened alert. I immediately sit up and lean forward, all attention focused on him.

"Down, down." He fans his hands toward me. "She still needs to hire another assistant, but I've also figured out Deckers don't like to ask for help, either. This album will take up most of my offseason since we'll try to finish the majority in the next two months. I won't be there to help her find balance and downtime. And she's stressed. I don't want her to get buried in work, you know. I want her to have fun. Preferably with me." He gives me a smile that lets me know he's not thinking pure thoughts about my sister.

I sigh. "I get it, I do. But tell her. Everything. Your concerns, your dreams, your wishes for her. She'll listen to you." Cole exhales and sits back on the couch, tossing his phone on the cushion beside him.

"Yeah, you're probably right." He looks around and sees we're still alone. "So, what's going on with Dani? You going to fix it?"

"I sure as fuck hope so. I'm about to be uncharacteristically Decker and ask for help. I hope Team True Love is up to the challenge."

Cole gives me a chuckle and gets a gleam in his eye. "We hoped that would be the case. Come on, I'll let them know the persuasion phase is unnecessary." He slaps me on the back.

"And they said Leigh was the only one who could do it. Jules owes me a hundred bucks!" I knew there was more going on in that group chat.

What the hell would the persuasion phase even look like? I'm not sure whether to be happy or terrified of the Decker Connection.

CHAPTER
FORTY-ONE

DANI

———

Jenny took Tyler to school this morning so I could have a few minutes to compose myself. She's meeting me at the courthouse with my parents. Even though I insisted I didn't want them there, I was overruled. I'm nervous. Nervous about the proceedings. Nervous about seeing Pauly Jackson and his evil smirk. Nervous about his lawyer making me look like a fool. Nervous the jury won't believe me. Nervous Alexander's name and reputation will be tarnished.

Admittedly, I'm a little surprised I haven't heard from him. I know he said he'd do anything I asked, but I also thought he wouldn't listen to me if he felt strongly. Maybe that's the case. Maybe he doesn't feel strongly. Then again, Courtney told me to stay away from him until this mess gets sorted, and I wonder if he's been told the same. Or were my words and lack of faith in him too damaging? I'm still haunted by the look on his face when I lashed out. I hurt him. My chest constricts thinking about it. About him.

I was told to meet the lawyers in a conference room down the hall from the courtroom. I steady myself with a deep breath and open the door. Courtney stands and hugs me. Despite her harsh, professional appearance, she's a real sweetheart. She's become a friend and advocate for me, and I appreciate her. She still hasn't told me how she came to my rescue, but I'm beyond grateful.

"You're going to be fine," she says, her hands on my shoulders. "I'll be right beside you, and if the prosecutor isn't doing his job, I'll be there to let him know. I can't speak up, but he'll know. I got you." She gives me a wink, and my shoulders relax a little.

"I don't want to mess this up. If he's not convicted, his other case becomes even more complicated and messy, and I can't handle more complicated." Complicated and complex.

"Just remember, you aren't alone. And you did nothing wrong. When they show that video, own it with pride. You were badass." I feel a glimmer of confidence for today's proceedings, thanks to her staunch belief in me.

There's a knock on the door, and the prosecutor sticks his head inside. "You ready?"

I smooth out the wrinkles in my skirt and take a deep breath. I'm dressed in a black sheath dress and heels, and I even broke out my special occasion purse. I hold my Kate Spade bag tight, willing it to protect me from the courtroom. I debated about what to wear today, but I wanted to look serious. Besides, black fits my mood these days. My hair is straightened for a more sophisticated appearance. Alexander would hate my look, and knowing that was enough to wear it. I need to put as much distance as possible between us. "Yep. Let's do this."

I was told to sit in the front row right behind the prosecutor. They'll call me when it's my time to testify. Courtney will stay beside me, probably ensuring I won't bolt. We open the doors and enter the courtroom. I focus my attention on the floor, not wanting to see Pauly Jackson again.

One side of the courtroom is packed, while the other side has a few scattered people throughout. I was told to expect media in the room because he's a high-profile defendant, but I didn't think the media would wear suits. Or sit together. It looks like a lopsided wedding.

As I pass the back row, they stand in unison. The movement catches my eye, and I look up to see familiar faces, all looking very stoic. As I take another step, the next row does the same. More familiar faces, all looking like they're angry or frustrated. Are they mad at me?

Casey Samuels reaches out and squeezes my hand. "You've got this, friend," she whispers. Her husband, Joey, puts his arm around her shoulder and gives me a wink. "I hope he rots in hell," he mumbles. No, they aren't mad at me. They're looking past me to Pauly Jackson sitting at the defendant's table, whispering with his lawyer. The looks they give him are terrifying.

In the next row, Tripp Stevenson stands and hands me a piece of paper. "For later," he whispers. I respond with a slight smile and put it into my purse. I don't know what to make of this. He's sitting beside Matt and Darcy. And Luis is beside Darcy. I thought he went home to Miami for the holidays. Why is he here? I scan the group. It looks like most of the team is here. Is that Corey, the intern? Why are so many of the Reapers here?

Then I see Alexander's friends. Trevor sits beside Cole and Matt.

Does that mean Alexander is here? I scan the group again and don't see him. My hopeful smile slips. Courtney wraps her arm around mine. "Sorry, no Deckers in the courtroom," she whispers, my desperation obvious. "Now go be a badass." She and I sit in the front row beside my parents.

"All rise." The judge gets seated, reads the charges, and we are underway.

My dad reaches over, puts his arm around me, and gives my shoulder a slight squeeze. The Colonel is not an affectionate man, so this gesture speaks volumes. I do my best to channel his strength.

I glance past him to Mom and Jenny and notice a man at the end of our row I don't recognize. He seems to take notes, his fingers moving rapidly on his phone. Probably a reporter. Then I notice a spot of yellow on his black jacket that catches my eye. It's a sun. I peek behind me, seeing more suns, and choke up a little as I get the message. They're his proxy. His team. His friends. His family. He's here in spirit. My confidence gets another boost.

The jury comes in, and they get instructions. The lawyers do a lot of talking and the defense attorney paints a picture of me leading Pauly Jackson on and then saying something to set him off. None of it is true. He makes me sound like a horrible person. My stomach flips. This isn't going well and my optimism vanishes.

Like at the deposition, I'm called to the stand and grilled by the lawyer. This time it's even worse because my friends and family are hearing this. I'm embarrassed and humiliated, but do my best to be strong. I celebrate a tiny victory because I don't cry.

The prosecutor objects at the things being said, but the hurtful words hang in the air. You can't unhear it. I'm referred to as the victim more times than I can count. They imply Alexander paid me to seduce Pauly. It's ridiculous and nauseating. I'm a teacher, not a paid escort.

I close my eyes when they play the video on the big screen. I can't look. Courtney wants me to own it, but I can't. When I risk a glance at my dad, I notice the team is shifting in their seats, clearly uncomfortable. Mumbling fills the courtroom, and Pauly Jackson looks over his shoulder at his ex-teammates, and for the first time, his smug look is gone. The Reapers are furious. It reminds me of the day I met Alexander after he realized who I was. Controlled anger and pity filled his face. I can't handle being seen like that again.

The judge bangs his gavel, and I jump with a start. He orders everyone to be quiet and settle down.

The defense called several of Pauly Jackson's ex-girlfriends to the stand, all stating he was never remotely violent, always the best boyfriend, implying I must have done something. I feel sick.

Pauly Jackson tells lies. He says I led him on. The defense attorney goes through the video frame by frame with Jackson, asking his version of what happened. It's all a lie, but I can do nothing now. I need this to be over.

The prosecutor tries to trip up Jackson, but he's too slick and his lies are well-rehearsed. Both sides are done with witnesses, and it's time for closing arguments. We're granted a ten-minute break, and I lean over to ask Courtney if I need to stay.

"I've gotta go," I tell her. She nods, grabs her bag, and nudges me to leave. I rush out of the courtroom, not looking at anyone, and run into a man standing outside the door. He grabs my arms to keep me from falling and I look up into familiar eyes and a kind smile.

"You okay, Ms. Franklin?"

"Mr. Decker?"

"Please, call me Sully. Can I speak to you for just a moment?"

I look at Courtney for guidance, but her expression is stern. "Um, I'm not sure. It'll look bad for your family to be seen with me."

"I don't give a hot damn about it. Let them come after me and my family. I dare them." His serious, defiant look is familiar. He puts his hand on my elbow and leads me back to the conference room I started in. Courtney is by my side, her stone face not giving anything away.

"This is not the best idea," Courtney starts.

Sully cocks his eyebrow at her, shutting her down. I don't think he's used to being challenged like that. "I want to apologize on behalf of my organization and my family," he says once the door closes.

"Oh, you don't have to do that. Alexander, Julian, and Ashleigh have done that ten times over. None of this is your responsibility." His blue eyes remind me of Alexander's, and I'm hit with a wave of sadness. A wave of loss.

"Well, I'm sorry I didn't recognize you when we met. I know you must be pretty special if you've captured my son's heart. He's right, you know. You are like bottled sunshine." He beams at me with adoration.

"I, um," I stutter. I don't know what to say. I don't feel like sunshine right now. Is that really what Alexander told his father about me?

"I'm sorry we weren't in there to support you, but I want you to know, I don't care about the PR fallout, the possible bad press, any of it. All I care about is my family, and I can tell you Alexander is a shell of a man without you. He won't admit it, but he's functioning without a heart because you, my dear, have it." He gives me the kindest smile.

My instinct kicks in and I hug him. He chuckles and hugs me back. For a billionaire businessman, he gives amazing hugs. His kindness and warmth comfort me, and a spark of hope lands in my chest. Maybe?

His hand slides down my arm and holds me at my elbow. "I'm just here to say, if this mess is why you aren't with him, then forget about it. We'll let the lawyers sort it out. If there are other reasons, then that's for you to decide, of course. But take this lawyer stuff off the table in your decision-making." He winks at Courtney. "That's what we're paying her for."

"Mr. Decker," Courtney interrupts. "I'm sure Dani appreciates this. We can sort out the personal stuff later. She still has a significant legal case hanging over her head, and this one isn't over. Depending on the verdict and sentencing, it's complicated."

My spark of hope is quickly doused with a shot of complicated. She's right. Complicated. I pull away from Sully Decker and wipe a tear away. With a slight sniffle, I say, "Thank you. I appreciate this, but Courtney's right. I've got a lot going on, and now is not the time for, well, anything. It was nice seeing you again, but I have to go."

I need to get home, lock my doors, and pull myself together before Tyler comes home. Courtney is beside me as we walk to my car, talking about the case, but I don't hear anything she's saying. I'm exhausted and want to crawl into bed and let the darkness surround me. As I drive home, I replay the day like an awful movie with all the major themes shining through. The shame, humiliation, frustration, anger. But there's one thing that keeps bothering me.

That's what we're paying her for?

CHAPTER
FORTY-TWO

ALEXANDER

———

Jules and Ashleigh are doing their best to distract me, but their efforts are worthless. I can't wait here while she's sitting in an uncomfortable courtroom facing down the man who assaulted her.

"I'm going for a drive." I grab my keys and head to the front door.

"I'll come with you," Ashleigh offers.

"No," I quickly say. I look at her, see the concern in her eyes, and soften my tone. "No thanks, Ash. I need to be alone. Just getting some fresh air."

"Don't do it, Xander," Jules warns. "Do not go to the courtroom."

I turn back to both of them, prepared to snap at his rebuke. They're worried about me and are trying to protect us. My shoulders drop in an acceptance of defeat.

"I won't, I promise. I wouldn't do anything to hurt her. I just need a few minutes." I turn and leave. "I'll be back."

Message delivered. We're all here.

We're all here. And while I'm more than grateful they are supporting her, I'm not there, and it's killing me. I know I can't go into the courtroom, but I have to be near her. I drive to the courthouse and park outside like a total stalker. I chuckle at the thought. She's accused me of stalking before, but when it comes to her, I do crazy things. I'd do anything for her, even go without contact, which goes against my very nature. So here I am, sitting in my car, phone in hand, waiting for the next text.

Jack's texting at regular intervals with courtroom updates. My chest hurts and my eye twitches. I'm physically pained not to be there for her, but Jack has assured me it's the right move. I told him I'd follow his orders, and I trust him. It's just so damn hard and goes against every instinct I have, but I'll do what's best for her.

Apparently, they're taking a break before closing arguments, so my texts are quiet for now. My phone vibrates again.

CHANCE
How r u doing?

Not good. He needs to pay for what he's done to her.

He will. Let Jack handle it.

I am.

I'm so focused on my phone, I almost miss her. Dani is rushing down the sidewalk, Courtney by her side, trying to keep up. She's not used to heels that high and her feet are going to hurt from them. Her curls are gone, her hair straight, flat, and boring. I almost didn't recognize her. She's wearing all black and looks hot as hell, but she's not my happy-go-lucky girl. She's too dark, all her sunshine erased from her presence, and it hurts me to see her like this. This is not my Dani. I hate Pauly Jackson for what he's done to her. I hate myself for what I've done to her because I'm not innocent here, either.

I reach for the door and catch myself. I can't. Fuck!

Where are they going? It isn't over, is it? Why isn't Jack keeping me posted?

I try to call Jack, and it goes directly to voicemail.

> Why the fuck is Dani outside? And where is her security?

JACK

> She's with Courtney, so she's okay. She said she didn't want to stay. She's holding it together, but the accusations were brutal. Probably messed with her head. Leave her be.

> I fucking hate this.

> I know.

> Court is back in session. Here we go with closing arguments.

I want to wrap her in my arms and apologize a million times. I hate that she's going through this and hate it even more because I can't be there for her.

We determined the PI was still following me, and I can't risk being there with her. As a precaution, we hired someone to watch her from a close distance, but so far, she's been fine. She'd lose her mind if she knew about that. It's just as much for my peace of mind as it is for her safety. She's too precious to risk anything happening to her. Tyler needs her. Her students need her. I need her.

I know she'd think I'm treating her like a victim. I'm not. She's so strong and independent. Unfortunately, there are horrible people in the world. Pauly Jackson, for one.

JACK

> It's with the jury now. I won't lie. They painted a questionable picture of her. I'm not sure how it's going to land.

FUCK! That doesn't bode well for the civil suit against Dani. And what Jack isn't saying is Dani's in worse shape than he wants to admit. To make matters worse, I'm sure the media will take this and smear her even more. They like to sensationalize stories, and this one has the potential to be messy.

I'll have my work cut out to convince her I'm worth all this. For a moment, I wonder if I am.

My desire to be near her is gone once she left the courthouse, so I go home and wait with Jules and Ash. Trevor, Tripp, Cole and Matt let themselves into my penthouse two hours later. It's over.

"Day drinking?" Tripp asks as he looks at us.

"Seems appropriate," I mumble.

Cole shrugs and grabs a few beers from the kitchen and hugs Ashleigh, holding her a little tighter. I give him an approving look. I appreciate he's not taking her love for granted.

Tripp pours himself a drink from my bar, and they all settle in. Everyone's keeping quiet, lost in their own thoughts or too afraid to ask me about mine. I'm unsure of which.

It took the jury forty-two minutes to return with a guilty verdict. Thank god the jury still found it wrong for a man to hit a woman. Maybe there's hope for us yet.

They sentenced Pauly Jackson to sixty days in jail or six hundred hours of community service. Being allowed to pick up trash is too good for that son of a bitch. The judge also ordered him to stay away from Dani. He'd better do that anyway if he values his life.

"She looked beautiful," Tripp says.

"Stunning," Trevor adds.

"She was a fucking rock star," Cole says. He loosens his tie and tosses it on his jacket. I smile at the sunshine pin on his lapel.

"She saw them," Trevor says, catching my gaze. "That was a great touch." They all nod. The subtle message was Darcy's idea. She's quickly become one of my favorite people.

"I wonder if she read my note," I say, more to myself than anyone. I'll be there, regardless.

"I don't know. She put it in her purse," Tripp says.

They all sit with me in silence.

"I don't know what to do next," I admit.

"You wait," Trevor says.

"You wait until Jack gives the all clear, and then we reconvene Team True Love," Jules adds.

"Oh, for fuck's sake," Cole mumbles.

My thoughts exactly.

CHAPTER
FORTY-THREE

DANI

―――

"You ready?" Jenny asks, as she steps into my house.

"Almost," I call from the bathroom. I fix my lipstick and take one more look in the mirror. I look presentable. Practically normal, but with a touch of extra makeup to hide the dark circles under my eyes. Sleep has not been my friend lately.

It's winter break, so I have way too much time on my hands since school's out. Dad got Tyler ice skating lessons for Christmas, and he takes him every afternoon, giving me more alone time than I want. Tyler may be a budding hockey player after these lessons, and that would make Chance happy.

Jenny and I are attending Matt and Darcy's housewarming this evening. Darcy asked me to come, and you can't say no to her. It'll be my first time seeing them since the trial. It's only been a few weeks, but it feels like a lifetime.

After that horrible day, I've avoided all things that remind me of the humiliation of those accusations. I asked Courtney about Mr. Decker's comment, and she admitted the Deckers were paying her, but she would have done it for free anyway. She assured me she worked for me and wasn't sharing information or anything I said with them. I believe her. It was just part of their charity case and PR clean-up, right?

Courtney got a second deposition scheduled with Pauly Jackson a week after the trial and absolutely shredded him. She counter-sued him for damages, and we received a hefty settlement from him without going to court again. I paid her for her services, insisted she pay the Deckers back, made an anonymous donation to the Reaper's Foundation, and set the rest aside for Tyler's education. I refuse to live off his dirty money. There's no way I can profit from this. I've gained so much and lost even more.

At least I'm free of that complication.

But I'm still complicated. I have a kid. I'm not used to the wealthy lifestyle. I'm still a victim in his eyes. I'm a PR nightmare. After the sentencing, I was in all the tabloids, and my picture was even on ESPN. The victim who tried to snag one of America's most eligible bachelors. All the gossip magazines made me look like a pathetic girl reaching beyond my station. Maybe I was? Either way, I messed up.

Sully Decker's words float in and out of my dreams. He's willing to let his family get dragged through the messy press for their happiness. They value family. It's what Alexander kept saying. Showing. Isn't that what I've always wanted for Tyler and me? A loving family. A family with Xander. But best to keep that where it belongs, in my dreams.

I've considered calling Alexander and started dozens of texts, but never followed through. What do I say? I'm sorry isn't enough to fix the damage I've inflicted. Now it's been six weeks since I asked him to leave, and it's just awkward. Too much time has passed. Has he moved on? He hasn't reached out to me, but then again, he isn't the one who needs to apologize this time. I'm the one who said hurtful things to him. I'm the one who didn't trust him enough to take him at his word. I'm the one who broke his heart.

And here I am, going to a housewarming for a mutual friend because I can't say no, and my best friend is now part of that circle. Jenny and Luis are officially a couple, and both are head over heels. They're perfect for each other and I'm so happy for them. And Luis has become a good friend to me and a fabulous room *tio*, just like he promised. My class loves him.

I grab my coat and black Kate Spade bag and meet Jenny and Luis in the foyer. I open my purse to add my lipstick and notice a piece of paper tucked in there. The one from Tripp. In the chaos and emotion of the day, I forgot about it. Now isn't the time.

Jenny pulls me out of my thoughts. Focus. Get through tonight. Note later.

"You look," Jenny hesitates, "cute."

"What, is this not okay?" I look down at my long black sweater and black jeans. My black booties have a slight heel. And I have my nice black purse I never use. It matches. I've dressed for my mood. Or a funeral. Which could be interchangeable.

"You always look great," Luis says diplomatically.

I quirk my eyebrow. "Always?"

He gives me a shrug and a smile. Since Luis has become a regular visitor, he's seen me in holey shirts, worn pajama bottoms, and mismatched socks. I've been a bit of a hot mess lately. But it's the new year, so I'm striving to up my game, and I thought I had today. But apparently not.

"I didn't know you owned so much black," Jenny says. "But you look great. If you feel comfortable, then let's go."

I think about changing, but I don't. I'm tired of trying to act like I'm okay. I'm not. I mean, I'm functional. I'm just different. I'm not sunshine anymore. I've embraced the darkness.

Darcy and Matt's house isn't that far from mine. It's in an

older, more historic, and therefore, more expensive neighborhood. The homes are charming craftsmen style with manicured yards, some still displaying tasteful Christmas decorations.

I clutch my purse during the short drive and I can't help but think about the note. Should I read the long-forgotten message now? Certainly, it can't be anything of significance, right? Just a hang-in-there kind of encouragement. I take it out and hold it in my hand. Okay, you can do this. Face your fears now because it's likely your biggest fear will be at this party. I don't know how to face him or keep myself from running into his arms and begging for forgiveness. How to smile and pretend I don't care if he's not there or, worse yet, with someone else.

I unfold it and immediately recognize the stationery. It reminds me of the note I left on Xander's desk the night of our first kiss. I wrote a quote from *Pretty Woman*, one of my favorite movies. He gave her a dream world, and come to think of it, I was living a little of that story, minus the prostitution part. Of course, after the trial, a few of the tabloids alluded to that, too. My note to him read, *In case I forget to tell you, I had a great time tonight.* I sealed it with a kiss. I faced my fears then. I can do it again tonight.

We pull into the driveway of a larger home, and it's lit up from the inside. Several luxury cars are parked along the street, and a few more are ahead of us in the driveway. There's a high privacy fence surrounding the wooded backyard. It looks like a perfect house to start a family. I'm so happy for Darcy and Matt. They're the sweetest young couple.

Before I get out of the car, I take a deep breath and unfold the note. Alexander's handwriting makes my heart shatter before I even read the words. I've been such a fool. He wanted us to meet clandestinely after the trial, listing a time and place. Now he thinks I stood him up on top of everything else. I assume it's another reason he hasn't contacted me. I ghosted him. I feel sick, nauseous, and this isn't a stomach bug. It's a consequence of my prideful independence. Why did I push him away when all I wanted was to run into his arms? I'm an idiot.

But now is not the time. Now is the time to smile and be happy for others. When I get home tonight, I'll let myself cry. I take a deep breath and plaster on my best fake-it-'til-you-make-it smile. It's time to celebrate with Darcy and Matt. Rainbows from storm clouds, I remind myself. My assault was the catalyst for Matt's call up to the Reapers, and that's an absolute rainbow. Remembering makes my smile a little more authentic.

Luis opens the car door for Jenny and me. As I get out of the back seat, I take in my surroundings. This gorgeous house screams happy family. From the welcoming front porch with the cozy swing to the colorful pansies that fill the planters. It's perfect, and I can see Darcy's touch from here. Focus on her and the beauty she creates. That shouldn't be hard.

Darcy greets us at the front door. Her smile fills her face, and she hugs me tightly. She looks like something from the runway, but is still casual and effortless. I don't know how she does it, but she's always got a style that slays.

She gives Jenny and Luis a quick hi, and they quickly disappear into the house, leaving me on the porch. Way to be my wingman, Jenny.

"I'm so glad you came! I've missed you." She steps back and looks at me from head to toe, another disapproving eye.

"This place is amazing." Awkward level just hit a ten. I should have insisted on driving myself so I could bail early, but Luis wouldn't hear of it. He gave me some bullshit line about climate change and saving the planet. I didn't have the energy to argue, and here I am.

She looks around, admiring her surroundings, almost like she doesn't live here and see it all the time. "It is, isn't it? I had fun getting it ready," she says. "It still needs a few finishing touches, but it's livable."

"Hank, get back here!" Matt calls as a rolly-polly English Bulldog puppy charges toward me. I reach down and scoop him up. A light brown spot covers one eye, giving him an abundance of character. His tongue lolls out of his mouth, his cuteness factor going off the charts. Bulldogs are the most adorable puppies, and I may want to steal this one and not give him back. It reminds me of the first time I met Courtney, and Joe and Mickey helped buffer the awkwardness. I'll take this buffer every day.

"This must be Hank?" I ask. I snuggle with the adorable dog, rubbing his face against mine, when his sandpaper tongue licks my cheek. He puts my sour mood on a temporary hiatus, and I allow the joy to pour into my heart. It hurts just a little less now.

"Yeah, Hank Aaron," Matt says as he stands beside Darcy. He kisses her on the top of the head, and you can practically see the love aura surround them. "Come on in, Dani. We're glad you're here." Matt motions for me to come in and takes my coat and purse.

"Most everyone is out back. We've got lots of heaters and the fire pit going. Why don't you let Darcy show you around, and you can join us when you're done," he says. He gives her a wink and heads to the back of the house with my coat.

Hank squirms. "Is it okay if I put him down?"

"Sure, it's his house." I put him on the floor, and he runs a quick circle around me and then plops down on my feet, exhausted from the sudden burst of energy. He hasn't quite grown into his skin, and his feet are too big for his body. His entire backside wiggles, and I can't help but smile and think how much Tyler would love him.

I take a minute to look around the house after we leave the welcoming entryway. It's homey, comfortable. The front room has a large sectional facing a fireplace, the gas logs burning bright. The massive TV is above the mantel, paused in the middle of a game, as if someone rushed out, with the controllers thrown on the ottoman. The video game systems are all neatly stacked on the bookshelves, which are pretty bare except for some empty frames, like they're waiting for future memories. It's a little more minimal than I would have thought for Darcy, but the multiple gaming systems for Matt tracks. She said it wasn't quite finished. It's probably those little details that take more thought and time.

"This is gorgeous. I love the colors." The walls are dark grey, but the accent chairs and pillows add a pop of color. It's dramatic and fun, both eye-catching and balanced. It's similar to what she did in my classroom. The darkness and the light.

I step in and run my hand along the back of the sofa, the soft fibers confirming its luxury fabric. It reminds me of the sofa in Xander's penthouse. That is the most comfortable piece of furniture I've ever seen. Yes, this house is comfy but expensive.

"Oh, I'm so glad. Wait until you see the kitchen. It's a dream." We walk deeper into the house to the gorgeous kitchen. A swear jar sits on the counter and a sense of pride blooms when I think of what I started. Matt must be working on his language too.

I see people laughing and enjoying themselves outside through the large window in the backyard. I wonder if he's out there. I've got butterflies thinking about seeing him.

"This is amazing, Darcy." Someday I'd love to get her help with my house. Looking around, I feel we have similar tastes. She's just a lot more high-end.

"It is. It's absolutely perfect."

I feel a tug at my ankle and look down to see Hank biting at the cuff of my jeans. I reach down and pick him up again. I scratch him behind his ears, and he looks at me with big puppy dog eyes, and I melt.

"Looks like you've made a friend." I tense, frozen in place at the sound of the deep voice behind me. The voice that haunts my dreams. Hank is climbing over my shoulder to get to him.

"I think Matt needs me." Darcy excuses herself. "Good luck," she says, although I'm not sure which one of us she's talking to.

"Hi, sunshine." His voice sounds a little different, his usual confidence and swagger missing.

I slowly turn and look up into those deep blue eyes, made

bluer by the sweater he's wearing. He looks good. Real good. A hesitant smile graces his face. He licks his lips like he's nervous and wants to say something, but bites his bottom lip to stop himself. I want to put those lips to mine, taste him, but that's not my place anymore.

Hank squirms on my shoulder, breaking our stare down and drawing my attention away from Alexander.

"Hank, stop." There's no hesitancy in Alexander's voice now and the dog obeys the command. "Here, I'll take him."

He reaches for Hank, and I instinctively lean in until I remember he wants the dog. He puts him down on the floor and says, "Go to your bed." The dog looks up at him, turns, and wobbles down the hall while we both watch him walk away.

He clears his throat, the silence a chasm between us. After a few seconds that feel like hours, he takes a deep breath, and he gives me a nervous smile. "How have you been? Tyler?" His voice brings me back to focus. This smile, the one I've only seen him use around me, warms me from the inside out. He looks at me like he's unsure of my response.

What do I say? Is this where I break down and tell him I'm miserable without him? I need to keep it simple. Not complicated, even if I am.

"Good, we're good. Winter break's almost over, so we're back to school soon." I can't believe we're doing small talk, but at least he's not mad. We're awkward, but that's on me. He seems hesitant with me, but pretty comfortable in these surroundings. "You?"

"I've been busy. Lots of things to get ready for this new season." He runs his hands through his hair, something he does when he's frustrated, but tousled haired Alexander is one of my favorite looks. He rushes to say what's been weighing on his mind. "Listen, I'm sorry I wasn't there for you when you needed me most. It absolutely gutted me. But Jack said it was best for you and, fuck." He shakes his head. "Fudge, I'm so sorry. I'm so, so sorry. I know you felt alone and abandoned, but..." He looks like he could cry, his pain and regret visible on his face. This is so unexpected, I'm shocked.

"Stop. Stop right there." I put my hand up to touch his chest, remember he's not mine to touch, and slowly drop it to my side. I take a deep breath. "I wasn't alone. You sent your family. I was the one who withdrew. I'm the one who screwed up and didn't tell you, didn't trust you. That's all on me. And it's me who needs to apologize to you. I was overwhelmed, self-conscious of our differences, and too self-reliant. So I'm sorry. And besides, I need to thank you. Courtney was a lifesaver. I was in way over my head. I'm terrified to think about where I'd be without her. So thank you."

He shakes his head at me like he disagrees. "Of course. You should have never been in that situation."

"But I was. And it's over now. And look at the blessings. I wouldn't have met you and your amazing friends. Your generous donations wouldn't have blessed our school. Darcy and her amazing talent wouldn't have brightened my room for my students and me. Jenny would have never met Luis. It was one of the best things that's ever happened to me. Rainbows from storm clouds." As much as it was a horrible experience, I mean it. It was the catalyst for meeting some amazing people. I put my half-full spin on it.

I consider apologizing for not meeting him. I can tell him I just found his note. But why bring that up? It's probably best he thinks I didn't want to meet him. It makes it easier to pretend I don't want us together. It would never work. I'm still complicated. He's still complex.

He processes what I said, mumbling "storm clouds and rainbows" under his breath. His look shifts from upset to resolve. I know this look. It's his determined, take-action look. He's made a decision about something. Probably grateful he's not with complicated anymore.

"Speaking of Darcy, what do you think of the house?" His question takes our conversation in an unexpected direction.

"It's great. She did an amazing job." I reach out and run my hand over the countertop.

"She did, didn't she? That girl is talented and so damn sweet. Hard to believe she's related to Cole." He laughs at his joke. He gives Cole a hard time, but I know he secretly likes the guy. "Let me finish giving you the tour." He reaches out and takes my hand, this time without hesitation. The connection is like a spark to my heart, warmth spreading through my veins. It feels natural. Right.

"The owner's suite is upstairs," he says as he points to stairs and pulls me down a hallway. His excitement about this house is unexpected. Or maybe it's just part of this awkward encounter. I'm not sure. "It's like its own oasis, with a separate sitting area and huge bath."

"Come on," He's acting like a child on Christmas morning, ready to show off all his toys. Only this isn't his to be excited about. It's confusing, yet I'm curious about why it excites him, so I follow.

Hank greets us again, gives a high-pitched puppy bark, and Alexander shakes his head at him. He points to the fireplace, where I notice the dog bed and realize that's where he's supposed to be. Those big eyes look at Alexander pleading to be part of the tour. Alexander exhales loudly, and says, "Come on, Hank, let's show her the rest."

He leads me down another hall. "Guest bedroom," he says. I barely have time to peek in because he pulls me deeper down the hall. "Another bedroom, laundry room, bathroom." He stops in front of a closed door and looks at me with an intensity of a thousand suns. I wish I could read his mind because I'm beyond confused.

He opens the door to another large bedroom, and I'm baffled. It's decorated in Reapers' colors. Signed team posters line the walls and a twin bed is placed off to one side in the corner. A child-size desk sits by the window, next to a low bookshelf filled with children's books. Why would Matt and Darcy have a child's bedroom in their house?

"I don't," I stutter. "I don't understand."

Hank plops next to Alexander, his legs sliding out from under him. He lets out an audible sigh. We both look down at him and snicker.

"What don't you understand, sunshine?" He cups my face, his thumb brushes against my bottom lip, his eyes gaze into mine. "I love you. I love you so fucking much. This is ours. When you're ready, that is. Tomorrow, next month, next year. It's a home for us, our family. You, me, Tyler. Because sunshine, that's what I want. It's what I've wanted, and I'm sorry, but I'm tired of waiting."

Do I understand him correctly? This isn't Matt and Darcy's house? He bought a house for us? He's been working on this for how long? The entire time we've been apart? Maybe before? A house isn't an overnight thing you can pick up at Target. It takes time.

It sinks in. He still wants me. Wants us. He wants complicated.

"What did I tell you about apologizing?" I tease. His lips turn into a slight smile at the reprimand.

I reach out and wrap my hand around his neck, pulling him down. Our lips meet, our mouths devour one another, our souls connect, and my body returns to life. I could kiss this man for the rest of eternity. Is that what he's asking?

I push him slightly to break our kiss because he's taken my breath away. "Are you sure? Won't you miss walking to work?" I can't believe he'd give up his fantastic penthouse for a house with a yard. Does this urban bachelor want to be a suburban dad?

"Sunshine, I want to wake up with you so much more." Hard to believe he wants to wake up with me every morning and live the chaotic domestic life.

It's time to take down the last barrier around my heart and

surrender to what I've known for months, but was too afraid to admit to myself. I put my hands on his cheeks and make sure his eyes look into mine. I need him to understand precisely how much saying these words means to me. "I love you, Alexander Decker. So fucking much." I repeat his words back to him. It's worth a hundred dollars in the swear jar. Hell, it's worth all the money I have, and I say it again. "So fucking much."

He gazes into my soul, grasps my message, and a literal twinkle shines in his eye. He gets it. I'm saying yes. Yes to him. Yes to us. Yes to family.

Our lips meet, our hands frantic, exploring, touching. I need to feel skin against skin. With that thought, I think we need to be upstairs. I'm not doing this in Tyler's room and move us toward the door.

He must read my mind or body language. Frankly, I'm practically climbing him like a tree, so it's easy to interpret. He kisses me behind my ear, sending chills down my spine. "As much as I'd love to christen this house, and oh baby, we're going to christen this house, we have guests here." He kisses me again, this time more chastely, and when I try to deepen it, he growls in the back of his throat, heating my core. I miss the sounds he makes. Sounds that make me feel desirable. Sounds that remind me he's insatiable. "Now that I think about it, that may have been the one flaw in Team True Love's plan," he murmurs against my lips.

"Team True Love? What's that?"

A chuckle reverberates through his chest. "My family. They've been pretty helpful when it comes to you and grand gestures. Darcy knew you'd come to her party." He rolls his eyes, but a genuine smile fills his face. I can't wait to hear this story. He runs his fingers through my curls, relishing my thoroughly kissed look. No reason to hide it now. I'm smiling too. "Come on, let's say hello and goodbye and send them home."

"I like that plan. I like all your plans." I kiss him again, melting into him. I don't want to let him go.

He picks me up and spins me around. "I was hoping you would say that. Because sunshine, do I have plans." His grin warms me from the inside out. He whispers into my ear. "Once they're gone, I'm going to get you out of this." He pulls at my sweater and scowls. "Because sunshine, black is, most definitely, not your color."

That's a plan I can live with.

EPILOGUE

ALEXANDER

———

It took four weeks to put a ring on her finger and six weeks to move them into our home. Eight weeks to saying "I do."

I'm not sure which Tyler is more excited about: Hank Aaron, the enormous play set in the backyard, his Reaper's bedroom, or his favorite baseball player living down the street.

I've modified my usual travel this season to have more time at home with my family. My family. I like the sound of that. I'll make a few trips, but promise I'll never be gone more than two nights without her. I'll take them with me when I can.

I want to solidify this family, and that includes adopting Tyler, making him mine. I'm his dad from here on out. We've started the paperwork to make that a reality. He's a Decker in my heart, but I want it on paper too. Alexander, Dani, and Tyler Decker. It has a nice ring to it.

I'm ready for a new title besides boss. I'm ready for husband and dad. I want this family, and we all know I'm not good at waiting. When I want something, I go for it head-on. I tried the subtle, indirect approach. While it did finally net the best result, I'm not a patient man, and when it comes to Dani and Tyler, I'll always be direct. They're willing to take me as I am. That's what people who love you do.

Today, we're at Chance's beach house, surrounded by family and friends, celebrating our wedding. We got married this afternoon at a beautiful church in Charleston and are having a casual beach cookout for a reception. She wanted small and simple. I wanted now. I'll give her anything she wants, but I'm glad this wedding checked both our boxes.

It's been a perfect day, and the party's winding down. Dani's parents took Tyler back to the hotel, and we'll see him next weekend when we include him in our familymoon.

"I would have never guessed you'd be the first of us to get married," Jules says, a slight disbelief in his tone. "But I must say, no one could be happier for you than I am. Family man looks good on you." He raises his glass in a salute and turns to lean on the railing overlooking the pool.

"It does," Ashleigh says as she joins us on the balcony. She kisses me on the cheek and sits on the swing, leaning into me. I wrap my arm around her shoulder and pull her in tight.

"It doesn't mean I'm not still watching out for you," I remind her.

"Oh, I'm aware. But Cole and I are good, you know, the forever kind of good. You get that, right?" She smiles up at me.

I think about Dani and Tyler. My son and my sunshine. They're my forever kind of good.

"I get it."

"You know, your journey with Dani started right here in this house at Darcy's launch party," Ashleigh says. "You thought that phone call was a low point. And look at you now." She grins up at me.

She sounds like Dani. Rainbows from storm clouds. "When I think about him putting his hands on her," I start and tense up.

"What did I tell you about that?" Dani asks. She joins us, looking absolutely stunning, practically glowing. It damn near killed me to see her walking down the aisle because I just wanted to abandon my spot at the altar and run to her. She was walking too damn slow. Not. A. Patient. Man. And her in that dress, hugging all her curves. She looked like a fucking, I mean, flocking, fairytale princess. She's perfect. My sunshine.

She settles down on my other side, and I wrap my arm around her. My two favorite girls beside me. I think I've unlocked a new level of happiness. This feeling is confusing, but I'm content. I still have mixed feelings when I think of her assault, but I'm working on seeing it through her lens. Storm clouds and rainbows.

She leans in to kiss me, and I immediately relax when her lips touch mine.

"We agreed to be grateful because I met you," I mumble. Her half-full attitude is something I'm working to accept. It's hard, but she's rubbing off on me. I'm very thankful to have them, but I'll never celebrate the how. Wrapping a curl around my finger grounds me and reminds me what a lucky man I am. I'm so in love with this woman. Yep. She's my forever kind of good.

We leave for our honeymoon tomorrow for a few married adult days in the Caribbean. If I have it my way, we'll never leave the suite. I want to be buried inside her as much as possible. Maybe even put a baby in her. We've talked about it, and I'm ready. Dani's warming to the idea. We're both excited about practicing a lot, either way.

We'll meet Tyler and her parents at Disney World for the weekend to celebrate being a family. I never thought I'd be the Disney World kind of guy, but I'm looking forward to watching my family enjoy themselves. She's finally letting her guard down so I can spoil them. I'm excited about all the ways I can shower them with love.

I look over at Jules as he watches the remnants of the party below us. "And that leaves one Decker solo."

Jules doesn't even turn around. "Yep. But it's not for lack of trying." He sounds despondent.

"Maybe you need to quit dating actresses and models," Ashleigh says.

"Hey, they're people too," Jules says defensively. He turns and looks back at us, leaning against the railing. "Maybe I'll give dating a time out and focus on other things for a while." His normally happy-go-lucky demeanor turns sullen. Is he taking my role as the grumpy sibling?

"What other things? Certainly not work?" I ask.

Julian's business has grown, and he's tripled his clientele in the past three years. His agency has grown so much that he personally handles less than ten clients, and I don't think he charges commission for all of them, like Cole and Matt. I'm sure Chance and Tripp get the best agent in the country for a bargain too. Not that he's broke. His agency is bringing in close to a billion dollars a year.

"No, not work. It practically runs itself. I've made sure my clients are low maintenance."

"Hey, who are you calling low maintenance?" Cole asks as he joins us. Ash gets up, and he wraps her in his arms, giving her a kiss that's a little steamy for my liking. She's still my sister, after all.

"You'd better stay low maintenance," I warn. I mean, that's always going to be my job. Even though Cole is a solid guy who would never find himself in a scandal, tabloid stories, or stupid things young guys with lots of money find themselves in, it takes one photo out of context to blow it all up. With his talent on and off the field and my sister's love, I have no doubt he'll be one of the greats. Not to mention the Decker Connection behind him.

Dani giggles next to me. She always finds it funny when I switch into protector mode with Ash.

"So what other things?" Ash asks.

Jules shrugs. I quirk my eyebrow at him. It's not like Jules to keep secrets, especially from Ashleigh.

"I don't know. I want to spend more time on something I'm passionate about." He clearly doesn't want to elaborate.

"I thought actresses were your passion," Ash teases him.

"Haha. Hilarious." He takes a sip from his drink. "Life's short. I want to spend more time doing things I enjoy, that's all."

"Is this an early mid-life crisis?" I've noticed Jules is spending more time alone, but I attributed it to Chance being in season and my contribution to the family drama this year. I may be protective of Ashleigh, but I worry equally for my brother.

His carefree and casual attitude is genuine, but that doesn't mean he doesn't have emotional depth. Honestly, Jules is the most sensitive and emotional of the three of us. He always puts others first, which sometimes means no one takes care of him. He's most like our mom in that way. Maybe it's the middle child thing?

He shakes his head at me. "I love you guys, but it's time for you to start your honeymoon."

Got it. Conversation over. I chuckle. "We'll talk about this when I get back."

"Can't wait," he mumbles.

I get up from the swing and extend my hand to my bride. "Shall we, Mrs. Decker?"

She takes my hand, and I pull her up and into my chest. I lean down for a chaste kiss, but as soon as my lips touch hers, I can barely control myself. I deepen the kiss, needing more of her. That happened in the church today too. Everyone cheered and clapped except the Colonel. I could hear him clear his throat over the catcalls.

"On that note," Jules says. He claps me on the shoulder, but I don't stop kissing my wife. "Congratulations. Love you guys."

Dani breaks our kiss and sighs. I notice Cole and Ash left the balcony too.

"I'm sorry. You know I can't resist your kiss."

"What did I tell you about apologizing, Mr. Decker?" Her smile is pure love and devotion. She wraps her arms around my neck and pulls me to her lips again, where I get lost in my sunshine.

Yeah. I can get used to this sweet life.

WHAT'S NEXT FOR THE DECKER CONNECTION?

I just adore Jules, don't you? He's kind, caring, thoughtful, successful, driven, and considerate. Did I mention he's *get the smelling salts out because OMG the swoon factor is off the charts*, hot?

Julian Decker's been keeping a secret from everyone, even his closest friends and family. As he continues to feel unsettled, maybe now is the time to lean into something new.

And what if this new adventure leads to an unexpected love connection? Even better.

But buckle up, because this one will take you on an unexpected journey of secrets and building trust, but with a twist. The leader of Team True Love might be in over his head with this woman, and they may not be enough to save him.

The Final Draft: Julian and Harper

ALSO BY CHERYL CAMPBELL

Trouble at First: Ashleigh and Cole

The Decker Connection series starts with Ashleigh and Cole 📖

All Ashleigh Decker wants this summer is to be the social media intern for the Savannah Pajamas. Is that too much to ask? She's off to a great start until she meets a player who is nothing but trouble.

This summer league is the perfect opportunity for Cole Davidson to impress the MLB scouts. His dream to play first base for the Carolina Reapers is within his grasp. An added bonus? A beautiful intern who steals his heart.

The only problem? She's hiding her identity. Her father is the owner of the Reapers, and her overprotective older brother is the General Manager. Can Ashleigh keep her secret and the guy without jeopardizing his career?

Sliding into Home: Matt and Darcy

Overwhelmed doesn't begin to describe my life. I'm in over my head remodeling a multi-million-dollar beach house. It's the only thing standing between me and college graduation. Then the guy I've crushed on since middle school offers to be my assistant. Did I mention he's my brother's best friend? Yep. Matt Hartman, swoony boy next door and professional baseball player, is working side by side with me this fall. It takes everything I have to keep my feelings for him contained, until, well, I don't. Can I put his friendship with my brother on the line for a relationship with me?

I've hit more milestones this year than most do in a decade. I graduated from college, got drafted into Major League Baseball, played on a triple-A team in my hometown, and now, for the first time in my life, I'm enjoying my off-season. But am I? When I'm presented with the opportunity to help Darcy Davidson with her senior project, I gladly volunteer my services. It's something to fill my time, and besides, my best friend's sister needs help. That's all it is, right? Then why do I want to be so much more than her assistant?

The Final Draft: Julian and Harper

Julian Decker's billion-dollar sports agency represents the top athletes in the world. His charm, success and sexy blue eyes have landed him on the hottest bachelor list for the past five years. He's a hopeless romantic, with money, fame, and a rotation of beautiful women on his arm each week. Some would say he has it all. But things aren't always as they seem. Behind the flashing lights and camera clicks, Julian has deep-seated trust issues and a secret he keeps hidden, even from his closest friends in the Decker Connection.

Harper Cartwright is tired of being known as "the hockey player's sister" and is ready to forge her own path. With her master's degree in hand, she's headed to New York to learn from the best and make her author dreams come true. It's a whole new ball game for her. A new city. A NHL goalie roommate and his adorable dog. An intense and demanding writing program. She has a lot on her plate. Harper's handling all these life challenges until she encounters Julian Decker, a handsome playboy with a panty-dropping smile. His intense pursuit of her has Harper excited and wary, especially after she discovers his secret.

LET'S CONNECT

Cheryl loves connecting with readers and talking about the Deckers. Join her in the conversation. Follow for sneak peeks and behind-the-scenes fun.

And don't forget to leave a review on Amazon 😃

Cheryl Campbell Facebook Cheryl Campbell Author

Cheryl Campbell Instagram @Cheryl_Campbell_Author

Cheryl Campbell TikTok @cherylcampbellbooks

CherylCampbellbooks@gmail.com

Want to hear the Living the Suite Life playlist? Check it out on Spotify.

Spotify - The Decker Connection: Living the Suite Life